INFINITY'S END:

INFINITY'S END BOOK 9

ERIC WARREN

Part of the Sovereign Coalition Universe

ERIC WARREN

INFINITY'S END – INFINITY'S END BOOK 9

Cover Design by Dan Van Oss www.covermint.design

Content Editor Tiffany Shand www.eclipseediting.com

ISBN 979-8-6093-7176-8

"Our history is not our Destiny."

- Alan Cohen

ERIC WARREN

<u>The Sovereign Coalition Series</u>

Short Stories

CASPIAN'S GAMBIT: An Infinity's End Story

SOON'S FOLLY: An Infinity's End Story

Novels

INFINITY'S END SAGA

CASPIAN'S FORTUNE (BOOK 1)

TEMPEST RISING (BOOK 2)

DARKEST REACH (BOOK 3)

JOURNEY'S EDGE (BOOK 4)

SECRETS PAST (BOOK 5)

PLANETFALL (BOOK 6)

BROKEN LINKS (BOOK 7)

MEMORY'S BLADE (BOOK 8)

INFINITY'S END (BOOK 9)

<u>The Quantum Gate Series</u>

Short Stories

PROGENY (BOOK 0)

Novels

SINGULAR (BOOK 1)

DUALITY (BOOK 2)

TRIALITY (BOOK 3)

DISPARITY (BOOK 4)

CAUSALITY (BOOK 5)

Special Offer

Sign up on my website and receive the first short story in the
INFINITY'S END SAGA absolutely free!

Go to www.ericwarrenauthor.com to download
CASPIAN'S GAMBIT!

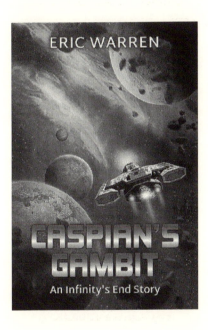

1

It was funny. Nothing looked different from this angle. Despite the fact *all of it* was different; alien in the truest sense of the word. Evelyn Diazal stared out at the vista. Were it not for the purple glow of the planet suspended before her in the blackness of space, she wouldn't even be able to tell she was far away from the stars of her home. This wasn't what she had once known as Coalition space. Nor was it the frontier of the Sargan Commonwealth or the non-aligned worlds. No, she was deep within Sil territory, in orbit of *their* home planet, one she had set foot on not more than three weeks ago. She hadn't expected to see it from above or to leave the surface alive. But somehow she had managed to convince the Sil governing body, otherwise known as the Sanctuary, that humanity was worth saving and they had agreed to assist in their fight with the species known as the Athru. She'd felt the thrill of victory when she'd been up on that stage, addressing their arrogance and watching the gears turn in their heads. To confront a species that had for so long discounted the human race, as nothing more than a nuisance to be ignored, and force them to acknowledge their mutual problems had been a significant accomplishment. She understood what Cas had felt when he came back from Zenfor's ship, victorious.

Evie stymied herself. She shouldn't feel pride at a time like this. As soon as she glanced down a surge of guilt ran through her, the casket before her reminding her despite all her success, it had come at too high a cost. Evie reached out and placed her hand on the top of the casket, its cold metal contrasting the warmth of her skin. She would do anything to take back her actions, to turn back the clock and fix it all. But despite all the advancements of science and technology, going back in time just wasn't possible. After it had first happened, she had wanted to return to how things were before, back as if nothing had happened at all. But now all she wanted was a chance to go back and tell Laura she was sorry.

Evie drew in a deep breath and placed her other hand on the casket, leaning over it as a tear fell from her eye. She didn't try to hold them back, nor did she sob uncontrollably. She allowed them to come and coat the top of the casket. "I know I don't deserve your forgiveness," she whispered. "But I hope somewhere you know how sorry I am. And…I hope, on some level, you're proud of me. I think I loved you more than I was even willing to admit to myself, and it took you being gone for me to see that." One more moment. That was all she needed. Though, if she was honest with herself, she would never truly be able to grasp the fact that Laura was gone. Part of her would always be with Evie, living on in her memory somewhere. The brief time they had together was etched in her mind as writing was carved into stone. Evie would persist, but it would be in honor of Laura; she wouldn't let what happened destroy her. Because it would…if she let it.

Evie glanced around at the empty cargo bay. This was the same place they'd held the ceremonies for Blohm and the others, and they had been packed houses. But she had wanted this to be a private ceremony. Laura hadn't had many acquaintances or friends on the ship as she had only been aboard a short time. And maybe it was selfish of her, but anyone else would be here just out of politeness, not because of their feelings for Laura. The truth was Evie had been putting it off. It had been difficult enough re-acclimating herself to the ship and the crew after everything that had happened, but now, seeing as they were on the brink of war, she wanted to make sure Laura had a proper send-off before there was no one left to honor her memory.

"Lieutenant Laura Yamashita," she whispered, "You have undertaken a journey we all must face one day. May it be helmed with a steady hand, a vigorous heart, and a sharp mind." As she said the final words of the typical Coalition discharge for a comrade who has died in the line of duty, the doors to the cargo bay opened and closed behind her. Without turning, Evie ran her hand over the casket one last time, then pressed the sequence of controls on the wall to eject the casket into open space.

Evie sensed the other person stop a few meters away, keeping their distance. Evie watched as the casket floated away from the ship, an auto thruster on the back making sure it was far enough not to be caught in the ship's tiny, but still present, gravitational field.

"I'm sorry to interrupt."

She wiped her eyes one more time before turning around. "It's no interruption." Caspian stood before her, a solemn look on his face.

"We're getting ready to start in a few minutes and he insisted you be there."

Evie furrowed her brow. "What time is it?" She glanced over at the comm panel and her stomach fell. She'd been in here over two hours. "I'm sorry, I lost track of time."

"Trust me, I know how it is," Cas replied. "Are you okay? You don't have to be there. I can tell him—"

She shook her head. "No. I promised." She glanced over her shoulder one last time at the casket which was now nothing but a gray dot in the distance, blending in with all the stars. "At least she'll have a good view."

He nodded. "Thislea is beautiful, I'll give them that. I had no idea. Zaal has been running every scan he can think of to collect all the astrometric data from this sector. You never know when or if we'll get another chance." He paused a moment. "Do you think we should hold the ceremony for Captain Greene here as well? While we have the time?"

"His directive was explicit. He wants to be returned home. Which means we owe it to him to get his body back to Earth."

Cas scoffed. "*If* Earth is still there. Until we get eyes on it, I'm not about to believe all the hearsay. We don't know—the Athru could have gone in and blown—"

She put her hand up. "I know. But we have to hope that didn't happen. Even with the invasion, there's a possibility there could still be survivors, fighting back from within. An underground resistance."

"I don't know, Evie. The Athru are thorough in their extermination techniques. How long have we been back and the only other humans we've seen have been from Samiya's group?"

He was referring to the fifty or so refugees they'd come upon after returning from open space, commanded by his old shipmate, Samiya Gysan. Finding them had been a blessing as they had been short on crew at the time, but he was right. Ever since they hadn't seen another human soul. "They're out there. We just have to find them. We're *not* the last. Hear me?" Cas gave her a begrudging acknowledgment. It was the best she would get.

Evie glanced over to the bit of cloth she'd brought with her to the cargo bay, laying at an angle on one of the engineering containers. Though she'd been dreading *and* anticipating this moment, she couldn't help but feel like she should just leave it there and never come back in here again.

Though, someone would inevitably find it, try to take it for themselves or return it to her. And that was the last thing she wanted. "Do you think his patience will hold?" She nodded to the cloth. Though it was what was wrapped inside the cloth that was the subject of her interest.

Cas eyed it. "Are you sure about this? There's no reason to rush—"

"I'm not rushing," she said. "I've had weeks to think about this. And every time I keep coming back to the same conclusion. It needs to be done."

Cas stepped out of her way. "Another two minutes won't make a difference."

Evie walked over and picked up the piece of cloth, which was an old uniform, from the crate she'd laid it on when she'd entered. She'd used the uniform because she couldn't bear to touch it again. The thing was cursed, and she didn't want any more of its dark energy leaking out and through her. She took the shroud over to the matter recycler and deposited it into the shelf. It made a loud *clang* when it hit the grate inside. Through the window Evie stared at her family's broadsword with a seething hatred she reserved for only the most atrocious of acts. And the sword had been the instrument of all the destruction in her life. It was time to be rid of it. She reached up to tap the recycler button and noticed Cas's hand moved to stop her, but then he pulled back. He was more of a sentimental person than she was; she no longer had any need for this weapon and was glad to be rid of it.

"Does Esterva know?"

His question stopped her hand millimeters from the button. She pulled back. "She wouldn't understand."

"Have you asked her?"

Evie cursed him under her breath. Esterva, her mother, had told her the true history of the sword and how it had come to be in Evie's possession. She would want Evie to keep it because it was Evie's one connection to her deceased father. But that had been a toxic connection, and Evie was quite literally cutting it out of her life. "It's not hers. It's mine…to do with as I please." She tapped the button.

The chamber glowed white and the sword began to disintegrate, atom by atom. In under thirty seconds there was nothing left, not even a mote of dust. Evie felt a giant weight leave her shoulders. She closed her eyes and took a deep breath. "Finally," she whispered, glancing at Cas. "Okay. We better get moving. He's not going to be happy if we have to keep making him wait."

Cas smiled. "I'm not sure I'm ready."

Evie returned the gesture. "I don't think anyone ever truly is."

2

The doors to the ship's refurbished bar stood in front of them but Caspian Robeaux hesitated. He hadn't been back in here ever since they'd returned from open space—not because he was afraid of what he might do—but more because he'd been so busy. This had been Martial's realm. Without him, it seemed…emptier somehow. The past few weeks had been calm, what with the Sil on the ship helping to upgrade their systems and Evie allowing herself to be subjected to more of their tests. They seemed obsessed with finding out the perfect combination of genes that created her from the human and Athru DNA. Esterva had kept her part in Evie's creation quiet, not wanting to get involved in their scrutiny. Cas hated her for that, because had she been willing to step forward and take some of the brunt of the Sil's requests, so much wouldn't fall on Evie's shoulders. But that was an internal family matter and it was best if he stayed out of it. Getting involved in her business again wasn't a good idea.

"Just get ready," Cas said as he and Evie stood shoulder to shoulder. "He's in rare form today."

"Oh, Kor," she replied. "You know it's times like this when I'm really glad I'm not the captain anymore."

Cas grumbled. She'd gotten out of this by the skin of her teeth. Evie was still the one who should take part in the ceremony since it had been her idea and her promise in the first place. "You know, I could always order you—"

Evie jolted forward so the doors opened for them, revealing the crowd of people. "Too late," she hissed back at him. They entered the crowded space which was beyond capacity. Had Box invited *everyone*?

"About time!" Box yelled over the din of people talking and milling about through the space. "You would think with limited lifespans humans would be more efficient about the use of their day." Cas watched Evie disappear into the crowd with a grin on her face as the rest of the people in the bar turned to look at him. "The most important day of my life and you're running to the altar with sweat on your brow and a guilty look on your face. Out flirting with the bridesmaids again?"

Cas felt his face go hot. "You're not getting married!" By Garth, he hated it when Box did this. Especially in front of the crew. Cas shot a look at Saturina, who was standing off to the side with Ryant, both were doing their best to conceal their smiles.

"You're right. This is *much* more important." Box moved to the front of the group. "I'm ready."

Cas sighed and walked up to the machine, pulling a small medallion from his pocket. The room quieted around them. Box stood in front of him with his chest puffed out, as much as that was possible for a machine, and his eyes blinking in a pattern Cas recognized as genuine pride. It was the same sequence Box used to blink when he'd done a spectacular job piloting the *Reasonable Excuse*, or getting them out of one of their skirmishes with the Sargans.

"Mr. Box." Cas did his best to sound sincere. "Because of your bravery and heroism in the face of imminent peril to yourself, and for the acts performed aboard this ship that saved the lives of your fellow crewmembers, I hereby present you with the Coalition's Medal of Honor. May it inspire others to follow in your deeds." Cas held out the sparking medallion. It was silver with gold inlays with the symbol of a star in the middle. "Congratulations."

"Put it on me," Box whispered, though he didn't do much to lower the timbre of his voice.

"No, put it on yourself," Cas hissed.

"Put. It. On. Me," Box hissed back.

Cas huffed, reached up and placed the medallion in the indentation Box had created on his superstructure. It magnetically locked onto his person. "Ohhhh, yeah. That feels sooo gooood," he moaned. "Take it off and put it back on again."

"I hate you," Cas said, as audible laughter came from the crowd.

"No one can do it like you can, Captain," Box replied.

Cas turned to Evie, who had her hand over her mouth. "See? This is why you should have done this." He turned and stomped over to the bar. There wasn't anyone behind the counter, so Cas hopped it and grabbed a bottle of scorb. He glanced up to Box admiring his medal. Other members of the crew had come up to him, giving him their congratulations. Cas even saw Ronde among the crowd, who wore a genuine smile and took Box's hand. Cas shook his head. He never thought he'd see the day.

He put the scorb back and instead pulled out the bottle Laska had introduced him to. After eighteen years it was bound to be even better than he'd remembered. Cas poured a drink then cleared his throat, raising his glass. "To Box, may we all strive to live by his example."

"To Box!" the crowd replied, those with drinks raising them. Cas couldn't help but smile. He didn't think he'd ever seen the robot so content. He stood in the middle of the crowd, beaming, while everyone around him cheered.

Zenfor stood on the far side, stoic as ever. She wasn't joining in the cheering, but he thought he could see the smallest upturn of her mouth.

Saturina approached the bar, her short, silver hair bouncing as she did. Cas had come to love that bounce, especially when it was walking toward him. "That was very gracious of you."

Cas shrugged, taking a sip of his drink. It *was* better than he remembered. "I figured he deserved at least one good day. And we have to take as many of those as we can get."

Her smile reached her eyes. "We sure do. Plans for later?"

The reminder of everything else he had to do came rushing back to him. "I've got to try and speak with the Sil again. This is taking longer than they originally estimated and I think they're stringing us along so they can keep examining Evie. But of course, she's the only one who ever talks to them so I'm going to be an intermediary. See if I can't move the process along a little further."

Saturina leaned over the counter, folding her arms under her. "Do you have a plan?"

"I think the only way we're going to get these bastards is with a surprise attack. They don't know we're amassing these kinds of numbers and I doubt they think we'll be bold enough to charge right into the inner systems. But we've got the advantage of speed and the element of surprise. If we can catch them off guard, I feel like we can deal a death-blow."

"Assuming the new weapons work" She scanned the room. "We've been working overtime in the Bay getting them installed on the wings, but we haven't actually tested them yet. For all I know they could burn out after one shot. Or not fire at all. They're going to need extensive testing."

Cas took another sip. "You're right. I need to speak to Zenfor about that. She's supposed to oversee coordinating the installation of these weapons." He finished the drink. "I'll take care of it now."

Saturina held out her hand, stopping him. "I wouldn't do it just now if I were you. She had another confrontation with one of the Sil teams in the corridors. It didn't go well."

Cas sighed. "How much damage this time?"

"I think the damage is more emotional than physical. How much verbal punishment can one person take from their own people? Let me tell you, the Sil are not kind to her."

Cas hated that. Zenfor was a good person. Hotheaded, quick to judge, sure. But she had saved this ship more than once, and she had always been there when they needed her. It wasn't fair she'd been ostracized from her own people for doing what she thought was right. He glanced over to Box reveling in the atmosphere of being celebrated and then back to Zenfor, off to the side by herself. She had done just as much for this ship as Box had. Perhaps it was time he finally recognized that.

"Isn't it weird?" Saturina asked.

The words pulled Cas from his thoughts. "What?"

"Being in here. Without Martial. Knowing he was spying on Diazal that whole time." Cas glanced over to Evie, who was engaged in discussion with her mother, just on the other side of Box. Over the past few weeks their relationship had improved. Or his perception of it had. Regardless, he wasn't about to disrupt the one familial connection she had left. He'd confided to Saturina about Martial's true mission one night over dinner. It seemed he was confiding a lot to her lately. And vice-versa. He hadn't known she'd had an uncle who had been in the Corps as well. She hadn't said much about him, which Cas could understand. She didn't want to linger on the probability he had died in the invasion.

"I guess. Though I think he always kept a sharp eye on me," Cas said. "He gave me a bit of advice once."

"What was that?"

"He said not to let my pain define me. Because it would ruin everything that came after what I lost."

Saturina took his hand. "I think he was right."

Cas squeezed her hand. "Esterva asked me if she could perform a traditional Athru ceremony for his body." He faked a laugh. "I wish I had known what I was agreeing to before I said yes." Saturina creased her brow as Cas leaned in close. "The Athru don't believe in waste. So, we fired him in the forge down on thirteen and then used a graviton emitter to compact his remains into the smallest amount of matter possible." He held up his hand and forefinger about a centimeter apart. "Which was then fused into one of the bulkheads."

"What?" Saturina exclaimed loudly enough so people turned and looked.

"Shh. It's no big deal. It's just—"

"—a dead person inside the hull of the ship," she finished.

"Okay, yes. It is that, but I think it's kind of a neat idea. Like you're taking your ancestors along with you. She said it was an ancient Athru tradition."

She shook her head. "You *have* to tell me where you put him. I'm not about to step foot on that deck again. Do you want to end up with ghosts roaming the corridors? Because this is how you end up with ghosts."

"Why? So, you can dig it out? You can't tell where it is, and it doesn't affect the integrity of the hull. It's designed to be innocuous."

She grabbed him by the collar, pulling him over the bar. "Tell me where it is, or I'll go over and ask Esterva myself."

Cas put up his hands. "Fine. Deck six, section twelve, corridor B. Three meters down, two up from the floor."

"Perfect, thank you." She let him go, then turned to head for the doors. He caught her by the arm.

"You're not going to remove it."

She faced him. "Two words. Ghost ship."

"Chief," Cas said, trying to make it sound like a warning, but it came out more like a playful jab.

"*Captain,*" she replied, the same tone in her voice.

"If I go down there and find a piece of bulkhead missing…"

Her eyes flashed and a mischievous grin appeared on her lips. "What are you gonna do?"

"Punishment."

Saturina arched an eyebrow. "Wow. I wasn't really going to remove it, but I think I have to now." She leaned in close like she was going to kiss him but stopped centimeters from his lips. "Just to see what happens." She turned again and left through the doors and a shiver ran up through Cas's spine as heat flushed his cheeks. He couldn't tell if she was serious or not. But now he had more pressing issues. Though he was looking forward to returning to his quarters more than he had been just a few minutes ago.

Across the room he caught Zenfor staring at him, her gaze unflinching. Great, she'd seen that entire encounter. His face grew even hotter. Now was as good a time as any. What did they say? Sometimes you just had to face your obstacles head-on.

That's just what he planned to do.

3

"Enjoying yourself?" Cas asked, sliding up beside Zenfor as she observed the party. Box was in full mode, regaling the crowd with some of his more outlandish stories. None of them were true but Cas supposed that wasn't the point, as long as they were entertaining.

"I assume this is fun." Zenfor crossed her arms.

"Do *you* find it fun?" Cas asked.

"It's fine," she replied.

"You know, the whole point of a party is to enjoy—" Her penetrating gaze cut him off. "Right. How are the weapon upgrades coming?"

"They'll be ready to test in another day. But that's not the primary concern."

Cas leaned forward. "What's the primary concern?"

"Another forty Sil ships are due to arrive today from the far side of the Hutakk sector. But the Sanctuary isn't being cooperative." Her face remained impassive.

"What do you mean? I thought Evie was negotiating—"

"Her efforts aren't as effective as we hoped. I've heard the Sil on the ship speaking. Some of them…taunting. The Sil won't move without evidence of Athru numbers and ship locations."

Cas cursed, setting aside the issue of the taunting for later. He'd never known anyone who could get under Zenfor's skin. "Does Evie know this?" Zenfor nodded. "Then why hasn't she said anything? She told me there wasn't anything to worry about."

"I believe Evelyn doesn't want to disappoint you. Or the crew. She knows there's a lot riding on her ability to convince my people to continue to assist in our efforts." She continued to stare at the people mingling in the party. Box had taken a bottle from a nearby shelf and doused himself in it, chanting something about winning the grand cup. Rare form indeed.

"I thought this was resolved a week ago. How are we supposed to move forward if we're the only ship willing to go into enemy territory?" Whether Zenfor sensed he was asking a rhetorical question, or she just didn't know, she remained silent. He should have seen this coming. The Sil were so infuriating in their desire to see all the *evidence* of a given situation before doing anything about it. No wonder they hadn't made any significant advancements in ten thousand years. By the time they decided on a given topic the time for action was long past. It was the same problem he'd had with them when he'd informed them of the Athru threat in the first place.

"I'm going to talk to them," Cas said, leaving Zenfor's side and storming out of the lounge.

"They won't speak with you," she called after him and Cas threw up his hand to dismiss what he already knew. Ever since her pronouncement on the planet, the Sil were adamant about only speaking with Evie for all the communication needs of the fleet. The teams that had transferred over and that were working with the Engineering teams weren't as discriminatory, though they regarded the rest of the crew with only the briefest of acknowledgments. The only time they would interact with anyone was when they had a question about a system they deemed too primitive to understand. But since Zenfor had been the one who had re-designed most of the systems they very rarely had a question. Cas had told the crew to stay out of their way and let them do their jobs. They'd be back on their own ships soon enough.

Cas made his way into a small room close to the lounge, but it had a comm terminal and a screen, that was all he needed. He tapped his comm. "Zaal?"

"Yes, Captain?"

"Can you patch me through to the Sanctuary? I need to speak with them."

"Of course," he replied, his trademark heavy voice even more threatening over the comm. "How is the party?"

"One of a kind, wish you could see it," Cas replied.

"Not for me. I don't do well in large gatherings. Coming up on your terminal now."

The screen before Cas flickered to reveal the image of a Sil Cas didn't know or recognize. He had to assume this was one of the Sanctuary. "Council member—"

"You are not the advanced human. Per our agreement, all communication will proceed through the superior human only." The faceless figure didn't move when they spoke, but the green aura above their head pulsed in time with their words.

"If you'll just permit me a moment of—" The screen went black. "Dammit!" Cas yelled.

"Sorry, Captain. It seems they are unwilling to speak to you," Zaal replied. "Would you like me to try again?"

Cas pinched the bridge of his nose. "No. I don't want to antagonize them. Just…let me know if there are any changes to the fleet."

"Aye, sir." Zaal cut the comm.

Cas left the small room and made his way back to the lounge. At last count they had nearly seven hundred Sil ships that had coalesced around Thislea, the Sil home world. An additional forty today would be helpful, but Cas wanted more. Zenfor had assured him the Sil had at least a hundred thousand ships spread throughout their territory, though some of them were so far away they could take a year or more to reach their current location. Cas suspected the Sil weren't bringing all these ships back for just their benefit. They'd broken their treaty with the Athru and expected some level of retribution.

As the doors slid open, Cas almost crashed head-first into Evie, who had been coming out at the same time. "Whoa, sorry." He held on to her arms, so he didn't run into her. He let go quickly. "I was just coming to find you."

"I saw you speaking with Zenfor," she said, pulling her dark brown ponytail over her shoulder. "She told you?" He nodded. "I asked her not to do that. I'll handle the Sil."

"Whatever you do, I hope you're better at it than I am. They won't even listen to me." Cas hated not being useful in this context. He'd been the one to make first contact with the Sil, he should be able to finish the deal.

"I'll take care of it," she replied. "But you see where they're coming from, right? They don't want to send a bunch of resources into an unknown situation. We can't fly in there blind and start shooting everything in sight."

"We can if the guns are big enough," he joked. But the look on her face told him she wasn't amused. He reset himself. "I get it. But there's no way to get that info. Not without being blown into a billion pieces before we get there. If there's one thing they're good at, it's hunting humans."

"Let me see what I can do." She sauntered past him. "Plus, I think you need to get back in there and get a hold of Box. He's enjoying this a bit *too* much."

"Oh hell," Cas said. "What's he done now?" She only shook her head and grinned, heading off in the other direction. Cas booked it back to the lounge.

***

Evie entered the small comm room not far from the lounge, taking a seat. She took a moment to compose herself, to clear her mind and focus her thoughts. She'd learned early on the Sil didn't tolerate *um's* and *ah's* as part of their discourse. Evie needed to be prepared and ready to speak so she wouldn't waste their time. She hated they had glommed on to her so vociferously, but what could she do about it now?

They'd been adamant about subjecting her to more scans, most from the additional teams that came over to work on *Tempest*. She hadn't minded at first, but after three weeks it was getting old. The only positive thing that seemed to have come out of the exchanges was the Sil weren't demanding all the rest of humanity rise to Evie's standard. As long as she existed, that seemed to be enough for the time being. She'd been worried they would only consider humanity worthy allies if *every* human went through a similar procedure. But as far as Esterva was concerned, it was something that could only be set in motion before conception, not after. None of the humans on the *Tempest* now would ever be able to rise to Evie's level. But that didn't mean the next generation couldn't.

"Zaal?" Evie tapped her comm.

"Commander," Zaal said. "Shall I put you in contact with the Sanctuary?"

"Please." She straightened her hair, though she didn't know why. It wasn't as if the Sil cared about hairstyles. "And it's just Evelyn from now on."

"Sorry. Old habits I suppose."

The screen flickered to life and she was face to face with Til-kes, one of the high-ranking members of the Sanctuary. Though face-to-face was a bit of a misnomer since she had on

24

her helmet above which glowed a green orb. "Please tell your human counterpart not to contact us again," she said.

"I apologize," Evie replied. "He is anxious. It's a failing of lesser humans." She didn't like throwing Cas under the bus like that, but it usually worked. The Sil loved discussing the failings of the "inferior" humans.

"If you cannot keep him under control, we will be forced to withdraw from our agreement."

"I implore you to stay, council member. You have seen the evidence. You know what will happen should the Athru be allowed to roam unchecked."

"Have you devised a way to determine their exact numbers, fleet positions and weapon capabilities? It does us no good to head directly into enemy territory only to be overrun as soon as we cross the border."

"We're working on it, council member. I should have something more concrete for you within the next few days."

The Sil fell silent for a moment. "One would think with that advanced mind of yours you would have come up with something sooner," Til-kes replied. "Are you sure you've as advanced as you say you are?"

Evie knew she was just fucking with her, trying to get her to flinch. "You've seen the evidence."

"I have. Do not contact us again until there has been a change. These pointless conversations are a waste of the Sanctuary's time."

She had to do her best not to raise her voice and tell the frigid alien where to shove her waste when the ship's proximity alert went off. The image of the Sil disappeared and Evie ran from the room. A proximity alert wouldn't register the Sil ships coming in, which meant it must be something else. As she dashed from the room, she turned the corner and caught up with Cas and the rest of the bridge crew who had been at the party sprinting for the nearest hypervator. Keeping up with them was undemanding. "What happened?" she yelled.

"A ship just came out of an undercurrent right beside the planet," Cas said as they reached the hypervator.

An unknown ship could only mean one thing. And their weapons weren't ready yet. "Athru?" she asked.

He shook his head. "No. It's a Coalition ship."

4

The doors to the bridge opened on chaos. The warning claxons blared while the crew scrambled to their stations. Cas assumed since things had been relatively quiet lately, the second shift weren't at their posts like they should have been. Except for Zaal. The Untuburu was unperturbed as ever, his gaze locked on his controls as he worked the problem. Just as Cas, Evie, Samiya, River, and Ronde stepped on the bridge, Ensigns Olguin and Handel jumped back up from the stations they'd just occupied, moving out of the way for the more seasoned officers. The newly-promoted Lieutenant Tileah entered through the other door to the bridge, taking her station at tactical. Cas's second-in-command, Hank Graydon, stood with his arms crossed at the first officer's chair, staring at the screen before them.

"You're not going to believe this," he said as everyone took their stations.

Cas glanced to the screen for the first time to see a familiar shape growing larger on the screen. It *was* a Coalition ship. "Identification?"

"Markings show *USCS Hiawatha*," Tileah said. "She's a warship. Or she was."

Cas exchanged glances with Evie, who had taken the specialist's position on the bridge. Her eyes flashed at him.

27

Volf. The *Hiawatha* had been her old posting. "What do you mean *was?*"

"Readings show the ship has been—modified," Zaal said. "The primary propulsion drive has been altered in a configuration I'm not familiar with. And the superstructure is covered in non-Coalition construction materials such as durax and heavy pyron."

"Sargan tech," Cas grumbled. He was well familiar with the types of construction materials the Sargans used, having ferried it back and forth on more than one occasion. Sometimes when his old ship had needed repairs, he didn't have a choice but to use their less-than-reliable materials.

"Sir, the Sil ships in orbit have all locked their weapons on the *Hiawatha*," Zaal said. "They're preparing to fire."

"Tell them to stand down!" Cas yelled. He didn't need the Sil blowing the *Hiawatha* out of the sky before they knew who was even aboard. If it was the Sargans, perhaps some were humans that had been in the Commonwealth and had survived when the Athru attacked. Much like the Coalition, the Sargan Commonwealth was made up of many different species, and humans had been a big part of that. He'd always assumed the Athru had gone after them just as hard, but what if they hadn't? What if that's where most humans sought refuge?

"They're not acknowledging our hails. It seems my attempts at communication—"

"I'll take care of it." Evie activated her station. "Sil ships, this is the advanced human *Diazal*. Do not fire on that ship until we know who is aboard. This is a direct request from me, personally." She rolled her eyes at Cas.

"They're standing down," Zaal replied.

Cas shook his head, taking the captain's chair. "Lieutenant, bring us up to the *Hiawatha*, let's put *Tempest* between us and all those Sil ships. To at least show them we're not a threat for the time being."

"How do we know that ship isn't full of Athru?" Hank asked.

He didn't know, but he didn't think the Athru were this sloppy. Bringing an old, broken-down ship deep into Sil territory to face off against hundreds of Sil ships? Not the best plan of action. "Are there any indications of any other ships?" Cas asked.

"None. As far as we can tell it is alone," Zaal replied.

The hypervator doors opened behind them and Zenfor stepped on to the bridge, but she kept to the back. Cas let her be, assuming she was just curious about this new ship. They all were. He shrugged. "Okay. Send them a comm. Let's see what they have to say."

"Aye," Zaal said. "The comm is open."

Cas stood and straightened his shirt. "*Hiawatha*, this is Captain Caspian Robeaux of the *USCS Tempest*. Please identify yourselves and your purpose here."

The screen flicked to life and Cas almost stumbled back because he thought he'd seen a ghost. Before him stood the weathered face of a man he never thought he'd see again. The man who was responsible for all the misery and destruction in Cas's life. The former Admiral Daniel Rutledge.

"No," Evie whispered.

"Well, well. Looks like you finally made captain after all," the grizzled man said. "I always said you couldn't keep a good officer down. Good for you, son." A smile spread across Rutledge's face. Though he was eighteen years older than when Cas had last seen him, he didn't look any frailer. Despite pushing eighty, he looked stronger than ever, as if he could go head-to-head with a bull and come out on top. He wore a modified version of the Coalition uniform, though the sleeves had been torn off to reveal his massive, muscled arms. His face was rough, his beard completely gray, and he'd gone bald, but it suited him. It made him look meaner. But the biggest difference was his right eye had been replaced with a cybernetic implant that glowed green. He'd done nothing to try and make it look like a normal, human eye. It seemed like he wanted to accentuate the fact that it wasn't natural, though it tracked seamlessly with his other eye.

"Evie, tell the Sil to lock weapons and destroy that ship," Cas said through gritted teeth. His fingernails cut into his palms and his breathing had shallowed. He was close to seething. How could Rutledge be here? Cas glanced at Samiya, she'd told him not to trust the info they'd received on Rutledge's "death", but he hadn't listened. He'd wanted it to be true too much. Still, she seemed as dumbfounded as he was, staring up at the screen with her mouth agape. By some miracle, he'd managed to survive the Athru attack. But coming here would be the last mistake he'd ever make.

"Why is it you're always in such a hurry to kill everyone?" Rutledge asked, unperturbed by Cas's order. "Don't you even want to know how I managed to get past the Sil border?"

Cas gritted his teeth. No, he wanted to blast the *Hiawatha* into a billion tiny pieces and then burn those in Thislea's sun. *That* would give him satisfaction more than anything else. Cas turned to see Zenfor standing almost right behind the command chairs and he took a step back. Her eyes were on fire and her normally reserved and composed demeanor was anything but. Her face was flushed so that it appeared more purple than the normal bluish color and a snarl covered her face like he'd never seen before. If Cas thought *he* was mad, it couldn't hold a candle to how Zenfor looked at the moment.

"Ah, I'm glad to see you're still working together," Rutledge said. "It looks like all that preparation wasn't for nothing after all. I knew you just needed a little encouragement." The smile left his face and Cas could have sworn Rutledge's muscles flexed.

"How did you breach the Sil defense net? Our detection methods would have seen you coming long before you reached our space." Though the words from Zenfor's mouth came out clear, there was an undercurrent of pure loathing beneath them.

"Not when you have one of these." Rutledge nodded to someone off-screen.

"Captain, the ship has disappeared from our scanners," Zaal said. "I believe they've entered a time bubble, if I'm reading this correctly."

"You are, Commander." Rutledge nodded again.

"The ship has returned to normal space," Zaal said. He looked up at Cas and the normally serene hard-light projection that was Zaal's face was now one of worry. It always unnerved Cas when Zaal changed his facial expressions. It meant something was very wrong.

"What the hell do you want, Daniel? And where did you get that technology?" Cas demanded.

"Daniel, huh? I guess you feel like now that the Coalition is in disarray, the chain of command isn't important anymore." Rutledge narrowed his eyes.

Cas's hands returned to fists once again. "What chain of command? You were relieved of your rank. You're a *criminal*."

"Ah," Rutledge said, warning in his voice. "I'd be careful who I was calling a criminal if I were you. *Mister* Robeaux." He took a breath and seemed to reset himself. "I'm here because I detected a buildup of Sil forces in this sector. That, combined with the Athru forces retreating along the Sil border led me to believe there had been a shift in the balance of power. Turns out I was right. Imagine my surprise to find the very same ship I sent out on a mission eighteen years ago back home again." He looked over the crew. "Though it seems most of you, unlike me, are immune to the effects of time for whatever reason." His eyes landed on Samiya, who continued to stare at him. "Commander."

"Rutledge." There was no emotion in her voice and Cas couldn't guess what she was feeling. Samiya had also lost an eye, but she'd never had hers replaced. Was she looking at his augmentation, or, more likely, was she trying to comprehend seeing her old commanding officer in the flesh again?

"If I didn't know better, I would think I'd have seen a ghost," he added. "Next thing I know, Captain Soon will come strolling on to your bridge."

"Enough of this. How did you get your worthless hands on Athru technology?" Zenfor growled, stepping forward.

Rutledge addressed her. "Salvage operation. Eighteen years is a long time. Athru ships can still be disabled by natural phenomena, or old gravitic mines they aren't aware of. We found one adrift near KPX Four, having succumbed to a quantum eddy. Their negators had failed and the entire crew was nothing but paint for the walls. We took it, studied it, and had it installed and working within a year."

"Typical human, just take whatever you want, even if it's not yours," Zenfor said.

"Listen *sweetie*, this is war. So yeah, we're going to take whatever we need to survive." He stared Zenfor down, but Cas's eyes had gone wide at the word *sweetie*. No doubt Rutledge was enjoying this turnabout in situations, given the last time they met, Zenfor had humiliated him in his jail cell. He could see her physically growing angrier. If Cas didn't do something, she could very well tear the bridge in two.

Cas stepped over so he was in front of Zenfor. Even though she was much taller than him, it put a physical barrier between her and the screen. It was better than nothing. "Cut the shit, Daniel. What do you want? With your technology you could have just stayed in the time bubble and we never would have known. The only reason you revealed yourself is because you want something."

"You're right," Rutledge said. "I want to win this war. And despite my excellent crew and all my enhancements, I can't do it alone. I will do anything to be victorious here, which means I need you."

Cas stared straight ahead. He didn't like this. Something about it felt off. Even if he could trust the man, he wouldn't want his help. Not after everything he'd done. Plus, it wasn't as if one more ship added to the cause would make any difference, even if it was a warship. "Fortunately for us, we don't need *you*. So, you can take your fancy toys, turn around and disappear before I decide keeping you alive is too much of a risk and send the Sil after you." Cas didn't care what Rutledge said, adding him into the mix was adding fire to a powder keg. If the rest of the Sil found out who he was they would probably kill him for retribution, and then Cas for agreeing to work with him again. He had a very tenuous balance here, and he needed to protect that at all costs.

"Are you sure about that?" Rutledge asked. "Nothing you need, like say, reconnaissance?"

"Not from you," Cas said, doing his best not to blow up in front of everyone.

Rutledge nodded, his lower lip protruding. "See if it were me, having been a soldier most of my life, I'd be a bit wary about charging head-first into an enemy camp I knew nothing about. They could have only a few patrols in there, or they could be walled up like a fortress. But I guess if you wouldn't find information like that valuable…"

"Cut the comm," Cas said. The screen went blank. He looked at his bridge staff. "How the hell does he know what we need? Has he been listening in on our conversations?"

"I don't detect any foreign signals interfering in our comms," Zaal said.

Cas looked at Tileah. "Nothing on my end. I don't know how he's doing it."

"I hate to say this," Samiya said. "But that might be his experience talking. He may not *need* to hear our conversations to know what's going on. We're building up all these forces and we have yet to attack. What would you assume?"

Cas fumed. He hated Rutledge having the upper hand. Out of everyone in the goddamn universe, why did it have to be *him*?

"Conference room," Cas said.

5

Cas stormed into the conference room, followed by Hank, Samiya, Evie, Zenfor, and Zaal. He'd left Tileah in charge on the bridge while they figured this out. He took his seat first, scanning the faces of everyone else as they gathered around the table. Zenfor, the most enraged of them all, stood to the side, the anger radiating off her in waves. She was feeling what Cas wanted to feel, but he had to keep a level head about this. He couldn't let his history with Rutledge, or all the emotions attached to the man override his better judgment. He had to be stronger than that. He needed to fit into this role of captain, and that meant staying calm and cool-headed.

"Opinions?" he asked once everyone was in their seats.

Hank moved to say something but Zenfor's booming voice drowned him out before the words left his lips. "You're a fool if you do anything other than annihilate him," she said. "Were this a Sil ship he'd be dragged into a judgment chamber, sentenced, and executed. The evidence is undeniable."

Cas couldn't disagree with her, but that wasn't how they operated. As much as he wanted to, he couldn't just execute Rutledge, especially not if he had valuable intel to share with them. "Anyone else?" Cas asked.

"This won't be the popular opinion," Samiya said. "But if he has something we can use, don't we have a duty to accept his help? Especially if it can help us win this battle? As far as we know, the Athru are one step ahead of us most of the time. This evens the playing field in a way they won't be expecting." She looked supplicant saying it, as if she'd done something wrong.

"Yeah, unless the Athru sent him," Hank said.

"They wouldn't do that," Evie replied. "They would have killed him given the chance. They're adamant about destroying all humans, no matter the cost."

"And what if he's the exception? We could be inviting an enemy right into our midst." Hank's stare was penetrating.

"I hate to say this, but I think Evie is right. As long as I knew the man, he only had one goal: the safety and security of the Coalition. I don't think he'd ever work with anyone else to undermine that. His methods may have been horrible—" Cas looked at Zenfor as he spoke "—but he loved the Coalition. I can't believe he'd be an agent."

"Eighteen years is a long time, Captain. You never know what might have happened," Hank said. "From what Samiya told me, he's ruthless in getting his way. Isn't that what you said?" Hank turned to Samiya, who seemed lost in thought.

After a beat she looked up. "Yes. If someone couldn't do a job, he'd remove them and go down the line until he found someone who could. But there's something else to consider too. Who else is aboard that ship?"

Cas had considered this as well. The *Hiawatha* was an *Exeter* class ship, which meant it could hold up to three thousand people in a pinch. That many couldn't survive on board for long without putting into a port-of-call, not without significant upgrades to the ship. And based on its appearance, there was no telling what Rutledge might have done to augment his vessel. Cas turned to Evie. "Could other Athru vessels detect him in that time bubble?"

A pained look came across her face. "I'm not sure. I'll have to ask my mother. But my feeling is they can hide from each other as well as from everyone else if they wish."

"I can't believe we're actually considering this," Hank said. "The man betrayed the Coalition, and if you've forgotten, at least two people at this very table!" It was clear he was getting as worked up as Zenfor, who continued to stare at Cas with accusing eyes. He found it hard to look away.

"Did he though?" Zaal spoke up for the first time.

"Excuse me?"

"Did the former Admiral Rutledge betray the Coalition? If I understand the sequence of events correctly, he anticipated a threat to the Coalition and implemented a plan to counter that threat. Now we can argue the morals of his plan, but ultimately, his desire was to protect the Coalition."

"Look," Cas said before Hank could start in on Zaal. "We're not going to sit here debating the morality of what's happened in the past. I think we can all agree Rutledge betrayed the spirit of the Coalition if not the letter of the law. The fact was, he was willing to kill to obtain his goals. And I see nothing in him that would make me think he's changed in the last eighteen years. Do you?" Samiya shook her head. "So, then we need to decide: is it worth the risk of trusting him to obtain what could be a crucial piece of technology, or do we try to go on our own?"

"Captain?" the voice came from Cas's personal comm.

He huffed, tapping it. "Go ahead, Xax."

"Captain, could you please report to sickbay?" his chief medical officer asked.

"I'm in the middle of something here. Is it important?"

"I'm afraid so."

Cas debated leaving it a moment, but gave in. "I'll be there in a minute." He ended the comm. "Hank, can you try to come to some kind of consensus on this? I'll be back as soon as I can."

"Yes, sir," Hank replied. Cas noticed Zenfor's color had returned to its regular hue, but she was giving him a strange look. What was that? Fear? He couldn't be sure, so he pushed it to the side until he could figure out what the hell could be so important down in sickbay.

***

Sickbay. Somehow, Zenfor knew it was bad news. And they were up here, arguing about something that should have not required any debate. Besides the fact this person had been convicted as a criminal in their own courts, he was an untrustworthy murderer. The worst humanity could offer, and the exact kind of person the Sil had assumed made up most of the people in the Coalition. It was what they always warned against: someone so self-centered they would do anything to achieve their goals. Half the reason she'd been willing to come on board was because she hadn't seen any evidence of that in the *Tempest's* crew. The people here were generally selfless, with aspirations to improve themselves and the lives of others, not violate their own rules for personal gain. She didn't care what they said about his motivations, working with Rutledge was dangerous, and if it were up to her, she would have already destroyed his ship and collected the body.

"You're all a gaggle of idiots," she interrupted whoever was talking. "This should not even be discussed."

"I agree," Hank said. "We're better off without him." He turned to Gysan, the one Zenfor had shoved against the wall for having been on Rutledge's ship. "I can't believe you're actually suggesting we let him help."

Gysan shook her head. "I know. He doesn't deserve it. But Hank…think about what one of those devices could mean for this cause. We'd finally have an advantage over those bastards. I don't like Rutledge any more than you do. But the Athru are worse. Much worse." She turned to Diazal. "No offense." Diazal didn't respond.

"Based on probabilities, Mr. Rutledge is only offering us part of the story. There is a good chance he has other capabilities he hasn't brought to light yet. I am not a card player, but if I were, I'd say this is his opening bet," Zaal said, impassive as ever. If there was one person Zenfor didn't understand, it was the Untuburu and his desire to fit in with the humans. Why make yourself to look like everyone else around you just for their comfort?

"Are you saying if we refuse, he might up the ante?" Hank asked.

"No," Diazal said. "We're not going to play his game. Either we agree we're going to trust him to help us by allowing us to use this technology, or we find another way to accomplish our goals. He's not going to goad us into his machinations." She seemed serious. Zenfor could only conclude she was as angry as Caspian about Rutledge's betrayal; she just wasn't showing it as much.

"What are we supposed to do, take a vote?" Hank asked.

"No," Zenfor offered.

"I say we can't let this opportunity pass us by. We might not get another," Samiya replied. "Yes."

"I wasn't serious, but okay," Hank said. "No."

"I agree with the commander. It is a serious tactical advantage," Zaal said. "Yes."

Everyone, including Zenfor looked at Evie. "It doesn't matter what we say," she said. "It's up to the captain. All we can do is present him with all viewpoints."

"Does that mean your vote is yes?" Hank asked.

Zenfor made a noise deep in her throat. "This bickering is pointless. Sit here and debate this all you want, it changes nothing. If you decide to work with him, I guarantee we will all regret it." She stormed from the room, barely waiting for the doors to open for her. She bypassed the bridge and went straight to the hypervator that could be used to access the conference room directly. If she had to return to the bridge and look at that ship on the screen again she might lose it this time. As it was, she'd done a fair job keeping herself together. If they weren't going to take care of this threat, she would have to do it herself. There was no other choice.

6

The corridors were busier than usual since the Sil had sent over teams of their engineers to help improve *Tempest's* systems. Due to Zenfor's upgrades while they were on the Athru planet, most of the big structural work was already done and left alone. Cas wasn't sure how he would have handled it if they needed to strip the ship down to its crossbeams and started over from scratch.

He couldn't get over the strange look she'd given him when he left for sickbay. He'd never seen that look before. Was it because she was angry at Rutledge's presence, or was there something else? Maybe he'd ask her about it if he felt the timing was right.

Cas skirted the edge of a Sil team working on one of the power conduits—neither acknowledging the other—and made his way to the primary sickbay entrance. Inside, Box was hunched over one of the consoles, cleaning whatever alcohol he'd poured all over himself out of his inner workings. Cas expected one of his trademark smart comments to greet him but when Box noticed him, Cas knew something was off. His eyes were dimmer than usual. That only meant something very bad. "What's wrong?"

"Captain." Cas turned to see Xax, standing at the entrance to her office adjacent to the main sickbay. "May we speak in private?"

Cas glanced at Box, then back at Xax and followed her in. He didn't allow them to settle. Now was not the time to tiptoe around their problems. "What is it? Is it a malfunction? Is he losing synaptic response? Maybe if I—" Xax's eyes narrowed at him.

"Captain, are you referring to—?"

Cas motioned to Box. "Him. That's why you wanted me down here, right? Something's gone wrong?"

Xax glanced at Box through her window that shared a wall between the two spaces. He feverishly scrubbed at his superstructure. "Box is fine," she said. "I've just returned from Engineering. It's Commander Sesster."

Cas's heart fell. He was relieved there was nothing wrong with Box, but he wasn't happy to hear Sesster might have a new problem. He'd been getting regular updates on him and everything had remained constant ever since they'd returned from Athru space. "Go ahead."

"I've started detecting cellular degradation all over his body. I'm afraid his condition is getting worse. If we don't find a way to wake him soon, he will die." Though her voice remained even and professional, Cas caught the hint of a twitch in her upper left eye.

"Xax, I don't mean to be insensitive, but how the hell do we do that? We've tried everything. At least, everything I know to try. You told me yourself you'd exhausted all of your remedies. What else is left?"

"Taking him back to be in the presence of other Claxians." She said it with such confidence, like it was a simple matter of moving him across the hall, despite the fact he was four meters tall and probably two hundred kilograms.

Cas scoffed. "I'm not sure you know this or not, but there are about a billion Athru between us and the only other place in the universe with Claxians." He bit his lip. "I'm sorry. That was unprofessional. I know I don't have to tell you the obstacles. But it's just not possible. Not until we've found a way to drive the Athru from Coalition space. And we can't do that until we have the full strength of the Sil fleet behind us."

She remained clinical. "I'm just giving you the facts. If Sesster stays on this ship another week, he'll be dead."

Cas cursed under his breath. "What good will taking him back to Claxia Prime do? Other than place him in the presence of other Claxians?"

Xax tapped a button on her desk and a 3-D image came up between them. It showed what looked like one of the Claxian tentacles in great detail. Cas could see the millions of nerve endings on the appendage. "The Claxians have an intricate neural network built into their bodies. Much like a human bloodstream carries red blood cells, it carries electrical impulses through their bodies at tremendous rates. It is how they prefer all their interactions, in-person and with physical contact. It's how they live and how they mate. It bypasses all known forms of communication, and yes, that even includes their ability to read and transmit thoughts. Quite frankly, it is an amazing evolutionary development."

Cas thought back to Sesster as he had been, all alone in his cradle in Engineering. Keeping the ship moving, making sure the crew could get to one place after another. All the while sacrificing his well-being, his mental health. "It must have been torture for him. All alone on this ship."

"I can't imagine it was pleasant. Though while he was in good health physically, his mental condition was deteriorating. I think when *Tempest* returned the first time under Volf's command, the mental stress finally got to him, and his mind went into a protection mode. But he's been this way for too long, and without the mind, the body just cannot survive any longer. The only way I know to wake him is to return him home. Every artificial remedy has been fruitless."

Zenfor. She had known this news was about Sesster. And Cas had made her a promise that he would get Sesster back home before something terrible happened. Which meant unless he was willing to let Sesster die, he might not have a choice but to accept Rutledge's help. At least with the time bubble technology they might be able to find a way to get Sesster home before it was too late.

"You say he has a week?"

Xax shook her head. "Maybe less. The cellular degradation is accelerating. Regardless of what happens, he will need rehabilitation services on Claxia Prime in order to regain his full functionality."

Cas stood. "Thanks for giving me a heads up. I'll…keep you updated. We might have a potential solution, but don't hold me to it yet."

Xax stood as well. "I know you'll do everything you can." Cas turned to leave. "If I may," she added, "the crew thinks you're doing a good job. Morale seems to be improving, despite our circumstances."

He was glad to know he wouldn't be facing a mutiny anytime soon. Deserting the Coalition seemed like a pretty minor thing when the entire future of their people was in jeopardy. "Thanks. That helps." Cas exited her office and approached Box, using one of the sonic brushes to blow liquid from his servos. "You heard?"

"She just uploaded the report into the computers. I download a backup copy of everything that comes through sickbay." Box scrubbed harder at his joint. "Damn scorb."

"Serves you right for making an ass of yourself over there. What were you thinking?"

"I was thinking: Box, these kinds of days don't come very often. If there's something you want to do, do it now. So that's what I did."

Cas arched an eyebrow. "You've always wanted to be doused in alcohol?"

"See, if you watched any net dramas at all you'd get it. When the hero wins a big race or even the guy who helped the hero, everyone comes around and celebrates by opening as many bottles of scorb as they can and dumping them all over each other. It's like a scorb orgy. I decided it was high time for a Box orgy."

Cas pinched the bridge of his nose. "Those are two words that should never be uttered together ever again."

"Plus, how many other machines do you know who have earned the Coalition medal of honor? None, that's how many." He stopped scrubbing and polished the medal affixed to his chest again. It reflected the lights from sickbay.

"I need to tell you something," Cas said, trying to ignore Box's self-indulgence. "That ship—it belongs to Rutledge. He wasn't killed on Eight. He's been hiding out in Sargan territory."

Box stopped what he was doing and stared at Cas. "What's he doing here?"

"He says he wants to help. Claims to have taken some of the Athru tech from their ships. He can make his own time bubble." Cas glanced around to make sure no one else was close enough to listen in. Nurse Menkel was on the other side of the sickbay and Xax was still in her office.

"Do you believe him?"

"He managed to get past the Sil border undetected, and you know how strict they are about monitoring their territory. Unless he managed to coerce the Sil to let him in and the probability of that scenario was one-hundred percent impossible."

"Agreed," Box said. "What are you going to do?"

Cas shook his head. "I don't want him involved. I don't even want him *alive*. I thought about stalling him out but given this situation with Sesster and the fact we're at a standstill with the Sil…I just don't know."

"You should talk to Captain Jann about it. Your thoughts are always clearer after one of your late-night trysts."

Cas stared at Box. "And just what the hell do you know about my…evening schedule?"

"Nothing! It was only a supposition. You're dating her, she's dating you…you spend time together off-duty. One can only assume you're making the beast with two backs at night."

Cas massaged his temples. "Please don't call it that."

"I'm only repeating what is a widely-accepted human euphemism. Don't get all prudish on me." He resumed cleaning his joints with the sonic brush.

"You haven't started up your experiments again?"

Box didn't even flinch. "Nope. Dead in the water. As ordered."

"Good. Make sure it stays that way. And leave the genetic manipulation to Esterva."

"Whatever you say, boss." Cas wasn't sure if Box was humoring him or not. Children of disparate species weren't common, and those who did survive often couldn't have their own children. Cas understood the desire from multi-species couples (and triples, etc) but he considered it a disservice to the child. Evie seemed to be the exception. He wasn't sure if it was because of the Athru's superior genetic skill, or if she'd just been lucky, but she'd managed to be a perfect fusion of the traits of both her parents; to the point it enhanced her physical and mental attributes beyond the source DNA. It was something that no other multi-species coupling had ever produced.

Cas left Box to his cleaning, making a mental note to send Vrij back into Box's room just for a routine sweep. Just in case.

7

Zenfor stomped down the corridor, not bothering to hide her anger. Those that saw her coming jumped out of her way, and those that didn't were rewarded by being knocked over or to the side with the swipe of a hand or collision of a shoulder. She didn't care. This ridiculous notion the captain had entertained had to be stopped. If she didn't do something, they could very well end up inviting this *man* on board. And Zenfor knew in her core it was a bad idea.

He was supposed to be in jail. Cas had *assured* her he would sit in a small cell for the rest of his life and rot there. And she was content with that. While Sil doctrine dictated he be killed for his actions, she liked the idea of allowing him to suffer another thirty or forty of their years, wasting away behind a cell, unable to experience anything beyond its four walls. According to human tradition, it was a life of misery, one many prisoners took their own lives to avoid. *That* would have been a fitting end.

Instead, the man who had betrayed her people, who had overseen a mission that had killed ten Sil civilians, including her second *Gla* Messtak, was captaining his own ship, roaming the galaxy as if nothing had happened. And that smug look on his face had told her everything she needed to know: he wasn't sorry. Not that it mattered if he were, he was a dead man either way. But at least to see some sort of change in the man would have given her greater confidence about the people she had aligned herself with. No Sil would act as Rutledge had. Most were much more like the crew of the *Tempest*, willing to accept responsibility for their deeds, regardless of the cost. But this man, this Rutledge, had broken his own system of rules, flaunted them in front of others and then not paid the appropriate price.

But he would pay now.

Zenfor entered the Bay, scanning the room for an empty shuttle. A series of the mid-size ones sat off to the side, the cowling on some of their engine components removed. She'd forgotten they had been upgrading the shuttles as well, in the event they were necessary for evacuations or support craft. Three Sil crew teams stood in different areas around the shuttles, using their expertise to enhance the shuttles' capability far beyond what the Coalition species could manage. Zenfor stood off to the side, not wanting to engage any of the teams in further insults. She knew she was a pariah and didn't need every Sil she to remind her that.

At first it had been hard. But at some point she'd become used to the idea, proud of it even, until she got into skirmishes with the other Sil regarding her status as an outsider. If there was one thing the Sil didn't like, it was those who violated their doctrines. Zenfor had been around humans long enough to realize those doctrines were rooted in millennia-old superstition. And she had no use for them anymore. The only upside was the other Sil were the only ones on board who could match her strength and give her a physical challenge. It was fortunate Xax was so proficient in repairing Sil biology.

"Come to watch?"

Zenfor turned to see Saturina Jann, standing off to her right with her arms crossed, staring at the Sil teams as they worked. "No."

"Me either. But seeing as they are taking apart every ship we have, I don't have much of a choice. I don't guess you could ask them if they could at least let my people *watch* what they're doing? If something goes wrong out there, I need to know we can fix it on our own."

"Nothing I say will make a difference," Zenfor said. "They consider us both inferior now."

"So that's how it is, huh?" She continued to stare at the shuttle teams.

Caspian had told Zenfor of Jann's resilience, especially in the face of dire circumstances. He'd described her as one of the most stalwart people he knew. "That ship out there," Zenfor nodded, beyond the Bay opening, even though nothing was visible other than a small section of her home planet, its purple hue glowing in the darkness of space. "Its captain is Daniel Rutledge."

Jann finally faced her. "What?"

"He should be dead," Zenfor growled. "I should have killed him the moment I set eyes on him."

"You're serious," Jann said.

"I came in here to steal a shuttle. I planned to fly over there, tear through his bulkheads and crush his windpipe between my fingers." She stared out at the planet beyond, willing herself to calm down.

Jann looked at her expectantly.

"But that is what they would do, isn't it?" she said, glancing at the Sil working on the ships. "They would want to exact revenge, to do whatever was necessary to kill those that had wronged them. They are ruthless in how they follow their prescribed roles, unable to waver. Unable to make their own decisions about their lives. They are tasked as warriors, they kill. If they are tasked as engineers they repair. And if they are tasked as leaders, they sit and squander all their time until they

50

are free from obligation." Upon seeing her people, her fury had been redirected.

"I'm not familiar with—"

"It is such a battle," she continued. "Maintaining this balance without guidelines. When I was a Consul, I knew what I had to do when I had to do it. And now…" She took a deep breath, the first she'd taken since learning Rutledge was still alive. "I refuse to be governed by my hatred of that man." She turned to Jann, who studied her, her face impassive. She saw what Cas liked about this woman—she didn't rush to judgment. "*I* choose how to respond. And I am done fighting this fight."

Leaving Jann standing there with a quizzical look on her face Zenfor stormed back into the corridors. Killing Rutledge would do them no good, other than to make her feel better. If Caspian decided they needed his help, she would abide by the decision. Leave the dutiful behavior to the rest of her people; there were more than enough Sil whose job it was to seek out threats and eliminate them. But that wasn't her role. Not anymore.

Zenfor made her way to Engineering in the hopes to take her mind off her people. She was proud of the fact the Sil had stayed away, not having anything further to contribute to the upgrades in this section, and she wondered what they thought when they knew a Consul had also acted as architect, engineer, and designer. No, she didn't *care* what they thought. What was done was done and there was no returning back. Her decision had been clear, and it had been the right one. Returning to Sil society would be suffocating. She couldn't fit back into a space she had outgrown.

"Morning," Lieutenant Tyler said as she passed, too chipper as always. She'd meant to avoid his station but being so lost in her thoughts she'd strolled right by. Every day it was the same greeting, and every day he was met with the same response from her: silence. It was an arcane tradition: stating the time of day on a starship which had no days, only hours. She refused to participate, to the point where it had become an expected ritual. If she *did* respond, his mind might explode.

"Hey, wait up," Tyler called. Zenfor grumbled to herself and stopped, turning to face him. "What's wrong?"

"What?" she asked.

"Something's the matter. I can tell. You're carrying yourself differently."

"I don't *carry* myself. This is how I ambulate."

Tyler shook his head. "No. Something's happened. What is it?"

Zenfor worked to contain her temper. "I am not in the business of involving other people in my personal affairs."

This produced a smile on Tyler's face. "Yeah. I know. You've never been one to express much, other than anger. But this is bothering you."

Zenfor was unnerved with how easily he seemed to be able to read her. She did her best to remain as impassive as possible most of the time. She didn't need other people concerning themselves with what were clearly her own personal issues. She had been slipping. Too much time around the humans, who, according to them, wore their *hearts on their sleeves.* "It's nothing I can't handle by myself."

"I have no doubt about that. But consider this, if you share your problem, you might find it easier to handle after speaking about it."

"I don't agree."

He nodded. "No problem. Just know if you ever do, I'm here to listen. I know things have been harder since the crew returned, but it's going to be okay." He gave her a soft smile and headed back to his station.

Zenfor watched him go for a moment, then headed to her own station. Tyler was a competent person, and a good engineer. She was glad he'd been there to assist in rebuilding the ship. In those very quiet moments, one extra voice was okay. Not that she'd ever give him the satisfaction of telling him that. He didn't deserve it that much.

But the one voice she craved to hear, the one who had broken through to her and provided her with comfort and solace in her darkest moments, was the one voice she feared she would never hear again. And after ten long years, she was beginning to give up hope.

***

Evie strolled into the simulator room and was struck with a sense of longing. It happened every time she came in here. She had to keep telling herself she'd never be able to go anywhere on the ship if she kept allowing herself to be overrun with all these memories, but the simulator was a little different. It had been where she had first dropped her guard around Laura. And where she'd first taken a peek into the woman's soul. There had been a time when she'd vowed never to come back in here, but this was a new start for her. A new beginning. She didn't want to face the Athru without knowing the full range of her capabilities, so she'd been coming in here to test her own personal limits once a day since they'd settled into orbit around Thislea. But no matter how many times she walked through that door, she was always struck with a wave of guilt and loss. She only hoped the feelings would ebb in time. Because even though part of her didn't want them to go—they were proof of something real and tangible—they could also be debilitating. She'd seen Cas go through something similar and she wasn't about to make the same journey.

"Activate Evie strength program zero one seven," she told the computer. All around her hard-light projections appeared, creating the appearance of large rocks and boulders, as if she was in the middle of a quarry. She glanced up. The blue sky that had replaced the barren room ended about twenty feet above her, which turned into black. It wasn't smart to forget this was just a simulation; most people needed a visual cue as a reminder.

"Let's start with the ninety kilos on a thirty-degree slope." She felt good after burning the sword. Liberated. Her previous record had been ninety-five kilos, but she usually started lighter than that to warm up. Not today.

Before her a hard-light projection of a rocky slope appeared along with boulders at the top. The first one rolled down on its own and Evie braced herself, holding her hands out. The rolling rock slammed into her, but she managed to stop it without too much effort. Evie rolled it to the side. "Increase to ninety-five kilos." Another rock launched itself down the hillside, tumbling much faster than the first one as its weight was compounded by the slope of the hill. Evie grimaced and braced for the impact, which came in no short order, sending her skidding back. But she'd stopped it. "Increase to a hundred kilos." She rolled the ninety-five to the side.

The rock at the top of the slope increased in size a bit before launching itself down the hill. Evie could swear she felt the vibrations in the room of the massive boulder still bouncing down toward her at a breakneck speed. For a moment she thought this might not have been a good idea as she tried to calculate the force of impact. But instead she bore down and placed both hands out in front of her as the boulder slammed into them, cracking right down the middle and shattering all around her. Evie lifted her head and confirmed she was still in the simulation; that had felt so real. Above her, the sky ended just as it should. She glanced around at the rubble surrounding her and felt a swell of pride. Her hands weren't even swollen. She turned back to the mountain, a wicked grin on her lips. "Increase to two hundred kilos."

"Is it true?" Evie spun in place to see Esterva had stepped into the simulator without announcing herself. "Did you destroy that sword?"

"Wha—?" Evie said before the ground rumbled. She turned to see the mammoth boulder screaming down the hill at the two of them faster than she could register. "End simulation!" The boulder disappeared along with the mountain, and the landscape all around them. They stood in a plain gray room. Damn. She'd been feeling really good too. She turned back to Esterva. "What are you doing here?"

"Please tell me you didn't. Tell me you're not that impulsive," Esterva said, concern on her gray face.

"As a matter of fact, I did. And it's not impulsive. That thing was cursed. I needed to be rid of it." Evie had lost her taste for training. Something about her mother watching her work put her off doing anything further today. She walked around Esterva and back out into the corridor. Her mother followed.

"I didn't tell you about the sword for you to go and destroy it," she said. "That was the last connection you had to your father. It was the last thing I had—"

"It was mine to do with as I pleased," Evie said. "I don't need a lecture from you about sentimentality."

Esterva drew herself up beside Evie. "No. You don't. You're right, it *was* yours to do with. I wish you'd spoken to me about it first."

"I don't owe you an explanation. And I don't need your permission," Evie said. "You're lucky I'm still talking to you." Esterva didn't reply, but she stayed in step beside her. Evie wasn't sure where she was going; she'd planned to spend at least an hour in the simulator until Cas figured out what he wanted to do about Rutledge. During the meeting she had tried to keep an open mind about the situation. The last time she'd seen Admiral Rutledge was when the public video service had shown him being led away to imprisonment. It felt like a thousand years ago, sitting back in Cas's quarters watching the newsfeed. After she'd learned what he'd done, she'd wanted nothing more to do with the man. To her, it was better if he stayed locked up forever. But this situation had forced him back into her life and she wasn't sure how she felt about it. Rutledge had put his faith in her, and she'd delivered. But she hadn't known the depth of his treachery at the time. Cas hated him for good reason and Zenfor *really* hated him, but Evie felt like they might be able to leverage this somehow. Maybe they could find a way to use him for once.

"You look lost in thought," Esterva said. Her mother had been overly insistent on trying to connect over the past three weeks and while Evie was happy to have her around, the ship felt a lot smaller these days.

"I'm trying to figure out what to do about this Rutledge situation," she replied.

"I heard." Esterva relaxed her body language, which told Evie she thought she was in safe territory with her daughter. But who would she have heard it from? Had news spread through the ship that fast? "If I'm not mistaken, he claims to have taken Athru technology from one of our ships."

"So he says. He wants to help."

"I will say this, Evelyn. The technology that can create a time bubble is not a simple piece of technology that can be easily removed. And our people do not leave our ships to be harvested by pirates."

"Are you saying we shouldn't trust him?" Evie glanced up at the woman.

Esterva grimaced. "I don't know. But something feels…wrong."

"I don't like it either." The fact Rutledge had just…appeared and was offering this help with little or no strings attached didn't sit right. But at the same time, they were low on options. Evie needed to figure out his endgame. She hadn't known him as well as Cas, or anyone for that matter, but maybe that gave her an edge. She might be able to see this without her opinions being colored by a history with the man.

"I have no doubt you'll figure out how to handle him. You've figured out everything else. In fact, I think you're the key to stopping our people. You're the one thing they don't expect. The thing they haven't prepared for."

Evie rolled her eyes. Putting aside her mother was calling her a "thing" for the time being, she'd heard this spiel before. It seemed the more time they spent together, the more Esterva became convinced Evie was the key to defeating the Athru and frankly it was getting a bit tiresome. "I think I'm going to grab some food," she said, turning and heading toward the mess hall knowing full well Esterva didn't like to eat in there as her food needed to be specially prepared.

Esterva paused. "Then I will see you later."

Evie did her best to ignore the hurt in Esterva's words and instead flashed her a smile and made her way down the corridor. As soon as she was out of view, she released the breath she hadn't realized she'd been holding. A hundred kilos. Maybe she'd try two hundred tomorrow.

8

Cas sat in his chair in the command room, spinning one way until the edge of the chair struck the desk, then spinning the other way until the same thing happened on the other side. All the while his eyes remained glazed over.

"You're going to start making a rut," Hank said.

Cas glanced up. "What?"

"Your chair." Hank pointed to the edge where the fabric had frayed from repeatedly being struck against the desk. Cas hadn't even realized he was doing it; he was lost in thought.

"Oh." Cas didn't care about the chair. He was more concerned about how to handle Rutledge. He'd come back from sickbay to find the conference room, sans Zenfor, locked in a debate about the merits of accepting help from the former admiral. It seemed they hadn't made much progress since he left. Shortly after he realized they weren't getting anywhere, Evie had left for "training"—whatever that meant—and Cas had adjourned the rest of them, retiring back to the command room with Hank to try and work this out.

"Do you think he might leave?" Hank asked. "Maybe he'll make the decision for us."

No way. Rutledge knew exactly what he was doing. "He's getting off on us sweating over here, trying to figure out what to do, I'd bet my map collection on it." Cas leaned forward on

58

his desk. "I'd like to tell that motherfucker to take his time bubble and shove it up his ass."

"You're going to accept his help," Hank said. It wasn't a question, just a straightforward statement, though Cas could hear the defeat in it.

"We have to take every advantage we can get. He knows that, otherwise he wouldn't be here. If Rutledge wasn't one hundred percent sure we'd bring him on board he would have stayed out of Sil territory and never taken the chance. The man doesn't take risks." Cas flopped back in his chair, feeling defeated himself. He'd hoped to never hear the name *Daniel Rutledge* again. But it seemed there were some parts of a person's past that just never went away.

Hank only stared at him, his face hardened by the knowledge they'd have to bring him and his people over if they wanted his help. Rutledge would insist on it; any attempt to get under Cas's skin.

Cas stood, leading Hank back onto the bridge. "Zaal, open the comms to the *Hiawatha*."

"Aye," Zaal replied.

A moment later the image of Rutledge reappeared. "Glad to see you haven't forgotten about me. I was thinking about leaving."

"Cut the bullshit, Daniel. Let's talk about this face to face. Just so I have a proper understanding of your terms."

"Terms? You make it sound like a hostage negotiation." *Not far from it,* Cas thought. "But I'd be happy to come over. It's been quite a while since I've seen another Coalition ship, especially one in as good of condition as yours. Though I can't help but wonder, what happened to Captain Greene?" He allowed the unspoken accusation to hang in the air between them. But Cas wasn't about to take the bait.

"Greene died in the service of the Coalition, defending it with his life. That's more than I can say for a lot of people." The eyes of his crewmates were on him, but he didn't flinch.

"I see," Rutledge replied. "I'll prepare a shuttle and be on my way over in a few minutes. I'll also be bringing two of my crew to accompany me."

"Then they'll stay in the shuttle, in the Bay while you're here," Cas said.

Rutledge's mouth tweaked. "Don't trust your old captain?"

"No one steps on this ship without my authorization and I don't know your crew. But to answer your question: no, I don't." Cas wasn't about to make this into a bickering situation. Rutledge would follow his rules because it suited his cause…for the moment. Cas feared what might happen when that situation changed.

"See you shortly," Rutledge said, and cut the comm.

Cas couldn't help but smile to himself. He'd at least irked the man a little. It seemed time had worn down Rutledge's patience, and that was something Cas could work with.

***

"Do not let him out of your sight. If you need a shift change, make sure you've got double the number of guards on him, got it?" Cas stood in Bay One with Vrij beside him and three more security personnel behind them both.

"I've got it," Vrij replied. "This one—Rutledge—he's slippery."

"He's…determined," Cas replied. "And he's not going to get the best of us. No matter what he thinks." Cas was confident Vrij could disable or subdue Rutledge, given the fact he had a built-in weapon on his body. The only other person that Cas would trust to physically hold the man would be

Zenfor, and that wasn't an option. Not unless he wanted Rutledge dead before he stepped off his shuttle. Though, Saturina had told him she'd seen Zenfor in here not long ago. She'd planned to hijack a shuttle but had changed her mind at the last minute. That gave Cas some hope she might not be as volatile as he thought.

The medium-sized shuttle passed through the force barrier into the Bay, flying low to the deck until it came to an empty space near the end and set down. It was the same type of undercurrent-capable shuttle as the *Tempest* carried, though it had been worn by the ravages of time. One of the primary engine pylons had been replaced with a Sargan booster, and the hull was covered in scratches, marks, and burns. It had probably seen more action than most Coalition ships saw in a lifetime. Cas motioned for Vrij and the security officers to move over beside the doors. They each drew their pulse pistols while Vrij's remained attached to his belt as his mandible blade extricated itself from his back and drew up beside his arm.

Opening with a hiss marking the change in pressure, the door slid away to reveal Rutledge, decked out in what Cas could only describe as renegade gear. While he still had his Coalition uniform shirt on with the sleeves removed, the rest of his clothes were black, and made from what looked like heavy-duty materials. His boots were definitely not Coalition issue. And he sported a bandolier across his chest that held capsules Cas didn't recognize. Behind him stood a two-meter tall Erustiaan, and a member of the Arc-N'gali race. The N'galian was shorter than Rutledge, but not by much. His rough skin was tinted reddish, but with orange tattoo patterns running down under his clothes. Cas couldn't tell if they were natural or not. He also wore a wide-brimmed hat with the top removed for his two eye stalks to poke out of. His other two eyes were hidden deep in sockets on his face.

"Robeaux," Rutledge said, his voice dripping with sarcasm. "I never thought I'd see you in the flesh again. But then, if someone had to survive the destruction of our species, I can't say I'm surprised it's you."

"Y-you will address him as Captain Robeaux." Vrij stepped forward. "Weapons. Now." The other security officers took up their places at the sides of the door, keeping the Erustiaan and Arc-N'gali inside the ship.

Rutledge shrugged and pulled an impressive looking blaster off his hip, handing it to Vrij. "Is...that attached to your back?" He eyed Vrij's mandible. "I've never seen an Ashkasian with such a deformity before."

"I am not Ashkasian. I am Bulaq." Vrij grabbed Rutledge with what Cas considered a fair amount of force, pulling him forward. "I s-said weapons. All."

Rutledge turned to Cas. "Is this what you do now? Collect species? First the Sil and now him?"

"Do as he says, Daniel. Trust me, you don't want to see him use that blade." Rutledge was trying to take ahold of the situation like he always did, and Cas wasn't about to let that happen.

Rutledge forced a grin then reached behind him, removing a smaller, more compact blaster and a foldable blade. Vrij took each and passed them to the security forces. "They will stay. You will follow the captain."

"Hell of a welcome party," Rutledge said.

Cas scoffed. "Oh, I'm sorry. Were you expecting balloons? Maybe a banner? Some testament to the great Daniel Rutledge, savior of the Coalition?" That shut him up. "Let's get this over with." He turned and headed back down the corridor, leading Vrij and Rutledge to the closest hypervator. Cas couldn't help glance back at Rutledge, whose attention was being pulled in all directions by the state of the ship itself. Compared to anything else he'd seen in the past eighteen years, Cas bet it was like stepping back in time for him, connecting him to a place that had long since been destroyed.

"I noticed you made another deal with the Sil. Laska must have done a job on you," Rutledge said as they stepped into the hypervator.

"That wasn't me. You can thank Evie for that."

"Evie," Rutledge said, rolling the name around in his mouth. "Not Commander Diazal?" He barked a laugh. "You are full of surprises. I never thought she'd last this long. Not with that bleeding heart of hers. I always said she took too much pity on you from the beginning. Anyone could see it when she brought you back to Eight. Hell, the only reason I sent her after you was because I knew you couldn't resist a good pair of legs."

Cas spun on the man. "Listen here, you walking piece of shit, Evelyn Diazal is one of the most competent, most compassionate and strongest people I know. And if you refer to her physical characteristics one more time, I will make sure Vrij impales you right through both your kneecaps. Then we will *drag* you back to your shuttle bleeding and crying. Do I make myself clear?"

"Crystal," Rutledge said, his gaze unwavering. He'd known which buttons to push and Cas hated himself for taking the bait. But he wouldn't stand here and allow someone to disparage a member of his crew. There was no world in which that was acceptable, he didn't care if they lost the technology or not.

The hypervator opened on the bridge and Cas escorted the man through, all of his bridge officers staring at Rutledge as he passed. He neglected to look at any of them in turn, instead staying right beside Cas until they'd entered the conference room. Cas hung back as Vrij showed Rutledge to a seat inside.

"Zaal, recall the senior staff. We need to hash this out. But don't notify Zenfor."

"Aye," Zaal said, putting the call out. Cas stepped into the conference room, allowing the doors to close behind him. However this went, it needed to be quick. For Sesster's sake.

Cas stared out the conference room window, seeing nothing beyond the pane. He was trying to maintain an air of aloofness but wasn't pulling it off. His mind was a jumble of thoughts. As the rest of the senior staff reported to the conference room, Cas gazed back to Rutledge who sat at the far end of the table while Vrij stood behind him, his blade still extended. Cas was glad to see Vrij was taking this threat seriously. He still hadn't been able to get a good read on Rutledge yet and there was no telling what he was capable of.

When Samiya and Hank entered, Samiya paused a moment upon seeing Rutledge and then took her seat on the far side of the table. "Gysan," Rutledge said.

She nodded but didn't reply. Zaal, Lieutenant Tyler, and Tileah joined as well. Cas wasn't sure why Evie had yet to show up, but he decided it was best to go ahead and begin. They were short on time as it was.

Cas turned from the window looking out on Thislea. "As you all know, *Mr.* Rutledge here has offered to assist us in our endeavors. Rather than debating the merits of his offer, I decided we should all hear it from him before we move forward with a course of action."

"Spoken like a true captain. I knew you'd make it one day, son," Rutledge said.

Cas let the comment wash over him. "How do you propose to help?"

"Gather info. Provide it to the fleet and make sure we destroy these bastards once and for all." Rutledge looked around the room, extending his arms out in front of him on the table. "I've been fighting against the Athru for nigh on twenty years. One human and a bunch of Sargans. There were some close calls, and some days when I thought we'd never make it through, but here I am. I don't know your story and I don't really care. You're here now and you've done what I never could: build an effective defense against the Athru. The Sil fleet is just the advantage we need to beat those fuckers."

"Except," Samiya interjected. "They won't attack until they know the Athru's troop positions." Cas grimaced. He didn't want to give anything away to Rutledge. He wanted the man to think they were completely in control. But now Rutledge knew he'd been right.

"I assumed as much. Which is where I come in," he says. "Using my resources, we can find out their capabilities before we commit one ship to fighting."

Hank leaned over to Cas. "Should we bring the Sil in on this? They are the ones risking their ships after all," he whispered. Cas shook his head and returned his attention to the table. If the Sil learned Rutledge was the one who sanctioned the original attack against their people eighteen years ago they wouldn't allow him to leave the system alive. Not to mention their shaky alliance would dissolve. Something Rutledge no doubt knew.

"What's your proposal?" Cas asked.

"I've collected a number of...ships—" The doors to the conference room slid open to reveal Evie, who hurried in and took the seat on the other side of Cas. She didn't even acknowledge Rutledge was there, instead her attention was focused on the rest of the senior staff. "As I was saying,"

Rutledge continued. "I have several non-Coalition ships in my hold. We can load a small reconnaissance party on board a few at a time, then send it out to gather intelligence. *Tempest* or Sil vessels would be identified. This is innocuous. No comm signals, no Coalition signatures anywhere."

"Except for one problem," Cas said. "We're not doing this piecemeal. We plan on striking the Horus system, where they're holed up and in the greatest numbers. If we try to start taking out the outlying systems first, they'll turn those star-killing weapons on us, and we'll be dead before we get to Starbase One."

"Ambitious," Rutledge said.

"What about the time bubble technology?" Tyler asked. "Isn't *that* the reason you're here?"

"It's true the time bubbles will provide protection from anything in normal space, but the Athru can detect ships that are out of sync with time. I know because we tried to get to Earth once, a few years ago. And you're right, it's a fortress. They have these…bioscanners that look for human life signs on anything coming in and out of the system. We'd barely crossed the border before we were found out." He motioned to the eye that had been replaced. "If you want to go that deep, you can't have any human life signs on the transport. With or without the time bubble. And you can't use their own technology." He leaned forward. "The better plan is to go in as a merchant vessel looking to trade with some of the inner planets." He looked around the room. "So far, they've left the other species alone, if cut off. There are no other humans on my crew. My people can do it. I'll stay behind with the fleet."

Cas shook his head. "It still won't work. It would take a hundred and forty days to get to Earth from here in your ships. We don't have that long." Cas glanced at Evie.

"Why not? What's the hurry?" Rutledge asked. "We've waited this long." A smug smile sat on his lips, as if he were waiting for some juicy tidbit.

"It's a classified matter." Cas cleared his throat. "Whatever we do, we'll have to use *Tempest*. We can make it in under a week."

"A *week*." Rutledge sat back, the smile growing. "You've been keeping secrets, Robeaux. Seven hundred light-years in a *week*. Imagine the possibilities." He stared at the group for a moment. "You'll never get close enough. This ship is too recognizable. I haven't seen another Coalition ship in seven years. The Athru aren't stupid."

Cas drew in a deep breath through his nose. Maybe he was right. He needed to speak to Zenfor, see if they could possibly modify one of these smaller ships Rutledge had with him. Ever since they'd returned, anything that even resembled a Coalition ship had thrown up red flags. And here, deep in Sil territory, it wasn't as if they had the option of finding a non-aligned species that could lend them a vessel. If Cas wanted to save Sesster, Rutledge's plan might be the only way.

"I'll need to go," Evie said, breaking Cas's train of thought. "We'll need someone we can trust to bring back credible information."

Rutledge bristled. "Did you not just hear what I said, darlin'? No humans. They'll destroy the ship before you get past the outer planets."

"That won't be a problem." Evie stared Rutledge down. The hard edge in her voice was apparent.

"You've gotten insubordinate in my absence. There was a time when you'd address me as *sir*." Rutledge tensed and Vrij's eyes flashed. He was right on top of the man.

"There was a time when I didn't know what a traitor you were," Evie countered. "If I had, I never would have taken your assignment."

Rutledge moved to get up. "I came here to offer my help. But I can see it's a waste—" A sharp blade appeared under Rutledge's throat. "Well, well." He eyed Cas and not the blade. "Pirate tactics."

"Sit down, Daniel," Cas said. "We don't have time for these games. We both know you're not going to walk away from us, and we need your help otherwise you wouldn't be on board. So, let's just cut the shit. You give us one of your support craft and we'll modify it to get us into the Horus system on schedule. When it returns, we can share the intel and form a plan of attack. Fair enough?"

Rutledge's gloved hands were in fists. "For now."

"Good enough for me," Cas said. "Vrij, take our guest back to the Bay and wait for me there. I'll join you in a few minutes."

"Yes, Captain Robeaux," Vrij replied, escorting Rutledge from the room. Cas's former commander took one last look at Evie before departing. The rest of the crew followed him out, but Cas motioned for Evie to hang back.

Once they were alone, he took his seat again. "Are you sure you want to go? Assuming we can make this work at all."

She nodded. "I need to see what my people have done. And I'm the best choice. If we have to take some of his people with us, I can get us out of any jams they get us into."

"How are you going to explain your presence and keep them from scanning you?"

Evie took a deep breath. "I need to talk to my mother. But something—happened back when Zenfor and I were trying to get aboard that Sil ship. I felt a change inside of me when the shuttle lost pressurization. And my skin changed color. I think I might have more control over my genes than I realized."

"That could have just been a reaction to the cold, or a dozen other things. We don't know," Cas said. Evie had told him a few times about her experience in the vacuum of space, though he didn't know what to make of it. Xax hadn't found anything out of the ordinary in her scans. But the Sil had spent a lot more time analyzing her genes. He wondered if he could glean some information from them.

"You can't send Zenfor because they'll detect her as Sil. Box could do it, but he's not a fighter and isn't very good in those kinds of situations. I'm the only one who could make sure the mission is a success if they decide to betray us."

Cas didn't like it. She was putting herself in harm's way for no reason he could see other than pride. "What's the real reason?" he asked.

She cut her eyes to the table, taking her seat again. "All this time—we've been one step behind the Athru, picking up where they left off. Vrij's home planet, the Athru planet, Starbase Five, Untu, Sissk. We're always a step behind, seeing the aftermath. I need to see them in person, get a good look at them myself to see just how terrible they are. I need to prove to myself they deserve this fate."

"And if they don't?" Cas asked.

"Then I just won't tell you, and I'll live with the guilt. I'm good at that."

He leaned on his elbows on the table. "It's a big risk. If something happens to the ship—"

"I know. But it's like you said, we're running out of time." She glanced at the door. "It's Sesster, isn't it? I can feel something is wrong." Cas didn't have to say anything, she already knew; it was written on her face. "How long does he have?"

Cas took a deep breath. "Doc says maybe a week. If we're lucky."

"Then this mission just went from reconnaissance to rescue."

10

"This is a terrible idea." Zenfor walked beside Cas as they made their way down the corridor. "You are placing me in a compromising position."

"I know and I'm sorry," Cas replied. "But we are running out of time and options. I don't have to tell you what—or who in this case—is at stake." He stopped her in the hall, and she turned to him, but her eyes were burning with fury. "We can save him, Zen. I know we can. But we have to make a deal with the devil to do it."

Her face crinkled. "Devil?"

"A human myth." Cas resumed their course to the Bay. "It means in order to get what we want; we have to compromise our morals and our standards. But in this case, I feel it's worth it. Otherwise, Sesster…"

"I hate this," she replied. "I hate him. And you want me to stand in the same space with him? To look him in the eye and not gouge it out? To not tear his head clean from his shoulders and—"

"I get the idea," Cas said. "I know this won't be easy, but I don't have anyone else on board who can evaluate one of his ships to see if we can even make these modifications. You're the expert in *Tempest's* undercurrent drive and you're the one who helped us reach these fantastic speeds. I'm hoping you can do that again."

"It won't be the same." She bristled. "Your ship already had a modified drive with Sesster at the helm. It took me years to build something else that could work without him, even without Volf hamstringing me. If this ship of his is nothing more than a simple merchant vessel the modifications may not even be possible."

"I trust you'll find a way. You always do," Cas replied.

They entered the Bay where Vrij and his security contingent stood beside Rutledge, who looked bored. Behind him was his shuttle and Cas could see his two companions still inside, watching everything happening in the bay. He didn't like the looks they were giving him, or the rest of his crew. It reminded Cas of the pirates he used to avoid in the Sargan Commonwealth; those who would do anything to get just a little bit richer, or a little bit more powerful. It didn't instill him with a lot of confidence.

Cas looked for Saturina but she wasn't to be seen. He assumed she was in Bay Two, still overseeing the spacewing refits. He tapped his comm. "Chief."

"Captain," she replied, her voice all-business. That was part of what he liked about her: she knew when to keep it business and when it was time to be personal.

"I need an escort. Do you have two or three ships you can spare?"

"We do. I'll pull Blackfield, Ryant and Beard. What's the mission?"

"Shuttle escort. Zenfor and I will be returning to Mr. Rutledge's ship with him to inspect some equipment. I'd like a little backup to make sure nothing goes wrong." He said this loud enough so he knew Rutledge could hear, though the man seemed unperturbed.

Zenfor was doing a very poor job of masking the fury on her face. But Saturina had told him she'd already decided not to kill him on sight. Cas was trusting that would hold, but he wasn't pushing his luck. He and Zenfor would be following Rutledge's shuttle over. The last thing he needed to do was put Zenfor inside a small, confined space with the man. She might have self-control for the moment, but sometimes things changed in small spaces.

"We'll be ready," she said.

"And I need one more pilot for our shuttle," Cas added.

"Utley will be happy to oblige," Saturina said. Cas had hoped she would have volunteered herself, but likely there was too much to do over here. The Sil were still in the process of upgrading all their ships, which included the shuttles and spacewings and it frustrated her to no end she couldn't get them to tell her exactly what they were doing. She'd stay and push until one side gave way.

"I thought you said you were short on time," Rutledge said, having snapped to attention.

Cas nodded, his signal for Vrij and the rest of the security force to allow Rutledge to board his shuttle again. "We'll be right behind you," Cas said.

"Sure I can't convince you to come with us? It would save fuel." Cas wanted to smack that smile right off his face but instead he just stared at the man. "Fine. We're headed to Bay Three."

"Nothing funny here, Daniel," Cas said just as Rutledge stepped over the threshold.

The man looked back. "Nothing funny." He disappeared inside and the door slid closed.

Captain Utley came trotting up to Cas from the other side of the bay. "Chief says you need a pilot."

"Any of these shuttles," Cas said. "Vrij, you and Folier come with us over to the *Hiawatha*. We're not going over there unarmed." He turned to Zenfor again. Her hands were balled in fists and he could tell she was grinding her teeth, but she had managed to keep herself under control for the time being. Honestly, Cas was impressed.

"We'll take *Gramos,*" Utley said and trotted over to the unattended shuttle close to the wall. Cas and the others followed, passing a Sil maintenance crew as they did. There was no acknowledgment to Zenfor from the Sil or vice-versa.

"Sir, are you sure you should go?" Vrij asked. "Putting yourself in danger."

"It has to be me," Cas said as Utley climbed inside, followed by Folier and Zenfor. "I need to be there to help Zen and to make sure we're not getting swindled. If he's stupid enough to try something, go to work on him."

Vrij slapped his chest twice then nodded. "You can count on me." He boarded the *Gramos*. Cas took one last look at the bay before climbing in himself. He hoped he wasn't making a huge mistake.

***

Evie lifted her hand to tap the call button beside the door, then dropped it again. Was she crazy for wanting to go into the Horus system? In the meeting it had seemed like the most natural thing in the world to suggest she was going, as if there was no outcome in which she didn't go. But thinking back, she wasn't feeling as sure as she had been when she'd first made the declaration. There was a pull inside her—something that she felt like was tugging her toward Horus—toward Earth—but she didn't know what that was or why. All she knew was she needed to find out.

She tapped the call button.

The doors opened, Esterva stood on the other side. Tall, gray-skinned and with a face that had little resemblance to a human, no one would have ever known she was Evie's biological mother. "Evelyn," she said, relief in her voice as if it had been years instead of an hour since she'd last seen her daughter. "Come in, come in." She shuffled to the side, her long, gossamer dress dragging on the ground so Evie couldn't see her feet. It gave her something of an ethereal quality. "What brings you by?"

Evie didn't miss the unspoken insinuation that she didn't come by enough, but what did the woman want? They already spent hours together each day and had been for weeks now. It was as if she couldn't get enough of Evie, like she was a drug of some sort and Esterva kept needing her hit.

"I need to ask you something," Evie said, stepping inside. The room was bright with color on the walls and fabrics covering most surfaces. It contrasted with the way most Coalition quarters looked, but Evie didn't hate it. She was glad her mother felt like she had the freedom to arrange her room in whatever way made her feel comfortable.

"Anything," Esterva said. She smiled and though her features were decidedly not human, Evie caught a glimpse of what she thought her father might have been attracted to in the woman. There was a warm presence about her, like an invitation to come and sit and have some tea, take a moment to stay a while and enjoy yourself. It had always been present, but Evie had been so angry with the woman it had taken time for the anger to give way to the true soul beneath. And while Evie had told Esterva she'd forgiven her, some days it was still hard, knowing what she did and what had happened to her father as a result. Regardless, there would be time to debate the merits of her mother's true nature later. Right now, she needed answers.

"Can I mask my human nature? Can I make myself more—like you?"

Esterva frowned, and the pink jewel embedded in her forehead dipped down with her features. "Mask your human nature?"

"Do you know about the bioscanners? The ones our people use?"

"I know they require a lot of power. They are generally used before the decision to destroy or spare a planet is made. Number of creatures, types, that kind of thing. Why are you asking about bioscanners? What is this all about?"

Evie took a seat at the small table by the room's only window. "We've spoken with Rutledge; he's informed us the Athru are using bioscanners on anything and everything coming in and out of the Horus system. We want to send in a team, but there can't be any humans aboard."

"Seems simple enough," she replied. "Though if they're protecting the system with the scanners it must mean they've got something important in there. Something they're willing to expend a lot of energy to protect." She took the seat beside her daughter, folding her hands in her lap. Evie couldn't help but notice Esterva never slouched, never broke her posture. She wasn't sure if that was an Athru thing or if her mother just had some archaic notions about manners.

"I want to go in," Evie said. "I need to see our people for myself. I need to see what they're capable of, how they live."

Esterva studied her for a moment. "You're not sure about going to war with them."

Evie stood, pacing the room. "I thought I was. Back when I was on that planet and that…thing infected me—"

"Emerged from you. You were never infected by Daingne," Esterva corrected.

"Whatever. After I'd pushed her away, I felt nothing but hatred for the Athru. And then, coming back to find out what they had done to the Coalition—how many they have killed. It's unconscionable. But at the same time I can't say *they're* deserving of genocide as well, that makes me no better than them. I need to see them, understand them before we make this decision." She paused a minute. "Of course, the decision is already made. I guess I just have to make sure we're doing the right thing so I can live with it."

Esterva went to her, taking her daughter by the shoulders with her long, slender fingers. "I understand. Just know you *are* doing the right thing. But if you need to see, if nothing will satisfy that burning fire within you, then that's what you should do." She let go of Evie. "I will go as well. Having a full Athru on board will only help the charade."

"What about the bioscanners?" Evie asked. "Can I alter myself to pass them?"

Esterva regarded her. "Alter yourself? I don't understand."

Evie sighed. She'd been putting this off because she wasn't sure how Esterva would react. But it was best to get it out in the open now, at least let her know what happened. "When Zenfor and I…when the shuttle exploded and we drifted through space, I felt something within me change. And when we landed on the hull of the ship my skin was the color of yours. It turned back soon after, but for those few moments something felt different."

"You're being serious," Esterva said, her eyes dancing over Evie's face. "Why didn't you tell me before?"

"I wasn't sure what was happening. I wanted to see if anything else would come up, but ever since I've felt normal. I just wonder if something didn't happen—inside."

"Don't worry about that," Esterva said. "Plus, I know how to fool the bioscanners. There's nothing you need to do. I'm sure it was nothing more than your body reacting to the extreme cold; it would have killed any normal human so let's just be glad you are who you are."

Evie didn't like it. Esterva was holding something back—something important about her internal makeup. "Mother. I need you to be honest with me."

Esterva turned away from her and stared out the window. Thislea had come into view and was marching across the black sky. Beyond the planet Evie saw another small squadron of Sil ships exit an undercurrent back into normal space, the green glow of the undercurrent appearing and disappearing just as fast. "I never meant for this to happen," she finally said. "When your father and I created you…all we wanted was a healthy child. But you came with so many surprises." She returned to Evie. "The truth is, I don't know what is happening to you or even how you can do all these things. But I'm grateful you can. I just wish I knew what to expect."

"That makes two of us," Evie said. Esterva seemed to genuine, so Evie couldn't accuse her of lying, but it still felt like there was something more. "How do you beat the bioscanners?"

"Oh, that's a simple matter. It will involve a series of injections though. Just as we managed to fool all the Coalition computers that you were always fully human, now we can do the opposite."

"Is that something you can do in sickbay?" Evie asked.

"Of course. But do you need—"

"C'mon." Evie opened the door. "Let's finish the conversation on the way. We're on a tight schedule."

11

In the history of bad ideas, this might have been the worst.

It was certainly *Cas's* worst and given any other choice, he never would have put them in this situation. He stood beside one of the most volatile people he'd ever encountered, about to put her in a position of extreme duress where she could be easily triggered. All the while attempting to prevent his convicted criminal of a former commander from A: getting under his skin and B: betraying them. It was a fine mess. In a way, Cas was almost proud.

Zenfor stood beside him, stone-faced with her arms crossed as she stared out the shuttle's window to the *Hiawatha*. Ahead of them was Rutledge's shuttle, entering the ship's Bay, while three spacewing fighters escorted Cas's shuttle along the same route. He had to admit, the *Hiawatha* was massive in comparison to *Tempest*. The ship was twice as long with three times the girth of their own. It had massive struts hanging off both the port and starboard sides of the ship, giving it the silhouette of a whale with gigantic fins on either side. A ship like that could house ten times as many staffing personnel as *Tempest* and probably carry an additional ten thousand in an emergency. But its size came with a disadvantage: it was slow to maneuver in high gravity and it couldn't enter a planet's atmosphere; not like *Tempest* could.

But as they approached, Cas couldn't help but think it wasn't coincidence Rutledge had commandeered one of the largest ships in the fleet.

"Shall I follow him in, sir?" Utley asked from the pilot's seat.

Cas snuck another glance at Zenfor. "Go ahead."

"Spacewings, hold position here," Utley said into the comm. "We're headed in for docking." Cas looked behind him at Vrij and Folier. Vrij was baring his sharp teeth, but Folier seemed solid as a rock. Cas had left instructions with Hank if he didn't hear from Cas within ten minutes of them disembarking, he was to tell Evie to order the Sil to blow the *Hiawatha* to hell and back. He didn't think Rutledge was that stupid; that he'd show his hand with such clumsiness. No, Cas was more concerned with Zenfor, who he'd expected to be a lot more reactive on the way over here. But instead she hadn't moved, hadn't said a word. And to be honest, that scared him even more. He hoped she could handle it.

"Set us down over there." Cas pointed to a space opposite where Rutledge's shuttle was headed, just as they passed through the Bay's force barrier. The bay itself was shorter and more compact than either of *Tempest's* bays, but then again Cas could tell it was little more than a repair facility, not a full launch bay. As Utley set the shuttle down Cas caught sight of at least a dozen different species working on various shuttles, ships and other jobs in the repair hangar. There was a Calgarian, a Goruffian and even a Derandar, standing a meter taller than the rest on his three tripod-like legs. Cas hadn't seen one since Kathora. He'd hoped never to see another one again.

But there were also at least four different types of robots working in the bay. Including a class 117 AMR that looked exactly like Box. Cas hadn't seen another one of those since Kathora either since the Sargans didn't use them. At least, they didn't *used* to.

The shuttle set down on the deck and Utley began the shutdown procedures. Cas turned to Zenfor. "This will be quick. We go inspect the ship, if it passes the smell test, Utley brings it back and you and I return on this shuttle. Agreed?"

"I don't have faith in your piloting skills," she replied.

"Zen, trust me, I can pilot out of a shuttle bay. You don't need to—"

"It was meant as a joke." Cas was about to say it sounded like anything but given the hard edge in her voice, but he elected to keep his mouth shut for once. The last time he said something smart to her he ended up on his ass with a fractured cheek.

"Captain, stay with the ship," he told Utley. "No need for you to be out there until we need you. Seal the shuttle as soon as we're out."

Utley turned to him. "Aren't they supposed to be our allies?"

"That's to be determined." Cas motioned for Vrij and Folier to follow them out. As soon as Cas stepped off the shuttle, the smells of the Bay hit him. It wasn't the clean, sanitized smell he'd become used to on *Tempest*. No, it was a dirty, rusty smell that permeated his nose. He caught traces of fuel, burnt metal, iron, steel, and cyclax. The air was thick with it.

"Ah, home sweet home," Rutledge said, approaching them from his own shuttle. The Erustiaan and N'galian followed him. "I didn't have a chance before, but these are my two most trusted associates, Tos-V'Sel," he motioned to the N'galian whose hat tipped just a bit while the eyes on the end of the stalks remained fixed on Cas. "And Snomsy, of Erustiaa."

Cas bit back a laugh but he couldn't hide the smile on his face. The Erustiaan's grimace turned into one of rage and he stormed in Cas's direction before Rutledge put out his hand.

"Snomes, we talked about this. You know how your name translates into universal. It's not Robeaux's fault."

"Es eckl es snom, las marech las mar*ich*," Snomsy said in his native language.

Rutledge turned back to Cas. "Sorry, he refuses the translator. Makes everyone learn Erustiaan. It's a pain in the ass, but he's a hell of a fighter, so it's worth it." He turned back to Snomsy. "Es mackl mack car marech, Robeaux. Es grindle Cas male mal."

Snomsy stared at Cas a moment more before huffing from his wide nostrils and turning the other way, the long bluish-white hair of his fur rustling as he did. He disappeared through a door near the back, ducking under the threshold to fit.

"He's had a long week," Rutledge replied. He glanced up to Zenfor, who had dwarfed even the Erustiaan. "Good to see you in person again, Consul." He extended his hand.

To Cas's surprise Zenfor reached out, looking as if she was about to shake it, but instead she slapped it away with a massive *crack*. Rutledge sucked in a breath as he pulled his hand back, cradling it in his other one. "I see some things haven't changed," he said in short, pained breaths. Cas bet Zen had broken Rutledge's hand, not that he could blame her. But hopefully they were all so committed now, it would only be seen as a minor infraction.

"Why don't you show us the ship so we can get the hell out of here," Cas said.

Rutledge exchanged glances with Tos and motioned they should follow him. He and the N'galian weaved their way through the various ships in the bay until they reached a part where the bay extended back further into the ship, opening it up beyond what they had seen when they'd entered. They passed a transport vessel that looked like it could have come off the same assembly line as the *Reasonable Excuse* and Cas sorely wished Box was here to see it. As Rutledge rounded that ship Cas saw their quarry straight ahead.

It sat by itself in the middle of the deck with only a few containers for supplies and repairs surrounding it. It was taller than it was wide and sat on four feet that protruded from the main body. Cas estimated it was only about two shuttles wide, though it was a good deal longer. In the front were two pilot stations, one directly above the other. It also had long wings that swept back from the center of the ship, meaning it could be used in an atmosphere if necessary.

"Here it is," Rutledge said. "A Hawking Class transport, circa 2575. Picked it up near Oxical; it had been abandoned sometime in the five years before we found it."

"It's old." Cas surveyed the ship. It looked the part, though they might need to do some cosmetic upgrades. It was *too* worn in places. Cas glanced over at Zenfor. Her attention was on the ship, but he could tell she wanted nothing more than to take a swing at Rutledge. Her hands were still in fists. "What do you think?" She grumbled something incoherent and walked up to the ship, performing a visual inspection.

"She's one of our faster ships," Tos said, one of his stalk eyes turning to look at Cas while the other remained on the ship. Below the brim of his hat his other two eyes sparkled in the darkness.

"Not fast enough." Zenfor ran her hand down the side until she got about halfway, drove her fingers in between two seams Cas hadn't seen and ripped the hull plating off, exposing the ship underneath.

"Hey now!" Tos stepped forward. Rutledge put his hand out to stop the N'galian.

"Just imagine if that was your face," Cas said under his breath. "What's the verdict?" he called to Zenfor.

"Unclear."

Rutledge smiled. "So, what's your big hurry in all this? Why not take some extra time to get to Horus? It isn't like the Athru will do anything in the next few weeks or seasons that they haven't already done. They're already entrenched."

"I told you, it's a personal matter," Cas said. Vrij and Folier stepped forward with him.

"Must be something serious if you're willing to go to all this trouble." Rutledge let him sit in that before continuing. "Lucky I happened to show up at just the right time."

"Coincidence, nothing more." A nervous rumble made its way up Cas's spine. Did Rutledge already know about Sesster? Was this another one of his inane tests? Or was he just testing the waters to see what was biting today?

"Yeah, funny thing, coincidence." They watched Zenfor make her way around the ship. Every now and again she would steal a glance at Rutledge and somehow each glance was filled with more hate than the last. "Don't believe in it myself."

"Good for you." Cas stepped forward again. "Well?"

Rutledge stepped up with him, his hands clasped behind his back. "It's the Claxian, isn't it?"

Cas did his best not to flinch, but the moment Rutledge said *Claxian*, it was all over. Still, it didn't mean he had to respond.

"I figured as much. I sanctioned hundreds of missions, approved thousands of transfers and yet I never seem to forget who was on board what ship and when. When your engineer showed up to the meeting, he didn't seem to be speaking for anyone else. And I happened to notice the undercurrent management on the Engineering station on the bridge had been configured to accept inputs from four different people, when your ship was only designated one. Which leads me to believe he's either injured or dead. How am I doing so far?"

Cas just shook his head.

"Don't want to talk about it, that's fine. Keep in mind, I know all about the Claxian exchange program. But your officer was the first of his kind to leave their home world on a semi-permanent basis. He's not exactly unknown, at least not to those of us higher-ups."

Cas scethed at Rutledge's words. He hated the man had figured it out. The more Rutledge knew, the more he could exploit it for his own gain.

"I'll assume he's injured, given your urgency."

"Yes," Cas replied. "If we don't get him back to Claxia Prime within a week, he may die."

"Then we've just found your way in. It will require some paintwork," Rutledge said, putting his hands on his hips. "But I instead of a merchant vessel, we'll send the ship in as a medical transport. It will be perfect; they'll provide direct access to Claxia Prime's surface. You won't get better intel than that."

"A medical transport?" Cas asked.

Rutledge ran his tongue over his teeth beneath his lips. "Yes. As long as they don't find any humans aboard, they'll let the ship right through. Your people will be able to scan the entire system for Athru ship deployments and capabilities. It's the ultimate weapon: information."

Cas hated to admit it, but he might be right. Going in disguised as a ship trying to return Sesster to his people would be riskier; but they were much less likely to be refused and could get close to Earth and the other planets in the system. Cas could even find out if the orbital outposts surrounding the inner planets were still active.

Zenfor stepped from around the edge of the ship. "Well?" Cas asked again.

"It can be done," she replied.

"Very good," Rutledge replied. "Tos." The N'galian stepped toward the ship.

"Wait, what's going on?" Cas asked.

"Tos will pilot the ship back to *Tempest* so you can begin modifications," Rutledge said. "And he'll be accompanying your crew on their journey."

Cas felt the heat rising in his cheeks. "That wasn't part of the original deal."

"Robeaux. You know me well enough to know I cover all my bets. You don't get the ship unless one of my people goes with yours. I'm not asking you; I'm *telling* you. That's how it is."

Cas ground his teeth, stealing a glance at Vrij then Zenfor. This was precisely what he hadn't wanted to happen. He'd wanted the crew to be comprised of only people he trusted—which was part of the reason he'd rebuked Evie. But what was he supposed to do, call the whole thing off? Now that Rutledge knew how badly they needed that ship he knew he could exploit them. But Rutledge didn't know about Evie's abilities—at least Cas hoped he didn't. Which meant they might still have the upper hand.

"Then I guess that's how it is." Cas stuck his hand out to shake Rutledge's. The former admiral's eyes flashed at Cas as he still cradled his injured appendage. "Oh, right. Sorry. I forgot."

12

Evie winced as the needle penetrated her shoulder. "Don't worry, this is *totally* benign," Box said. "I mean, I assume it is. Your mother is a genius at genetic manipulation. Did you know she could have engineered you to come out with two more arms? Just like Xax over there! The amount of power she yielded in—"

"That's enough, Box." Xax walked over.

"I know, I know," Box replied. "It's just the violation of all this genetic material is fascinating. She's been giving me some great insight into what really makes—"

"Box," Xax snapped, inspecting Evie's injection site. He finally shut up. She turned back to the display showing Evie's vitals. "I've never seen DNA like this before. Tell me again how you managed to keep this from us?"

Esterva stood at the foot of the bed, her hands interlaced in front of her. She scoffed. "I didn't do anything to her DNA. It was all about fooling your scanning techniques. Osborn helped me understand how Coalition systems work and we devised a way to subvert them. It was a simple matter of installing the correct hardware to counteract your equipment with a false signal."

"Oh yes, of course," Xax said, but there was something hard in her voice. Evie guessed she didn't like being deceived, especially not in her given profession. This was the first she'd heard of *hardware* being installed. She didn't like the sound of that. "And these new devices will obscure her from the Athru bio scanners?"

"Fortunately for you, I know how the scanners work," she replied. "And because they scan organic tissue using a different method from yours, we must use a different type of bio blocker to inhibit them. If they do not see her in-person, all their instruments will tell them she's a full-blooded Athru."

Evie rubbed the place on her arm where she'd been injected. "And once we're done?"

"We can deactivate them any time," Esterva said, her lips in a fine line. Evie bet *she* didn't like someone questioning her capability in her chosen field either. It was strange sitting between these two, being pulled back and forth. She looked to Box for support, but he was too engrossed in the medical reports Esterva's technology had uncovered.

"The Coalition used to use nanites for medical purposes. Some of the outer worlds still do—did," Xax said. "It's not like we don't know how to look for them."

"Nanites is too cumbersome a word," Esterva replied. "These are much more sophisticated as they cannot be discerned from the cells in her body. Go on, attempt to take her pulse. You'll find your equipment is very confused. But their equipment will only show one possibility."

"Can anyone use this technology?" Xax asked. "Could we provide them to the entire ship, make it look like the rest of the crew are Athru as well?"

Esterva narrowed her eyes. "I don't know about some of the other species, but I know humans do not handle it well. They become sick easily and prolonged exposure can lead to permanent damage."

"But not Evelyn."

"No," Esterva replied, pride replacing her annoyance. "Because I engineered her that way."

Xax grumbled something about ethics as she turned away from Evie to monitor the distribution of the signal blockers through Evie's body. Evie couldn't say she blamed her. The Coalition used to have strict guidelines about genetic manipulation. What Esterva had done spit in the face of everything Xax believed in.

Evie was ready to be done with this. For the past hour she'd felt like little more than a science experiment being passed back and forth and she was tired of being talked over. Cas had commed down to let her know Zenfor was working on the ship and if she was serious about going on this mission, she needed to get her team together. She swung her legs off the bed, feeling no different other than a patch of soreness from where she'd been injected.

"Doc, we're going to need to get Sesster on that transport once Zenfor finishes the modifications," she said, rubbing her shoulder.

"I know," Xax said still examining the display. "I've already lined up some anti-grav generators to help us move him. We'll have to use the access corridors to get him down to the bay due to his size. He won't fit in the hypervators." She turned to face Evie. "By the way, I'm coming with you."

Evie furrowed her brow, then shot a quick glance to Esterva. The woman's face didn't betray a hint of emotion. "Do you really think that's necessary?"

"What if something goes wrong, or his condition worsens on the way? You need someone who is versed in Claxian physiology. I want to make sure you get him to Claxia Prime without any hiccups. I'll just be along to monitor and assist if anything goes wrong. Plus, I have always wanted to see the planet; it is said to contain some of the vastest libraries anywhere in the Coalition."

"There's really no need," Esterva replied. "I'll be accompanying my daughter and can watch over the Claxian. I have detailed notes on their species and will make sure he arrives intact."

Xax stared at the woman. "*Showdown*," Box whispered without taking his attention from what he was doing.

"With all due respect, you're not a member of this crew and I cannot turn over a sick patient to someone I have not vetted. Especially when that patient *is* a crew member," Xax said, the strain apparent in her voice.

Evie needed to step in before this blew up in her face. "Okay, fine. Doctor, you'll accompany us on the ship. Mother, you'll stay out of Xax's way. Sesster is *her* patient, understand?"

"Of course," she replied, a sweetness in her voice Evie decided she didn't like. With both of them on the ship it would make for an interesting trip.

"Wait, does that mean while you're gone...*I'm* the Chief Medical Officer for the ship?" Box asked, his eyes shuttering.

Xax huffed. "I suppose, since you have more combined knowledge than any of the rest of the medical staff—but it's just temporary, you understand. This will be a *trial run*. If I get reports from Menkel or any of the others you're abusing your power—"

"Doctor, I am shocked," Box said, pushing his chest out again. "You're looking at the recipient for the Coalition medal of honor. I would never abuse my position."

"I'm not questioning your ethics, Box, just your demeanor. Remember all the work you've done on your bedside manner. I don't want to come back and find you've regressed in less than a week."

"Not possible," Box replied. "They are deeply encoded into my cortex. You can trust me; I'll perform my duties to my best ability. When you return, you'll be so impressed you'll want me to take over for you full time."

"Somehow I doubt that." Xax returned her attention to Evie. "You'll notify me when we're ready to move Sesster?"

Evie nodded. "As soon as we know something." Now that the procedure had been completed this was becoming more real. Evie couldn't decide whether she was excited or terrified. One way or the other, she was going to see her own people for the first time since being taken prisoner on that planet. She needed to make sure she was ready. Not for the first time she was thankful the sword had been destroyed.

As she and Esterva exited sickbay her mother leaned down. "You handled that well. And I believe you will handle our people just as deftly. You're the one thing they'll never see coming."

Evie wasn't sure how to take that. But instead of dwelling on it, she forged ahead, intent on making sure this operation went off without a hitch.

***

Zenfor was on her back, elbow deep in engine components when she heard the approaching footsteps. At first, she thought it was Tyler or maybe Lieutenant Sophie Denna, coming to ask if they could help. Sophie had been on her team to redesign the hand-held weapons and Zenfor got the feeling she'd felt scorned after being dismissed from the team. The truth was Zenfor had dismissed everyone from the team because she just couldn't think with so many different voices arguing all the time. But in the end, she had finally decided on a design and sent it down to matter processing so they could begin upgrading all the weapons. In the three weeks since she'd finished, Lieutenant Tileah reported every weapon on the ship now had the capability to fire both projectiles and energy weapons, which gave them a lot of versatility and should prove harmful, if not lethal, against the Athru, should they need them.

But as the footsteps grew closer, she realized they were too heavy-footed to belong to a human. Or any Coalition species that was, except for perhaps those long Derandar. No, they could only belong to her own people and Zenfor cursed over and over as she replaced one of the primary undercurrent emitter coils in the guts of the ship.

"Zenfor of Kantor, move or be moved." The words came across in her native language. Zen drew in a deep breath, closed her eyes for a moment, then extricated herself out from under the ship's engine. Before her stood two Sil, neither of whom she knew, and both with impassive looks on their faces.

"I am working," she said as calmly as she could.

"You are to be relieved. The humans have communicated to the Sil the desire to have this ship match the capabilities of *Tempest* and the reasons why. We're here to make sure that technology is installed properly and in as little time as possible." The two Sil were shorter than Zenfor, but not by much. She could tell they were both engineers by birth; that they'd been bred for specifically that purpose and no other. It was clear the Sanctuary didn't trust her to do the job, since she'd been bred a Consul.

"I've already replaced one of the primary undercurrent emitters," Zenfor said, knowing arguing with them was useless but pursued it anyway.

"Your work will be stripped. This mission is too important to be left to hands that may not be…experienced," the one on the left said. Zenfor couldn't place her accent, but she could tell she was an on-worlder. Sil designated to ships generally didn't like to be without their artificial suits, no matter where they went. She'd always found the suit comforting, but also— if she admitted it to herself—suffocating. Ever since she'd removed it, she'd felt better, though anyone would have had a hard time convincing her of that in the beginning. Returning to all her normal bodily functions after so long in the suit was…jarring. At least for the first few hundred sqirms.

"Move," the other Sil snapped.

She considered for a moment what might happen if she raised a hand to them. The Sanctuary would no doubt change its mind about allowing her to remain on *Tempest* and would bring her in for judgment. They would probably bring up all the charges against her and she'd be summarily killed in a judgment chamber within hours of the infraction. There was little she could do, except step aside and allow the Sil to work.

She complied, moving out of the way and the two Sil shoved past her, one maneuvering himself under the ship where she'd just been while the other walked aboard and disappeared inside. Zenfor glanced around to see some of the Coalition maintenance crews in the bay staring at the confrontation. A deep scowl forming on her face, Zen stormed from the Bay to the closest hypervator.

"Bridge," she shouted as soon as she was inside. As the hypervator moved she could feel the anger bubbling up inside her and she couldn't tamp it down. All the peace and tranquility she'd found while the ship had been hers was gone, replaced with nothing but fury and frustration. Before she might have cared, but no longer.

The doors slid open and she took in the bridge for a moment, not seeing her quarry. "Where is he?" she demanded.

Graydon, the first officer turned to her. "He's in the Command room, but he's—"

In three steps she was across the bridge and at the door. She didn't bother using the call button, instead she forced her fingers between the slits in the door and shoved them open. Inside, Cas was staring at a display of tactical information. He glanced up, but when he saw her his eyes went wide. Good, she wanted him afraid.

"I'm sorry, sir, she just—" Zenfor spun around. Graydon had followed her in. While he was large for a human, she still dwarfed him and could easily dispatch him from her sight.

"Zen!" Cas yelled. She glanced over her shoulder to see he'd stood, a scowl on his face. "It's okay, Commander, you can return to the bridge."

"Are you sure?" Graydon asked. She didn't see fear in his eyes, only resolve. This was a human she liked.

"Yes, it's fine," Cas said.

Graydon backed away, not taking his eyes off Zenfor until the doors closed between them again. She noticed there was a small dent where she'd forced them open.

"What's the problem?" Cas asked.

She faced him again. "You know what the problem is; I was just removed from my job."

Cas's face fell and he took his seat again, turning off his display. "Dammit. I was hoping they wouldn't do that."

"I knew this was your doing." She approached his desk. It would be so easy to reach across and yank him up by his throat.

"What was I supposed to do? The Sanctuary sent Evie a message asking why we'd been transferring ships back and forth. I had to tell them our plan because it's the only way we're going to get their full support on this. When the ship comes back with the tactical data—"

"I don't *care* about tactical data," she yelled, smashing her hand on his desk. A spiderweb crack spread out on the glass from the impact. "This was supposed to be *my* job, so *I* could make sure he gets there safely."

Cas gave her a hard stare for a moment. There was a time when he would have shrunken away from an outburst like that, but either he'd seen it enough to expect it, or he was being reckless. "I know it was your job," he said, his voice soft. "And I hoped the Sil wouldn't interfere in what is an internal issue for us, but the fact is we need them. And if they think they can make the modifications faster then I'm not going to argue. Every minute we save here is another minute closer to getting Sesster back home."

"You took away my involvement!" she yelled. "*I* was supposed to be the one who helped him, who woke him back up. He trusted *me*. And then you tell me I can't go on the mission because they will detect me, despite the fact that Athru woman has some kind of technology to confuse their scanners—"

"Listen to me. We don't know how Esterva's bio blockers would work with your system. They could be harmless, or they could kill you. And right now, we have too much on the line to be taking stupid risks. I'm *sorry* you can't go with them, but *we* need you, here, alive and functioning. We can't do this without you."

She leaned over his desk. "How would *you* feel, if Chief Jann was sick and you were barred from helping her in every way possible? How do humans deal with that sort of disconnection? Do you just shrug it aside?"

"That would be terrible. And I would hate every minute of it," Cas admitted. "But this is the only way we have to help him. I know you two were very close. You don't have to tell me about losing someone." A memory of the onboard funerals hit Zenfor. She remembered seeing Cas, hunched over in one of the front rows as people gave their favorite memories of Commander Blohm. It had taken him a long time to process his guilt over losing her. Maybe he did understand, at least in some superficial way. Trying to explain to everyone the connection she'd formed with Sesster was like trying to take a hold of smoke…or fire. It was impossible and burned every time.

She stepped back. "I'm holding you to your promise."

"I expect you to. No matter what happens I'm getting him back, alive. He's not going to die, Zen. That is my solemn oath."

She regarded him a moment, then left the command room without another word. She could feel the eyes of everyone on the bridge on her back as she waited for the hypervator, and when it arrived she stepped inside without turning around. "Engineering," she said as the doors closed. If she couldn't help to upgrade the shuttle, she could at least take some time to say goodbye. She needed it, if for no other reason than to close that chapter of her life, knowing they would never again be in each other's presence.

As the hypervator descended, a rogue tear escaped her eye and struck the deck plating at her feet.

13

Cas watched as four anti-grav generators hovered below the form of Commander Sesster as he was guided up the ramp on the newly-modified medical ship. It had been repainted all white to emphasize it was nothing more than a medical vessel, but any other insignia had been left off.

The bay was a flurry of activity as maintenance workers loaded supplies in the other, smaller cargo hold and the two Sil engineers continued to perform checks and evaluations of the ship's readiness. Back at the door leading to the corridors stood Zenfor, leaning against the wall with her arms crossed and a scowl on her face a kilometer wide. Xax and Box stood beside the anti-grav generators, making sure to guide Sesster inside safely. He was still curled up in his oval shape and Cas couldn't detect any movement from him. He'd been down to see their chief engineer a few different times, trying to reach out with his mind and finding nothing. He just hoped they weren't too late.

"Solemn occasion."

Cas turned to see Evie and Esterva had come up beside him. Lately they seemed nigh-inseparable. Where one went— usually Evie—the other followed. He wasn't sure if it was creepy, or if the woman was just trying to catch up on all the time she'd missed with her daughter. "Yeah, now if only our pilot would get here," Cas replied.

Evie looked around the bay. "Where is he?"

"Oh, he's been enjoying the fruits of our bar ever since he brought the ship over from the *Hiawatha*," Cas replied. "Which doesn't give me a lot of confidence about his abilities." Tos, the N'galian, had exited the ship as soon as it had landed and made a beeline for the bar, ignoring any attempts for Cas to get him into some crew quarters. Eventually Cas gave up and had Vrij post a guard outside the lounge doors. As far as he knew, Tos was still in there.

"Wait," Evie said. "This is too good. You're telling me it's your job to get a drunk Sargan mercenary to accept his mission and take a ship back into Coalition territory?" A huge smile had formed on her lips.

"Yes, very funny. See how I'm doubled over with laughter?" He cut his eyes toward her. No doubt she was referring to their very first encounter, when she'd gone undercover in the Sargan Commonwealth to retrieve him. Though he had to admit, there was some irony in there somewhere. "It's not the same. The N'galian was never an officer."

"Still, maybe his inebriation is for the best. If he's drunk enough, we can drug him, and *I'll* pilot the ship."

"I'm not too worried," Cas replied. "Between you and…" He nodded to Esterva, "…I don't think you'll have any trouble keeping him in line. Rutledge said something about listening outposts, so it may be better to take an indirect route around those, if you have the time. I assume Tos knows where they are."

"He better," Esterva said, having been listening in. "Otherwise he's little more than dead weight to me."

Cas's comm beeped. "Go ahead."

"Captain. Mister Rutledge on the *Hiawatha* is attempting to contact you. He wishes to discuss strategy once the ship has departed for Horus."

"Tell him he better get his pilot down to the Bay unless he wants the ship to leave without his representative aboard," Cas replied.

"Yes, sir," Zaal replied. "What would you like me to relay about your meeting?"

Cas rolled his eyes, shooting another glance at Evie. "Tell him I'll call once the ship is away." He didn't want to talk strategy with Rutledge. But considering they were something of partners now, he had little choice. Since Evie would be coming back with the intel, they needed to start planning out the next steps. If they got too complacent the Athru might take advantage of their apathy. "And I'm serious about the N'galian. Get him—"

Evie tapped him on the shoulder. "Look."

The N'galian came stumbling into the bay, a dazed look on his face and his eye stalks swinging back and forth as he walked. Zenfor stared at him as he passed her and made his way to the ship. "You watch your back around him, got me?" Cas said. "Just in case he's decided to put on a performance."

"Yeah," she said, eyeing him. "Got it."

Tos strode by Cas and the others and gave a short, two-fingered salute before walking up the ramp into the ship behind Xax and Box. "I'll see you on board," Esterva said, following him. "Good luck, Captain."

"Thanks," Cas replied, but she was already on her way to the ship, gliding across the deck. She passed Box who, presumably, had finished helping Xax secure Sesster inside. Cas turned to Evie. "Good luck to you too." Now that he was really looking at her, he couldn't help but notice she looked paler than normal. Maybe it was the light. He couldn't tell.

"Yeah," she said, her voice distant. "I'll see you when I get back." Something struck him, like a phantom or an afterimage, but it was as if he was looking down on the two of them standing there, facing each other, instead of actually being there with her. It was a very strange sensation and he couldn't help but wonder if this might be the last time he ever saw her. It was a dangerous mission, but they'd been through worse together. Cas shook the thoughts and the feeling from his mind. He stuck out his hand and she took it, giving it a shake. Cas couldn't decide if he should hug her or not, but before he could decide the moment was gone and she was making her way over to the shuttle. She too passed Box on the way and he offered her luck as well. Box came up to Cas and stood beside him, watching as Evie walked up the ramp. As the ramp retracted and the doors began to close, she turned one last time and offered a wave, which both Cas and Box returned.

"I guess that's that," Box said. The ground crews which had been seeing to the ship's maintenance decoupled all the fuel and sensor equipment. Cas was about to respond when he felt another presence beside him. Zenfor had come up on his other side, watching along with them.

"This is the right decision," she said.

"It is," Cas replied. "Did you make sure the Sil made all the necessary adjustments before they left?"

"I did," Zen said. "It was curious though. The ship was already outfitted with the same technology of the *Tempest*. It may at one time have had a Claxian on board regulating the undercurrent flow."

Cas's brow creased. "Are you sure?" A Sargan vessel with room for a Claxian. That didn't sound right. As far as he knew, no other Claxians had ever served aboard a ship—any ship— the way Sesster had. But then again, it had been eighteen years since he'd been up on the most current news. Perhaps in that time some disgruntled individuals left Claxia Prime in pursuit of something else. Rutledge had given them the perfect ship at the perfect time. And that didn't sit right with Cas, no matter if everything checked out or not.

The ship fired its main thrusters and lifted off the deck. Within seconds it was already through *Tempest's* force barrier and into open space. Cas and the others watched until they could no longer see the ship, at which point Zenfor walked away without another word.

"Well," Cas said, feeling an empty pit in his stomach. "I guess I have a call to make."

14

"Robeaux," Rutledge boomed, his face taking up most of the display. Cas had come back to the Command room to make the call once they confirmed Evie's ship entered the undercurrent. "Did they depart?"

"You know they did, Daniel. You were monitoring." Cas had no patience for Rutledge's games. Cas sat back in his chair, doing his best to contain his annoyance.

"What did you do, leave a tracker on my ship when you were over here?"

Cas ran his hand through his hair. He needed a shower. "Of course not. Do you think I don't know you're monitoring everything we're doing? Enough of this, Zaal said something about strategy."

"I've been going over my old tactical strategies—it's been a long time since I've been able to command a *fleet* of ships— and I think we need to consider our options." He glanced down at something outside the range of Cas's display.

"You realize *you're* not commanding anything, right? The only reason you're still here is because I haven't ordered the Sil fleet to destroy you."

Rutledge *tsked.* "Empty threats aren't like you, Robeaux. I taught you better than that. Regardless, assuming the mission is a success and they return with our enemy's locations, we need to think about our attack strategy."

Cas suppressed the urge to rebuke him. Instead, he tried to decide if Rutledge's thought process had any merit. "How are we supposed to devise a strategy before we know the location of their ships?"

"I'm speaking of an overall strategy. We can't make any concrete plans until we know the details, but this is higher level, more global, not all the detail." By Kor, would he just spit it out already? The man could talk a Vurn back into its hole again. How did he ever accomplish anything when he had to draw it out like this?

"Daniel, I have a lot of work to do over here," Cas said.

"What I'm talking about, Robeaux, is we need to catch the Athru off guard, no matter what. Surprise will be the biggest and most powerful weapon we have. I assume the Sil have weapons that can disable their ships."

"We think so," Cas replied. "But they're untested."

"Regardless," Rutledge replied. "We need to move the fleet."

Cas sat up. "What?"

"Move the fleet. They have to assume an attack is coming. And which direction do you think they'll plan for? Which direction will they set up blockades and mines and all sorts of goodies for us?"

"The direction of Sil space," Cas said, realizing Rutledge might be right.

"Exactly. They know the Sil are the only real threat to them anywhere around here. So, they're going to be prepared for a confrontation. What we need to do is circle around, hit them from the back or the side. Where they won't see it coming. But we can't do a full-on frontal attack; they'll be prepared for that no matter how much intel we collect."

Dammit. He hated to admit it, but he was probably right. Even though there hadn't been a formal dissolution of the treaty between the Athru and the Sil, they had to know something was up. The Sil had closed off all borders, and hadn't responded to any Athru communiques, despite Cas's insistence they keep up the charade. The Sanctuary had told him—Evie really—there was no need. And unnecessary actions were not tolerated or sanctioned. Their hubris infuriated him. Didn't they understand the concept of subterfuge? Or had it been so long since they'd been in any meaningful confrontation they'd forgotten? Things got dirty in war, and he didn't want to be in the middle of a confrontation when the Sil finally realized it. Cas wondered, when the Coalition launched its attack over a hundred years ago, if they weren't as unmatched as they'd originally been led to believe.

"So, what do you say? Agree?" Rutledge asked.

"You're not wrong," Cas replied.

"While I'll take what I can get," he said, a smile on his face. "It's okay to say I'm right, you know."

"Don't push your luck."

Rutledge cleared his throat. "As I understand it, the Sil won't move against the Athru until we've got all the intel. But will they move the fleet? Allow us to get into position so as soon as Diazal returns we can strike and strike hard."

Cas ran his hand down his face. Damn he was tired. When was the last time he'd slept? "I don't know. But without Evie here it's a moot point. They won't talk to anyone but her."

"That's inconvenient," Rutledge replied. Something in his voice had changed, it had become softer in some way, less combative. Or was Cas just imagining it? He couldn't be sure.

"Where would we take the fleet anyway? And how would we tell Evie and the others where we are? No comms, remember?"

Rutledge sat back, thinking. "What's the top speed of the Sil ships?"

Cas shook his head. "They're comparable in speed to *Tempest*. I'll have to check with Zenfor for specifics. What are you thinking?"

"Sargan space," Rutledge replied. "It's been in disarray ever since the Athru came in. We could move a fleet there with little to no confrontation and then strike the heart of the Athru stronghold from a direction they'd never expect. They don't have anything out near Sargan space."

"Nothing?" Cas asked. They couldn't be that complacent.

"Other than a few patrol vessels, no. They keep mostly within Coalition-held territory. Though I've seen them chase down and destroy ships coming from Coalition space into what used to be the Sargan Commonwealth. When the Athru attacked, most of the warlords dissolved their formal operations, preferring instead to work from the shadows." Rutledge's voice was weary, as if he'd witnessed this for a long time.

"What about humans? The Commonwealth was full of them when I left." Cas was thinking specifically of Veena and her operations on Devil's Gate. She'd been semi-important in the Commonwealth; her family controlling a large swath of the southern borders.

"They're around, but you won't see their faces," he replied. "Some took ships and headed out into open space, willing to take their chances. Most went into hiding. But some, like me, decided to fight back in the best way they could. Using whatever tools they had."

"But you said you don't have any other humans on your crew."

"Personal liability." Rutledge produced a smug smile. "It's better to limit our exposure. A ship like yours, full of humans, will do nothing but light you up like a beacon. But mine…they might just pass by if I get into trouble. There are ways to mask the fact I'm on board. Which reminds me…" Ah, shit. Cas knew this was coming. "…how did Diazal disguise her biosignature? That would be useful information."

"That's classified," Cas said, aware he was using the same excuse to keep a lot from the man. But what choice did he have, tell him about her dual nature? About Esterva? That wouldn't go over well and he was willing to bet Rutledge would try to find a way to use Evie for his own personal gain once she got back.

He rubbed his graying beard. "Very well. But keep in mind I'm trusting you here. I'm taking your word the Athru won't detect any humans aboard because if they do—they'll kill everyone, not just her."

"Yeah," Cas replied. "I know the drill. We've been to Sissk."

"Ah. Planet of a thousand voices." He sat back, reflective. "From your demeanor, I won't assume they're sympathetic to our cause."

Cas had to choke back a laugh. "Not exactly."

"It's a shame most worlds have written us off," Rutledge said. "Us, the founding members of the Coalition. And when we turn to them for help, they banish us. It's wrong. I thought we had a stronger union."

"Maybe that was part of the problem," Cas replied. But he wasn't thinking of the other member worlds of the Coalition. He was focused on exactly how he was going to convince the Sanctuary to let him move their fleet to Sargan space. With Evie gone, talking to them would be difficult, if not impossible. But he had to try.

"Always the optimist," Rutledge's human eye squinted while the artificial one remained completely open. It put Cas off, and he decided he didn't want to be in this conversation anymore.

"Was there anything else?"

"Just strategy. Contact me when you have the Sil's approval. I'll begin planning where we can stage the fleet. And don't forget to get me the info on the speed of the Sil ships. We'll want to make sure we can circumvent enough of Coalition space, so we catch them completely off guard."

Why did Cas feel like he was back in his old post on the *Achlys*? He didn't take orders from this man anymore, despite what the former admiral might think. In fact, it was the opposite. But before Cas could raise his objections, Rutledge cut the comm leaving Cas starting at a blank display. "Goddammit," he said under his breath. He tapped a few different controls and the image of their Sanctuary contact came up.

"You were told never to contact us again," the Sil said and moved to cut off the comm.

"Wait! Diazal is gone, we have no way to communicate."

"Then that is your own fault. Contact us again when Diazal returns." The screen went blank.

Cas fumed; all thoughts of his former exhaustion gone. These people were the most infuriating, hard-headed—

He tapped his personal comm. "Zen?"

"Captain," Zenfor replied.

"I need a favor."

"I don't do favors."

Cas clenched his jaw. "I wouldn't be asking if it weren't important. But it's been pointed out to me we may be in a tactical disadvantage. I need you to speak to the Sanctuary about moving the fleet." There was silence on the other end. "Listen, I tried, but they won't talk to me. And Evie's radio silent. If I thought anyone else could do this I would ask."

"They won't listen to me," she replied.

"They'll listen to you before they'll listen to anyone else on this ship. Tell them if they don't pay attention, we'll leave

Thislea while their people are still aboard." It wasn't his intention to say "their" instead of "your" but Cas hadn't thought of Zenfor as one of the Sil for a while now. She had grown so far beyond them he had a hard time believing she could have ever been that closed-minded. But if it bothered her, she didn't say anything.

"Try and the reaction won't be pleasant, believe me."

"Zen, we're not really going to do it. But I just need you to get them to listen. They'll expect an attack from the direction of Sil space. But not from somewhere else."

"Such as?" He heard genuine interest in her voice.

"Sargan territory."

"Interesting proposal. It's a gambit, but I believe it's better than a head-on attack. Perceptive planning." He shouldn't tell her where the idea came from, but he wasn't going to lie to her, not when she was tenuous on trust as it was.

"I wish I could take the credit," Cas replied.

"Rutledge?" The word came out with a volley of hatred attached to it. Cas couldn't blame her; he felt the same, he just hid it better. She huffed. "If they do listen, they'll want assurances."

Cas racked his brain. What kind of assurances? There were no assurances in war. Other than people would die. "I'm not sure I can provide them."

The other end of the comm was silent for a moment. "I will do what I can."

"Thank you, you don't know—"

"Thank me when it's over," she replied and cut the comm.

15

Had she known it was going to be this rough of a trip, Evie might have thought twice about coming. The ship—which in her mind she'd dubbed the *Vengeance*, though she'd neglected to tell anyone else this—wasn't built as well as *Tempest*. It shook and rattled as it traveled through the modified undercurrent. When it was in the normal undercurrent space things were relatively quiet, but every time they made a jump through one of the micro wormholes that propelled them tens of light-years forward, the ship vibrated as if it were going to come apart at the seams. While nothing had fallen apart yet, the decks were scattered with debris from shelves that seemed pointless to restock as it would all just end up back on the floor in another thirty minutes anyway.

"Never thought I'd be goin' this fast," Tos said from the pilot's seat. He'd plopped down while they were still in *Tempest's* bay and hadn't moved from that spot, despite the fact they'd traveled for six hours so far. Evie wasn't sure if N'galians had large bladders or what, but from what Cas had said about the man drinking at the bar she'd figured he would have had to get up at some point. She'd been hovering over him the past three hours, hoping to get a chance at the helm just to give her something to do. Ever since she'd been a pilot, it was always easier to endure the turbulence from the driver's seat than it was as a passenger. She suspected Tos might know this as well, and was holding all his liquid in.

Then again, for all she knew, N'galians didn't even have a bladder. She'd had precious little contact with the species since most of them confined themselves to the Sargan Commonwealth considering their home planet was in Sargan space. She'd seen one, from a distance when she'd been on Devil's Gate, and none before that. According to what she knew, no self-respecting N'galian would find themselves applying for citizenship with the Coalition. And definitely not in any branch of the military.

The ship began to rumble again, and Evie grabbed hold of the nearest bulkhead. The green tinge of the undercurrent out the main viewer turned into a bright bluish-white light, held for a few seconds, then turned back to green again. The rumble stopped.

"I think ah'm gettin' used to it." Tos burped, and not for the first time. He'd been burping since they'd taken off. Evie wondered if it was something all Arc-N'gali did, or if it was just this darling.

"I'm going to check on the others, let me know if you need a break," Evie said, sensing he wouldn't be getting up anytime soon.

"Yup." Tos didn't bother to glance back at her, instead keeping all four of his eyes straight forward. Evie suppressed an unfavorable comment. And Cas thought this guy might be a threat? Even if he was, she was pretty sure she could take him down faster than he could get out of that chair. "Might get stopped," he added just as she reached the door.

She turned back to him. "What do you mean?"

"Athru patrols—always lookin' for humans. Might do a routine stop, just givin' you a heads up. They might not be able to scan ya, but if they see your face, that's it. Stay in the back. It's nothin' I haven't dealt with a hundred times with Rutledge. I'll keep 'em from boardin'."

"Yeah…okay," Evie said, unsure of what to make of him. She made her way down the narrow corridor that connected the small "bridge" to the rest of the ship, climbing down the ladder into a small hold, which then opened up into a larger one. There, up against the side of the wall sat Sesster's immobile form, a little more than a pile of tentacles and flesh. Xax sat beside him, the equipment she'd brought on board monitoring his vitals.

"Any change?" Evie asked.

Xax shook her head. "And that's a good thing. If he gets much worse this entire trip will be wasted."

"Except for all the intel we gather," Evie said.

Xax slid her gaze up to Evie with all six of her eyes. "This war won't be good for anyone. Especially not us. If their behavior on their own planet is any indication, the Athru won't let go of their territory easily. And what's left of the Coalition may destroy themselves trying to make them."

Evie put her hands on her hips. "You don't think we should try to remove them from Coalition territory? That we should liberate all these worlds that are too afraid to leave their own systems? Yours included?"

"I didn't say that. I only meant—" Xax stopped, staring at Evie in a way that made her uncomfortable.

"What? Why are you looking at me like that?"

"Are you feeling alright?" she asked.

Evie shrugged. "No better or worse than any other day. Why?"

Xax took Evie's hand, and held it up to her face. Evie could feel her eyes going wide. "What the…?" Her hand was at least five shades paler than it had ever been and was an ashy gray color. Xax flipped her palm over, which was still more pinkish-beige and felt her pulse.

"Normal." Xax turned her scanning equipment on Evie. "Dammit, my readings are all over the place because of those *things* in your system."

"Is…something wrong?" Evie asked.

"I don't know. Where's your mother? I need to ask her."

"I don't—" Evie's heart pounded. "In the back maybe?"

"Grab her, I don't want to leave him in case something happens," Xax said, releasing her hand.

Evie felt like the wind had been knocked out of her. She glanced around for a moment as if trying to remember what she was doing, then headed for the back of the ship, where the crew quarters were located. She navigated another narrow hall, passing the room she'd designated as her own before stopping short. Evie stepped inside, ignored her bag on the small bed and went straight for the washroom. As soon as she saw her own reflection in the mirror she almost cried out, but took two steps back instead, her back hitting the bulkheads of the room.

Her chest heaved and her pulse raced, but she forced herself to stare at her own reflection. Instead of her normal skin color, she'd gone an ashy gray, almost matching her mother's skin tone. Her eyes seemed further sunken in, though she couldn't tell if they'd moved or if it was nothing more than the fact her face resembled a skull now, so any contrast was exaggerated. She stepped forward, taking a close look at her features. It was still her face, the shape and arrangement of everything on it hadn't changed, just the color. The more she looked the more she started to relax. It wasn't as big of a deal as she'd first thought; though it had been jarring. She pushed on her cheeks and the skin blanched, then blushed a soft pink when she let them go, just like before. The only difference was they returned to the ashy gray color shortly after.

Evie stomped from the room down to her mother's quarters, banging on the metal door twice. The second bang had been muffled and she glanced up to see a small dent in the door where her fist had hit it. What was going *on*?

The door slid open to reveal Esterva, whose eyes momentarily went wide before returning to their normal, serene state as the woman smiled. "Evelyn. Is everything on schedule? What—"

"Mother," Evie said through clenched teeth. "What is happening to me?"

Esterva paused. "I'm not sure I know—"

"Yes, you do. Look at my skin. I want an explanation and I want it now," she said, bunching her shoulders.

Esterva held out a hand. "I understand this might be frightening. But everything is okay. You're okay. Come in." She stood to the side so Evie could enter, which she did with reluctance. Esterva walked around her, and took the only seat in the room, bringing her eye level just below Evie's due to her height. "Come here, let me see."

Evie walked up to her as Esterva reached out with her long fingers, running them over Evie's face, her hair, and down her arms. "What is it? Did something go wrong with the bio blockers?"

"I don't think so," she replied. "I'm not sure what's going on, as the blockers shouldn't result in any physical effects. What did Xax say?"

"She can't scan me because of the blockers. She says they're scrambling her system."

Esterva nodded, her gaze going past Evie as if she was barely listening. "How do you feel?"

"Other than freaked out, fine," she replied, already sick of the question. "I don't understand. I had bio blockers in my system most of my entire life, and they never did anything like this. And now, six hours after they're injected…" Evie couldn't finish because she wasn't even sure what was going on; all she knew was she was changing.

"Those blockers were to keep your Athru nature from being discovered," Esterva said. "Much how these are meant to keep your human nature a secret. But they aren't supposed to create physical changes." She pressed a finger to her lips and tapped, lost in thought. "The only thing I can speculate on is that because I engineered you to accept the blockers into your system, they're filtering out some of your more human characteristics. Kind of like a safety mechanism."

"Does that mean I'm going to change into an Athru?" Evie asked.

"I don't think so," she replied. "They can't make you grow taller or modify the arrangement of your internal organs. But superficial changes…such as the levels of blood supplied to your skin and how you react to certain stimuli—there may be a few more small surprises to come."

"Great," Evie said, turning her back to her. "You couldn't have given me a little warning?"

"I wasn't aware of it," Esterva said. "I didn't—and still don't think it is anything you need to worry about, nor do I believe it is permanent. Think of it like an allergic reaction." The ship rumbled again, and Evie held on to the closest bulkhead. It lasted a little longer this time, but gradually faded.

"I don't suppose there's anything you can do about that," Esterva asked. When Evie turned back to her, both hands gripped the sides of the chair she was still perched in.

"I would have already done it," Evie said. "I guess we'll both just have to live with a little discomfort for a while." She left her mother alone in her room, furious as she made her way back down the narrow corridor. She had a nagging sensation Esterva suspected something like this might happen and had neglected to tell her. Not that it mattered now; the blockers were in her system and the ship was already underway. But that didn't mean she couldn't be upset.

She'd barely reached her own room again, planning to lie down for a nap when the ship shuddered and Tos came on over the comm. "Got a patrol ship comin' in. Don't nobody do nothin', I'll take care of this."

Evie jumped up, bolting from her room and back toward the bridge.

16

Zenfor stood in front of the display, cursing Cas, his ancestors and anyone or anything else contributing to the unique set of circumstances that created the man. She cursed the planet he was born on, the parents who'd raised him, and the unfathomable *genius* who'd permitted him to step off his homeworld into the depths of space. All of which had led up to this moment. She was supposed to try and convince the people whom she'd renounced and who, in turn, wanted nothing to do with her, to listen for five minutes while she tried to explain a strategy that came from a human responsible for ten Sil deaths and the loss of one of their sentient ships.

Yes, an excellent set of circumstances. She was very optimistic about how this would go.

Zenfor took a deep breath and tapped the controls in front of her, steeling her resolve.

"Human, these interruptions are becoming—" The Sil on the other side stopped speaking as soon as he realized Cas wasn't the one calling. "*You.* What do you want?"

"Dracsal, I need five minutes," Zenfor said.

"You do not have it," he replied. Of course, he would be the one to answer. Out of all four hundred and twenty-six members of the Sil High Sanctuary, it *had to be* Dracsal. The man who had approved her for Consul after the completion of her training at the camp fields of Sharak. "I'm ending the transmission."

"You *owe* me," Zenfor said, losing her composure.

He stopped. "I owe nothing. You renounced your commission. Renounced our people. It is as if you do not exist."

"Just like Zakria then," Zenfor said, recalling her old companion on the training fields. The one who had sung those beautiful songs every night…until they took her away. "Those who do not reach their potential are recycled. Isn't that right?"

Dracsal stiffened. "That's how it has always been."

"No, I refuse to accept that. Not always. Not forever. It is an archaic and barbaric rule and *you know it*."

"*I* do not presume to fly in the face of our traditions, Zenfor. *You* have broken your covenant with our people. Your words and your actions no longer matter. You are lucky the Sanctuary did not vote to pursue judgment against you." Though he tried to hide it, Zenfor could tell she'd gotten to him. Dracsal was one of the most composed Sil she'd ever met, always keeping his emotions in check. But Zakria's mistreatment and subsequent death had been stewing in the back of her mind for years and this might be the only chance she ever had to confront the person foremost responsible.

She wasn't going to waste it. "At least I was not responsible for the execution of Sil who did not meet some ancient standard. Zakria was good at what she did, even if it wasn't what she was bred for. I even heard test scores in the program went down after you decided to have her killed."

"I did not—"

"Don't try to hide the truth, Dracsal. You had her *killed* because she wasn't advancing in the Consul program. You know it, I know it, and the Sanctuary knows it. The difference is you and I know it was wrong. The Sanctuary has become so apathetic they don't even care anymore. When I stood in front of you with the human, that was the most volatile reaction I'd ever seen. And you know what? It filled my heart with pride to see my people passionate again."

"She had reached the mandatory age limit. What was I supposed to do? Not fulfill my duty to the Sil? I would be just as—if not more so—guilty as her."

"She did nothing wrong!" Zenfor yelled. "She helped others through the program. She was a mentor. Her only crime was not being adept at the job she'd been bred for. And you *murdered* her for it."

Dracsal sat back. "You always have been too passionate."

She was heaving. Zenfor hadn't meant to get that upset. But it had been a long time since she'd spoken of Zakria. The only other people on the ship who knew had been Caspian and Sesster. "It comes from my family. You know that better than anyone. Passion isn't a crime. Yet."

"You realize I am putting myself in jeopardy by even speaking with you at length," Dracsal said.

"I realize. But as I said, you owe me. You owe Zakria. Now sit there and listen." To her astonishment, he motioned for her to continue. "It has been brought to my attention any attack against the Athru will be anticipated. We suggest moving the fleet to a less conspicuous location before launching the offensive."

His eyes narrowed. Dracsal had never served aboard a Sil ship, he'd been a Sanctuary member ever since emerging from his own specialized academy. Zenfor often wondered how it had differed from her own, since Sanctuary members were rare and only one or two per year were added to the group. But regardless, he had never felt the ship's consciousness with the crew, working in tandem. He had no concept of how to understand her position. He could only work in hypotheticals.

"It's a sound position," Dracsal finally said. "But without the tactical data from the Horus system, the Sanctuary won't want to take the chance."

"The longer we wait the more opportunity we give the Athru to build a defense against us. They aren't stupid. They know something is happening. If a one-time ally cut off relations with the Sil, how would we respond?"

"By setting up blockades along our common border," Dracsal replied. He wasn't as stupid as she'd thought. Perhaps he did have some insight into actual battle tactics.

"Exactly. We propose to circumvent that. While the Athru commit their forces to protecting what was once the Coalition border closest to Sil space, we move the fleet to Sargan territory, move in from there."

He shook his head. "The Sanctuary will want to wait until the information has returned."

"Waiting is what got us in this mess, Dracsal. Had the Sanctuary acted instead of debated when the threat was first established—"

"I'm not going to participate in conjecture with you, Zenfor. The past is past, we cannot change it." He sighed, glancing off-screen. "I will speak with the council, but I will tell them the human, Diazal, brought this to us. Your name will not come up."

"Thank you. Just make sure they understand the urgency. Time may be shorter than we realize." Underneath the table, off the screen, Zenfor's fists were clenched tight. She was almost done.

"There will be a lot of pushback. The new negative-mass weapons haven't even been tested against the Athru yet."

"We still have the interdimensional weapons, and we know those work," she replied.

"But they are clumsy and unreliable," Dracsal said. "Not to mention the damage they do to the fabric of space."

"Which is why we needed the new weapon systems. Do you not consider the destruction of a star an equal, if not more destructive force?"

He threw a hand up, as if he'd heard enough. "I am done with this conversation. I will present the argument. You will hear from the Sanctuary within four sqirms. And it will be a broadcast message, no more direct contact. If you message here again, I will inform the Sanctuary and you will be arrested." He cut the comm and the display went dark.

Zenfor stared at it a few moments before collecting herself. It hadn't been perfect, but she felt like in some way, Zakria's sacrifice had found retribution. It had at least forced Dracsal to listen long enough to consider the operation. But it didn't mean they would be convinced. For that it might take more than every Sil sacrifice combined.

***

"What kind of patrol ship?" Evie shouted. They had dropped from the undercurrent and were cruising along at sublight speeds. She saw the answer to her question before Tos could respond. Outside the main window was a large Athru ship to starboard, having come up alongside them.

"What are you doin'?" Tos yelled. "Git out of sight!"

Evie ducked back, stepping down the ladder so she could still hear, but not be seen through the windows of the bridge. She had expected the Athru eventually, but not so fast.

"Lach ma cha, est ma enlach," a female voice said over the comms.

"Damn 'thru," Tos said. She could hear him tapping controls and levers. "Nobody understands this language around here. Woulda thought by now…" he trailed off.

"Unmarked vessel, identify and open communication," the same voice—processed this time into universal—said.

120

"This is medical transport Kyro," Tos said. "Transportin' wounded back to Claxia Prime."

"Claxia Prime," the voice said. "Enable visual communication." Evie heard the flicker of the display that would take up the whole main window. "N'galian, identify yourself."

"Rak-D'stavis, out of Landox. I've got wounded here. You gonna let me pass or what?"

There was silence for a moment. "Explain the Claxian."

Tos uttered what sounded to Evie like an annoyance. "I don't know. He booked passage on my ship out of Landox and went into some kind of coma when he got on board. He had a Yax-Inax doctor takin' care of 'em and she came along. I was just hired to transport 'em."

More silence. Evie listened carefully. "You have two Athru on board as well."

"Yeah, so?" Tos asked. Evie couldn't believe how cavalier he was being with the Athru. Was it better to act like you weren't afraid at all rather than feign reverence to them, as Run'ak had?

"I wish to speak with them," the Athru said.

"They're in…whaddaya call it? Meditation?"

"Wake them." Evie's heart jumped up in her chest. She glanced down to see Esterva standing at the bottom of the ladder. She had one finger to her lips.

"Look, they paid for this passage just like the Claxian. I was given instructions not to wake 'em from whatever it is they're doin'. Somethin' about hallowed time. I don't get it, I'm a simple driver. But ah'm not wakin' my clients. You want to do that; you're welcome to come over and explain it."

"Their destination is Claxia Prime?"

"No, Earth. Quick jump right next door. And you're makin' me late."

There was a long pause, long enough that Evie thought they'd been found out. "Very well, proceed medical transport." The comm went silent. Evie felt the ship rumble as it re-entered the undercurrent. She stuck her head up above the ladder.

"All clear," Tos said, one of his eyes turned around to see her peeking up. "But we'll have to stay out of the wormholes for a while until they're outta range. Don't wanna try an' explain how we jump so fast."

"What the hell was that? Inviting them on board?" Evie said, climbing up over the rungs onto the catwalk that connected to the bridge.

"They never take the bait," Tos said. "Not worth their time. Looks like your little trick worked. I knew it had as soon as they came in range. They never would have contacted us if they'd detected a human."

"Even with another Athru aboard?" Evie took the seat beside him.

"Nah," he replied, all four eyes back on the course. "Consider 'em collaborators. Not worth sparin'."

Evie hadn't realized that. She'd figured Esterva was their insurance policy. That even if her human nature did show through, Esterva's obvious nature would give them time to escape any confrontation.

"You better git comfortable," Tos said. "It's gonna be a long week ahead and there's a good chance that wasn't the only stop. But they're all the same. Head down, git some rest and stay outta sight. It's that easy."

"Don't you need to be relieved?" Evie asked. "You can't fly the ship for an entire week."

"Sure can. N'galians don't sleep. An' we can postpone food or drink for long periods of time. I ain't movin' from this spot until we reach Claxia Prime."

Evie turned, mouthing "o-kay" to herself, and headed back for the ladder where her mother still waited at the bottom. Once she was back down and face to face with Esterva she glared at the woman. "Did you know? That the Athru would just destroy this ship if they detected me?"

"I...was aware of that possibility, yes," Esterva said.

"Why didn't you say anything?" Evie spat.

"There didn't seem to be a need. Why make you worry?" She brushed it off as if she hadn't just deceived her daughter. Which made Evie wonder.

She stared daggers at the pale Athru. "What else aren't you telling me?"

Esterva held up her hands in defense. "Nothing." But Evie didn't buy it.

"Mother. Tell me."

Esterva grimaced, breaking eye contact with Evie. "Well, there is another small matter. But it's hardly worth mentioning."

Evie's fingernails dug into her newly pale skin. "Mention it. Now."

"I might not have been honest about why I accompanied you."

"Which means what? Why did you come then?"

Esterva hesitated a moment, tapping her fingers together. "In a word: Dulthar."

17

Cas lay flat on his back with his arm draped over his eyes, despite the fact the room was already dark as night without any of the lights on. He hadn't been sleeping well lately and no matter how tired he was during the day; insomnia would always follow him into the night. So he'd taken a few hours off to try and fall asleep when he felt the most tired, but as soon as he'd laid down on the bed it was like a firecracker had gone off in his brain and he couldn't stop it from exploding over and over in his mind.

Regardless, he lay there, as still as possible, willing himself to fall into sleep. He didn't want to think about more drastic options, such as asking Box for a sedative. But if this kept up, he'd have no choice. He couldn't lead a fleet of ships into harm's way while he was falling asleep at his job.

The door to his quarters slid open and the dull light from the corridor tried to breach his arm and eyelids before disappearing again. He sat up only to find a shadowy figure moving around in the darkness on the other side of the room. "It's okay, you can turn on the light."

One of the small desk lights in the kitchen went on, revealing Saturina, her uniform half covered in grime. "Sorry, I didn't know you'd be in here right now. I thought I might have left a clean uniform top in here." She glanced around;

her mouth twisted in disappointment. "But I guess I'll have to talk to the quartermaster."

Cas rubbed his eyes. "What are you doing down there?"

"Ryant and I are taking one of the spacewings back apart, trying to figure out what the Sil did to them. I'm not flying a ship until I know exactly how it works and what kind of components are in it," she said. Saturina placed her hands on her hips. "Shit. I was hoping there was one here." She paused a moment. "Are you okay? Why aren't you on the bridge?"

He waved her off. "It's nothing."

Saturina shook her head, approaching the bed. "That's the tone of voice you use when you're lying," she replied. Then, "It's *fine*, don't worry about *me*."

"I wasn't—you're on duty, I don't need—"

She sat down beside him on the bed. "Is it Rutledge?"

Cas sighed. "I don't know. Maybe. Probably. I just really thought that chapter of my life was over. It's like no matter what I do, I can't get away from the man." His face darkened. "I should have just told the Sil to destroy his ship. I should have told them who he was."

"But then we wouldn't have a way into Coalition territory," she replied. "I'm not a fan of the man either. I don't like that he's here, I don't like that you have to work with him."

"I just feel like the same junior officer he pulled out of the ranks to serve with him on the *Achlys*," Cas replied. "It's like no matter what I do, he'll always have this superiority over me. To him, I'm nothing more than an officer gone rogue."

Saturina *tsked*. "That's how he wants you to feel. He wants it to seem like he's the better person because then he has all the power. Don't let him put you in that box. Don't give him permission to determine who you are. Only you can do that."

"How the hell are you so damn smart?"

She flashed him a grin. "It comes with the territory. You don't stay on a team like Rafnkell's without learning how to defend yourself." Before he knew it, she'd leaned in and kissed him on the cheek. She stood, holding on to his shoulder for a moment. "Just be careful around him. I don't trust his motives."

Cas shook his head. "Neither do I. But he's coming aboard again shortly. In anticipation of the Sil agreeing to move the fleet." He placed his hand on top of hers.

"Then you make sure you keep a sharp eye on him at all times."

"Already arranged." Cas had spoken with Vrij who had agreed to keep a security detail on Rutledge while he was aboard.

"Okay. I gotta head back, we need to know what's in these spacewings if we're going to depart soon."

She tried to pull away and Cas held on, guiding her arm down until her face was level with his. He pressed his lips to hers. "Thanks for the advice."

She grinned. "Anytime. Keep this up and maybe I'll apply for ship's counselor." He arched an eyebrow and she laughed. "Nope, not in a million years. Can't give up piloting."

"I don't blame you," he replied, thinking back to when he'd been grounded or in jail. Both had been terrible. Cas let go of her hand and she gave him a wink before leaving. Cas laid back on the bed again, except Saturina had left the desk light on, which threw shadows on the ceiling beside the window. He took a deep breath, trying to focus his mind. He needed to take his emotions out of this. Why was it every time he was around Rutledge his logic centers just went haywire? If it was anyone else he'd be able to make an easy, rational decision…but with Rutledge it was always different. Always harder. He hated that.

He was about to get up and turn off the light when his comm chirped. "Captain."

"Zen? Did you hear back? What's going on?"

"We need to talk," Zenfor replied.

***

"They want to do what?" Cas asked, leaning over the conference table. Zenfor stood at the other end, while Zaal, Tileah, Hank, and Samiya sat in various chairs around the table itself.

Frustration crossed Zenfor's face. "Why must I explain the same circumstances over and over? It isn't as if it will change them." She sighed. "The Sil have only agreed to move half the fleet. They feel leaving Thislea unprotected at a time when we might be vulnerable is too large of a risk."

Cas did the mental calculation. That would leave them with less than four hundred ships. Granted they were four hundred Sil warships, but still. He needed the *entire* fleet. "Is there no way to negotiate with them?"

"I was told not to contact the Sanctuary again," she replied. "So no." Cas glanced to Tileah.

"Half the fleet is still a significant number," she said. "But I'll have to make some modifications to our attack plan if we're headed into Coalition space with less of a force than we planned."

"What are they going to do with the rest of them, leave them in orbit around the planet?" Hank asked.

"I wasn't given that information," Zenfor replied, crossing her arms.

Hank turned to Cas. "Is it better to split the force like this? If they outnumber us in there, this battle could be over real quick."

"Don't worry," Cas replied. "We'll still wait for Evie's report before we head in. But my concern is time. It's going to take us at least a week at full speed to get over to Sargan territory without going straight through Coalition space and possibly alerting them to what we're doing. If we leave half the fleet here and Evie comes back telling us they're vulnerable, it's going to take another week to get the other half of the fleet in place before we can attack. I don't want to leave something like this up to chance." He turned back to Zenfor. "What are the odds the Athru actually break through Sil space and reach Thislea with any kind of credible threat?"

"Low, but possible," she replied.

"So, they're just dicking us around," Samiya said.

Zenfor bristled. "They don't like the fact that Evelyn is the only one to exhibit their desired traits. It limits their trust in you. They'd prefer the rest of you begin to advance as well. Or at least show steps in that direction. And without her in front of them, they're less inclined to act."

Cas put his head in his hands and rubbed his eyes. His comm chirped. "Sir?"

"Go ahead, River."

"Incoming transmission from the *Hiawatha*, sir. Mr. Rutledge would like to speak to you. He sounds upset."

Cas glanced up. "How did you hear back from the Sanctuary?" Cas asked Zenfor.

"It was a broad transmission to the fleet itself," she replied.

"Christ." Rutledge had received the transmission as well then. Which meant he already knew and was probably pissed. "River, transfer it through to in here."

"Aye."

The 3-D display in the middle of the table lit up with Rutledge's image. "Robeaux! What is the meaning behind that transmission? Only half the fleet?"

"Calm down, Daniel. We're discussing it now," Cas said.

"I don't want you to discuss it, I want you to *fix* it," the man said.

Cas took a deep breath. "Unless you've forgotten, you're not in charge here. This is what the Sil are willing to do. Neither I, nor anyone else on my ship can convince them otherwise, unless we'd like to put the whole operation into jeopardy. Am I clear?"

He crossed his arms; a move Cas knew to mean he was preparing to argue. It was that stubborn streak in him. "Very clear, *Mr.* Robeaux." He let the accusation hang there for a moment. "When can we depart?"

Cas looked up at Zenfor. She made a motion that signaled the fleet would be ready to leave when he was. "As soon as we transfer you over. The *Hiawatha* won't be able to keep up."

"Fine," Rutledge said. "I'll leave her here with the *other half*." He ended the transmission.

"Child," Cas said under his breath. He didn't care if Rutledge was pissed off or not, in fact he kinda preferred it. It was better than that smarmy superiority complex he liked to walk around with. "Lieutenant, work with Vrij on that man's transportation and as soon as he is aboard let me know. I want him under constant surveillance. Hank, let's signal the fleet to prepare to leave." Cas glanced over to Zenfor. "I assume they'll respond to automated battle plans coming over the comms?"

She nodded. "Just broadcast the battle plans and the strategies you've drawn up; they'll handle the rest."

This was maddening. He couldn't even communicate with his own fleet of ships. He swore the Sil did it just to be contrarian. Like they divined sick pleasure from making things as difficult as possible. "Samiya, double-check everything with Tyler. And make sure the auto sequence is solid for the undercurrents, I don't want to run into a problem out there in the middle of an operation. Let's get everything checked, rechecked and checked again. We've had three weeks to sit on our butts, now is the time to make it count. Dismissed."

Everyone at the table stood, except for Cas. He glanced to his left, missing Evie's presence. At least this way she wouldn't come back to an empty planet. And once she was here and could relay the information, the rest of the Sil would fall in line.

As Cas stood, he realized he was pinning a lot of his hopes on her. They had better not be in vain.

18

Evie woke with a start. The ship rumbled through a micro wormhole then back out again, the vibration lessening. She figured she would have gotten used to it after six and a half days of continuous jumps but instead it seemed to have the opposite effect. She'd come to dread every time they did a jump—even subconsciously training herself to wake just before them and hold on to something, though it did little good. She didn't know why it was grating on her so much, but it had become like a high-pitched noise that was ever-present in the back of her mind. She couldn't wait to get off this ship and she had no idea how she was supposed to make the trip back. She wondered if Xax could put her under, maybe keep her from experiencing the continuous stress of dealing with these.

The ship lurched again, and the vibrations started, then lessened. Two in a row. They must be getting close. Evie rubbed her eyes and swung her legs off the short bed. Because of the cramped quarters she hadn't been able to stretch out on the bed, instead having to keep her knees bent in order to lay completely flat. If she didn't know better, she would say the crew quarters were built by the Val. She didn't know how her mother was faring considering she was a good deal taller than Evie, and at the moment she didn't care. The woman had straight out lied about her intentions on this trip and if Evie could help it, she wasn't going to speak to her again until after they were off this Kor-forsaken ship and she could clear her head.

She should have known from the start something was off about Esterva wanting to come along, considering the woman had built her life on lies. She'd just hoped as her daughter, they'd moved past that.

Apparently not.

Evie stood and stretched as much as she could in the small space, her back popping in places she'd never felt before. As had become customary every time she woke, she performed a quick physical inspection of her body to make sure she hadn't grown another pair of ears in the middle of the night. So far, the changes had been limited to the color of her skin. She thought her face looked tighter, but it was difficult to tell and could have just been a trick of the light. Most importantly, she didn't feel any different. She didn't feel like she was changing in any meaningful way and that was something to be thankful for. The gray skin had taken some getting used to, but Esterva had said it would return to its normal color once they removed the bio blockers. But then again, she lied about everything else, she might be lying about them as well.

Slipping on her civilian clothes, Evie pulled her hair back and tucked it into a neat bun. She'd done away with the long ponytail over the shoulder for the trip as she didn't want to draw any attention to her human-like appearance. And since Athru had no hair, it was best if she kept it pulled back and out of sight. Just in case.

They'd been stopped four more times and true to what Tos said, each one had been a near carbon-copy of the last. The script from the Athru might have varied by a few words, but the meaning behind it was clear. And Tos, cool as ever, played it nonchalant and easy. He said the number of stops was up, but that was probably because they kept detecting Sesster, and were curious since there weren't supposed to be any Claxians off-world. Evie didn't care. As long as he kept doing what he was doing and got them there as quickly as possible was all that mattered.

She made her way down the narrow corridor into the larger space of the ship where Sesster lay. Xax, ever-present, was asleep beside him. She'd barely moved the entire trip, electing to stay by his side in the event something went wrong. Evie, on occasion, would try and reach out with her mind, but found nothing there to grab on to. She could only pray they weren't too late.

"Morning," she whispered as Xax stirred, probably in response to her presence in the room.

"Is it?" Xax asked, blinking all six eyes in succession and checking one of her instruments for the time. "Where are we?"

"I was just about to check," Evie said. "Want anything to eat?"

Xax shook her head. "I'll grab something later. Thank you though."

Evie patted her shoulder as she walked past. "Back in a second." She continued on down the other side of the ship, past the stores and over to the ladder which led to the bridge. Taking it two at a time gave her another opportunity to stretch, which she relished. Something else deep inside popped when she hoisted her leg up three rungs. *Too much*, her inner voice said.

As she climbed over the edge to speak with Tos, she stopped short. Her mother sat in the other main seat, engaged in conversation with Tos.

"...not worth the Kassope. I'd much rather try the Harmonious Halls near Grum."

Tos scoffed. "That place is a hole. You want real entertainment, head to The Elongorium. They got shows that'll blow your mind. There's these wind walkers that can—"

"Ahem," Evie said, standing at the end of the catwalk.

Esterva turned to her. "Evelyn. Good morning." She produced a small smile but kept it under control. Evie hadn't made it a secret her mother was on her shit list. "Coffee?"

"No," Evie replied, walking over to one of the control stations on the small bridge. "How close are we?"

"Not far, I was jus' about to comm you. We should be gettin' data from Horus any minute now," Tos said.

My ass. You would have just let me sleep until we reached Claxia Prime. Tos had been consistent about one thing: he was in this for Tos. He didn't really concern himself with what anyone else on the ship wanted or needed. If it didn't affect him, he was unlikely to do it. Typical Sargan scum in Evie's opinion. She would be happy when this mission was over and she could get back to life on *Tempest*.

"Sleep well?" Esterva asked. Evie *harrumphed*. Same questions, different morning. Esterva seemed to get the hint as she didn't say anything else. Evie pulled up the astrometric data on their location. They *were* close. Another wormhole jump, or two and they would be there in less than thirty minutes. They'd just passed Alpha Onias and were coming up on Jurest. Horus would be next.

"Are we getting any data from the inner systems yet?" she asked. "Anything on their capabilities?"

"So far nothin' but patrol ships," Tos replied. "If they're fortified, it isn't this far out."

"Can we see Earth yet?" It had been years since she'd been this close. Even though she'd grown up on Sissk, her father had always talked about Earth like it was this utopia paradise, having grown up there himself. And when she'd finally arrived to go to the academy, she'd found he'd been right; it was magnificent. She'd almost taken an assignment at

Coalition Central as soon as she'd graduated but had declined as it never would have led to a command position. As beautiful and welcoming as the planet was, she didn't want to sacrifice her future for it. She had planned to return every few years, catch up with her old friends from school, bask in the serenity of it all, but that hadn't happened. Evie been too focused on her career and eventually had lost touch with most everyone she'd graduated with. She figured there was always time for that kind of stuff later.

"Hang on, one more jump," Tos said. The ship vibrated and the green glow of the undercurrent flashed a bright white. Evie closed her eyes and held on to the closest railing. When it was over they were back in the regular undercurrent. "Best not ta raise any suspicions this close," he said. "We'll be goin' the rest of the way slow. But we're close enough to pull data now."

Evie tapped the controls, focusing the long-range scanners on the Horus system. "What the..." she said as the visual of the system came up.

"What's wrong?" Evie felt Esterva come up behind her, but it barely registered. It didn't even matter anymore.

"This can't be right," Evie said, resetting the scanners. When the information displayed again, it was unchanged.

"Well? What is it?" Tos asked.

"The scanners have counted over five thousand Athru ships in the Horus system alone, and it keeps adding more." She spun on Esterva. "How can they have that many ships?"

"I have no idea," Esterva replied. "They left our planet with fewer than two hundred, and most of those were smaller support craft. Whatever they've been doing in this system for the past eighteen years, it has been extensive." Her face darkened. "Dulthar."

Evie grimaced. She didn't want to hear that name again. Instead, she returned her attention to the display, bringing up an image of Earth. She gasped at what the display showed. "This...can't be right." Instead of the blue and green world she'd been expecting there was nothing but a brown sphere, covered in black and gray splotches. As best she could tell, the planet still had oceans, but they were no longer blue. They were kind of a sickly green. And all around the planet were artificial structures, some of them huge.

"That bastard," Esterva said. "He's terraformed it into a construction platform. *That's* how he's built up such an armada. He's been siphoning the natural resources of the planet and using them to build more ships. I should have known he'd pull something like this."

"You never knew?" Evie asked, tears welling in her eyes. She couldn't believe the beautiful planet she'd lived on for four years was just...gone. As if someone had snapped their fingers and destroyed it, in one, fell swoop. "In all that time you were looking for me, you never came here?"

"I never got this close," Esterva admitted. "I knew if you were this close, you were probably dead."

"By Garth Almighty," Tos said. "Never seen anythin' like that before."

"Is this what the Athru do?" Evie demanded. "Do they just come and destroy?"

"They don't see it as destruction," Esterva said. "They'll see it as creation. That the planet was changed to serve their own needs. Dulthar is relentless in his pursuit of—"

"Stop saying that name!" Evie yelled. Every time was like a slap in the face, because it did nothing but remind Evie that her mother had lied about her true intentions of coming on this trip. After Evie had practically dragged it out of her, she learned Dulthar was the Athru-in-chief. The one who made the final decision, despite the Athru ruling body having a part in the say. He had been her mother's commander at one point, and had been the one to discover Esterva's treachery, hunting down and killing the rest of her team. Esterva had finally admitted she'd come along to determine where he was, how fortified his position, and if possible, break in and kill him before the rest of the Athru ever knew she was there. It didn't matter that one action could destabilize everything, including their attack plans. She was driven purely by a need for revenge, but Evie had shut that down. She'd forbade Esterva from leaving the ship without her, and under no circumstances was she to have contact with any Athru while they delivered Sesster home.

The computer beeped and Evie turned to it. "It's up to seven thousand," she said, her voice small now. How were they supposed to go up against a fleet this big? Even if they did have the element of surprise, if each of those ships had a planet-killing weapon on board, their fleet wouldn't survive a day.

"We'll be at Claxia Prime in a few minutes," Tos said.

Evie's heart jumped in her throat. She hadn't even considered what the Athru might have done to Sesster's home world. She altered the scanners to look at Earth's closest planetary neighbor and was greeted with a sea-green planet, a wide band of bluish rings circling the equator. She let out an audible sigh. At least the Athru had left Claxia Prime alone. Evie did a double-check of all the rest of the planets in the system: Osiris, Ra, Isis, Amun & Mut, and Set…they all seemed unchanged. The only planet they'd decided to destroy was Earth. And they hadn't even destroyed it, not in the traditional sense. Instead, they'd debased it, stripped it of everything good and useful, all in the name of building a bigger defense. "Dulthar did this?" she finally asked.

"Most certainly. He has the final say on all general operations. Including construction and military."

"Then we need to make him pay," Evie said through her teeth, seething.

"I know," Esterva replied. "Which is why I'm here."

"We're coming out of the undercurrent," Tos said. Evie glanced to the side. The green of the undercurrent disappeared to reveal the cool glow of Claxia Prime beyond. It didn't escape her notice at least four Athru ships were in patrol around the planet.

She wiped her eyes. "Let's do what we came to do first. And hope it's not too late." She tapped her comm. "Xax, get ready, we're going down."

19

Samiya took a deep breath and pressed the comm button beside the door. Behind her Vrij stood at attention. Cas didn't need to know she was down here, but she wasn't about to confront him alone. She'd had this nagging sensation ever since he'd first appeared on that screen, and even after he'd come on board she thought she could resist. But it had been almost seven days, and she couldn't put it off any longer. Vrij had been understanding.

Despite the fact he was close to eighty, somehow Rutledge *seemed* younger now. Stronger in some way. She couldn't understand how, as she already felt the weight of time on her own body, despite being nearly twenty years his junior. Maybe it was that hit from Zenfor that really drove it home. The loss of the eye—that had been unfortunate, but something like that could happen at any age. But being batted around like a piece of raw meat had given her a new perspective on just what her body was capable of these days. And if Rutledge decided to try something, she wasn't confident she could stop him in time.

But that blade on Vrij's back could do it.

The doors slid open to reveal the large man, still clad in his "uniform" from the *Hiawatha,* with one glaring difference.

There was a Coalition captain's emblem on his chest, shiny and new.

"Commander," Rutledge said, surprise in his voice. "I didn't expect a visit from you."

"Life is full of surprises. I didn't expect to see you alive again," she replied.

"Does that mean you're glad to see me?" he asked.

"I'm confused. You're supposed to be dead. All this time, you and I have been hiding out in Coalition space, helping other humans and we've never come across each other's paths? Don't you find that strange?"

Rutledge made a dismissive motion with his hand. "It's a big galaxy. And the key word there is *hiding*." He paused. "Though, you are supposed to be dead as well. I thought we lost you on the *Achlys*."

"That was the idea," she replied.

"Where have you been keeping yourself?"

She shifted. "Most recently? Starbase Five. Or what was left of it. Before that we were all over the place. We stayed out of the core worlds, kept to the fringes when we could."

"Impressive. I didn't know there were any others still alive." His eyes narrowed.

Samiya nodded at his new piece of hardware. "You better not let the captain catch you wearing that."

He glanced down in feigned ignorance. "Why not? I am the captain of my own ship, after all."

"You know why. You're technically a civilian. You were given a dishonorable discharge. You're not an officer."

He stared at her a moment, then removed the emblem and tossed it into the room. "It's been a while since I've had enough resources to print what I want. I had to indulge."

"I know how you feel," Samiya replied. When *Tempest* first showed up she couldn't believe the resources of this ship.

But in the following weeks she'd come to take it for granted without even realizing it.

"What can I do for you, Commander?" Rutledge asked.

She took a deep breath. Coming here, standing in front of this man she'd once seen as a mentor and a leader, Samiya found it harder to begin than she'd anticipated. Was she still concerned with his opinion of her? "I thought you should know, we're close to Sargan territory. A few more hours until our destination." The fleet had spent the last seven days micro-jumping through the undercurrents without incident. Samiya wasn't even sure the Athru could detect them during micro-jumps.

"Thank you for telling me. Robeaux is keeping me sequestered. I don't know if he thinks I'm a threat to his authority or what, but it's a tight leash."

"Are you?" she asked.

"If he finds he can't deal with the pressure, I'm always here to help." He glanced over to Vrij. "Where are we stopping?"

"Close to Devil's Gate. There's not a lot of traffic in that area anymore. Anything close to the Coalition border has been abandoned." Cas had initially had reservations about this area, but scans had shown it was a good location. Close to Coalition space, but in neutral territory, but also devoid of a lot of traffic. Back when Samiya had left the *Achlys*, she'd navigated this area, bartering her and John through to stay off the Coalition's radar until they could get further away. It was strange being back. Starbase Eight—or what was left of it—was less than a day away. She had a strong desire to go find it, see what had become of her old stomping grounds, but that meant entering Coalition space. And even with their dampener installed, it was too big of a risk. But it did bring up something she'd had a hard time getting off her mind. And it gave her an excuse not to get to the real reason why she was here. "How did you do it?"

His face crinkled. "What?"

"How did you make it off Eight alive? We heard from a trader you'd been killed when the Athru invaded."

He scoffed. "Would you like to come inside? As much as I enjoy conversing in the middle of the hall, I'm an old man and prefer to sit more than I stand."

Samiya exchanged glances with Vrij. "Yeah. Sure." Rutledge stepped to the side as she stepped inside with Vrij behind her, keeping a barrier between her and her former commander.

The room was sparse, unremarkable. Rutledge hadn't taken the time to make any changes, though Samiya did notice an admiral's emblem laying on the table beside the door. She guessed it said something he'd tried the lower rank rather than trying to *completely* reinstate his former position. Though the fact he'd printed it off at all was troublesome.

Rutledge walked around them, pulling one of the plush lounge chairs in the room, and taking a seat, apparently unconcerned whether they did the same.

"Commander," Vrij began but Samiya shook her head. She needed to hear this, if for no reason other than to satisfy her curiosity.

"Did Robeaux tell you they were holding me on Eight, then?" the older man asked, brushing the front of his uniform with his hands, as if he were looking for stray motes of dust. His bandolier lay on the bed behind him.

"I knew," she replied. "I saw the vid of them taking you away. We were still in Sargan space at the time, but it broadcast everywhere."

"Which begs the question." He stopped the brushing. "Why weren't you on the *Achlys* when it malfunctioned?"

Her heart jumped in her chest. Could he see the change on her face, or was her reaction just in her mind? "You first."

"Very well." He cleared his throat. "I wasn't the only officer Robeaux managed to get locked up. Across the cells from me was a man named Page. He'd had a good career ahead of him before he'd run into my former apprentice." She scoffed but said nothing further. "But the circumstances of my survival came down more to luck than anything else. The only thing I did was kept moving."

"Luck?" She'd never known Rutledge to be one who relied on anything other than his own guile. To hear him speak in such terms was…odd.

"Keep in mind, without comms in the cells, we had no idea what was going on. When the first attack came, I thought maybe the operation with the Sil had backfired. In fact, I kind of expected it. I never thought Robeaux would be able to tame those people in any way. Turns out I was wrong.

"I didn't know it at the time, but the first blast from the Athru blew the station in half. But because we were in the cells deep in the station, the damage wasn't too bad in our section. The force barriers dropped and the emergency power came on, lighting ways to escape pods. Page and I moved…as fast as we could. I admit I wasn't as fast as I should have been—those seasons in the cell were hell on the psyche and I hadn't been keeping up with my physical regimen."

"I hope you don't expect pity from me," Samiya said, feeling the boldness in her blood. If anything, Rutledge's recollection reminded her he was a *criminal*, and she should have no compunction about telling him the truth.

"I don't want it," he replied, his voice hard. "But had I been quicker, I wouldn't be here now. Page was scouting ahead of me, trying to figure out what was going on, when the structural integrity of his section failed, and he was sucked out into open space. The emergency force barrier went up just in time to keep me from being sucked out as well. It was there where I finally saw the extent of the damage and realized if it was the Sil, they were using ships we'd never seen before. As for Page...there was nothing I could do except watch as he tumbled through open space toward the other side of the burning station. I doubled-back, and eventually made my way to one of the cargo bays."

"And meanwhile the Athru just let you go about your business?" Samiya hadn't been on Five when they'd attacked it, but it had looked like they'd sent down shock troops to flush out any remaining survivors.

He shook his head. "No, but I got off on a cargo shuttle. There was no one else around otherwise I would have taken them with me. I think they were all busy going for the escape pods and what few starships that had survived the initial attack. I made my launch look like an automated response."

"Then how did they not detect you?" It wasn't like the Athru to be sloppy either. They didn't leave survivors.

He grinned. "I didn't realize until much later—the cargo in the ship acted as a natural shield for my bio sign. Magesnest emits a kind of radiation that obscures life signs."

She knew. It was one of the key components to the dampener they'd been using for years against the Athru. She'd heard about it from a friendly Untuburu before things had gotten really bad and they'd managed to build the dampener, which had probably saved them more times than she'd been willing to admit. But at the same time she had difficulty believing Rutledge *and no one else* had made it off Eight alive. It was convenient.

"Pretty simple really. Just plain luck. Like I said." He leaned forward in his chair. "Now. Your turn."

Samiya shot another glance at Vrij, who remained stoic but also looked ready if the occasion rose. Which it might. Rutledge had always had something of a temper, which he managed to keep down for the most part. But she'd also seen him at his most vulnerable. And in those moments his "true" self had emerged. "Fine. You deserve to know. It was me."

He didn't react. "What was you?"

"I sabotaged the Sil weapon on board the *Achlys*. Me and John. We made it so it would backfire on anyone that used it."

He stared at her a moment, and she could almost see the gears in his head spinning, putting it all together. Cas, the Court Martial, Soon's promotion, the new assignment and eventually the *Achlys* coming back successful in her mission. "*You*," he growled. "I knew you weren't that incompetent. But as you didn't leave anyone left alive on that ship, I had no choice but to determine it was a malfunction or improper understanding of the technology."

"I understood it just fine," she replied. "And I tried to tell them. I tried to tell Soon before we left the ship. I begged her not to use it. But she was adamant—she had to impress *you*. She had to succeed where Cas failed. You never should have betrayed him like that."

Rutledge stood and stepped toward her. She felt Vrij come around to her side, his presence protective. Rutledge stopped where he was. "You realize if you'd followed your orders none of this would have ever happened?"

Heat rose in her cheeks. "Nor would it had you listened to your first officer. You don't save the Coalition by violating one of its most basic tenets. This is as much your fault as it is mine."

Rutledge stared her down. "I should have known you and your husband were too close to Robeaux. But when you didn't say anything at the Court Martial, I figured I was in the clear. Little did I know you were plotting behind my back."

"You always said it was important to trust your crewmates. That we were each other's backbone and if we didn't have the trust of our crew, we didn't have anything.

When you turned on Cas, you broke that trust. You fractured us."

"I have to say, Commander, you've surprised me. I didn't suspect you at all. I thought you were dust along with the rest of them." In another context it could have been a compliment, but the vitriol coming across in his voice made it anything but. "Is that what you really needed, then? To clear your conscience?"

"At least I have one to clear," she shot back.

"Then I suggest you leave." He stared at both her and Vrij, the glare from his artificial eye unescapable. Heart thrumming in her chest, Samiya turned and left, with Vrij close behind. Once the doors were closed behind them she let out a long sigh and leaned up against the closest wall.

"Are y-you alright?" Vrij asked.

She took a few deep breaths. She'd done it. She'd faced the man head on and come through the other side. "I think I will be. In time."

20

As the ship descended through the atmosphere, it occasionally caught gusts of strong winds which would temporarily cause it to stall and hover a moment before continuing on its path to the planet's surface. To Evie it felt like the ship had become a feather, only moving and floating with the breeze. She could have ordered Tos to burn through the currents but given the age of the ship there was always the risk it could do some damage. Claxia Prime had always had a strong atmosphere, which helped protect the surface; if a ship didn't ride the currents properly, they could break apart before reaching the troposphere.

Evie descended the ladder back into the main hold just as they hit another gust, causing the ship to shift for a moment before experiencing the controlled fall again. Xax glanced up as she approached. "Anything?"

Xax shook her head. "At least he's still alive. You did it, you got him back home."

"It doesn't matter if he dies on the landing pad," Evie replied. "Tos has already sent an emergency message to the Claxians. They're supposed to meet us there."

"Where are we landing?" Xax asked.

"High Town," Evie said. There was no sense in not getting Sesster immediate help, and there was no better place to do that than the planet's capital city. The ship shuddered again, and Evie gritted her teeth. Being onboard this ship was doing nothing for her patience. She needed off.

"Landin' now," Tos called from above them, ignoring the use of the comms.

"Okay," Evie said. "Let's get him prepped." She placed her hands on Sesster, hoping to feel something but still there was nothing. She'd thought perhaps Sesster might have felt the close proximity of his home planet but there was no such luck yet.

Xax gathered her equipment, disconnecting the monitoring devices from Sesster's body. Evie felt the ship touch down on something solid and silently thanked Kor for small miracles as Tos began the shutdown procedures. She ran over to the main hold door, checking the pressurization and then sliding it open. She was greeted with a blistering cold blast of wind and she bristled. She'd heard it was cold on Claxia Prime, but she hadn't really thought to expect it.

"He's ready," Xax said, stepping out of the way.

"Do you need help?" Esterva asked. She'd appeared from the crew quarters where she'd retreated shortly after they'd arrived at Claxia Prime.

"I can manage," Evie replied, stepping over to Sesster. Perhaps it wasn't quite dignified but rolling him out was the easiest way to move him. She could probably pick him up if she had to, but his form was so massive and cumbersome it didn't make sense to carry him. But before she could even begin a notion tickled her brain.

Please step away.

We can do that.

Thank you for returning.

Evie turned to see three Claxians approaching, cartwheeling toward them on the pad. She was so struck by the image she froze in place. Two of the Claxians were about the same size as Sesster but the third was a good deal larger. She hadn't realized they all weren't similar in size like most humanoid species.

We will take him, a voice said in her mind. It was a voice very much like Sesster's, smooth and gentle, but it had an air of authority to it.

What happened? asked another voice. She wasn't sure which voice was coming from with Claxian. The three of them reached the ship and stopped.

"Gaw' damn," Tos said behind her. She glanced over her shoulder to see he'd finally left his chair and descended the ladder as well.

"Can anyone else hear them or is it just me?" she asked. Looking around, the indication seemed to be the Claxians were speaking to her alone. "Xax, can you tell them what happened?"

Xax stepped forward as the three Claxians halted in front of the shuttle. One of the smaller of the two reached in, wrapping its long arms around Sesster and lifting him up and out of the hold of the ship, like he was a piece of cargo. "We weren't there when…whatever it is happened. But from what I can tell, he's gone into some kind of coma or shocked state, and he's deteriorating."

How long?

"About ten years," Evie said. "Standard Coalition time."

Do not speak of the Coalition here, a different voice said. *Please come with us.*

Evie stepped into the brisk, clean air and was struck by the beauty beyond the landing pad that had been obscured while she was in the shuttle. The sky was a bright, sea-green, full of wispy clouds which staggered down until they reached the snow-capped peaks of mountains in the distance, their hue a bluish-gray. Beyond the clouds hung three of Claxia Prime's moons, each nothing but a white plate against the sky. The landing pad itself sat on the edge of a precipice under which water flowed and cascaded down a two-hundred-meter waterfall into the dense, lush forests below. Before them was the gleaming city of High Town. Its bright, steel spires rising out of the city itself, each at least a hundred and fifty floors high. Some ended in points, others seemed upside down as they were wider at the top than at the bottom, and all of them were peppered with small dots of light indicating windows. Below, the rest of the city stood in small blocks over a wide, open space, ornate bridges spanning the shallow rivers running between the buildings or squares.

The second, smaller Claxian helped the first to lift Sesster on to what looked to Evie like a gurney, with the exception that it had a divot in the middle to hold Sesster's rolled-up form.

Tell us, one of them said.

We must know how this occurred.

"Is no one else hearing them?" Evie asked.

Esterva and Xax stood beside her, watching them load Sesster on the gurney, while Tos stayed back at the ship. Evie noticed Esterva glancing around, her eyes sharp. She was keeping a lookout for any Athru, which Evie hadn't even considered when she'd walked out of the ship. She'd been too concerned with Sesster. She shied back, heading for the ship again.

Do not worry, there are no Athru here, one of the Claxians said. Evie glanced up to see the largest of the three standing before them, his large form blocking out the sun. She could tell he was a he, by the way his voice sounded in her own head.

Evie reached out and took Esterva's hand. "He says we're safe. They're not here." She nodded but didn't relinquish her suspicious look.

"We think Sesster went into shock, after seeing what happened to the Coalition. He just…folded in on himself. We were…away. We didn't see it happen."

You left him alone?

"No, he was with others on the ship. But only one of them was with him when it happened. She couldn't come, she's a Sil," Evie said before he asked. The other two Claxians rolled away beside the gurney as it hovered off down the pad's connecting ramp. "Hey, wait," Evie said.

Come along, the Claxian said. *I am R'resst, duly elected leader in High Town.*

"Is he going to be okay?" Xax asked.

We don't know. Had he been here, among the company of others, we could have prevented this. Many of our people experienced the same reaction at the time of the changing. *But since it has been so long, I cannot say.* R'resst began to cartwheel behind the others.

Evie relayed the message. Now she knew how Tyler felt all the time as she and the others jogged to keep up with the Claxians. She'd never seen a Claxian move outside before and only now did she comprehend just how claustrophobic that must have been for Sesster, squeezed into that tiny room, despite the fact it was plenty large for the rest of the crew. For him *Tempest* must have seemed much more like a prison than an assignment. But out here R'resst and the other Claxians moved with a simplified grace. It was like watching a dance.

"What are they going to do?" Xax asked, breathing hard as she tried to keep up.

"I don't know. Help him, I hope." Evie glanced back at her mother who moved swiftly, her gaze still darting all over the area. "Mom?"

"Just making sure," she replied, turning to Evie. "I can't help but think this planet looks a lot like one of your father's paintings."

Now that she thought about it, Evie knew exactly which one she was talking about. Her father might have visited Claxia Prime at some time in his career, so it made sense in the cobwebs of his mind while he tried to prevent himself from going crazy he'd painted something very similar. It was a beautiful, peaceful world and for a moment Evie could understand why the Claxians never fought invaders off to defend it: they were too afraid of destroying paradise to save it. And thus, their solution was to always let it go with the knowledge that nothing lasts forever, and any occupation of their world would eventually die out.

It was an interesting philosophy, but it was one Evie couldn't ascribe to. After everything the Athru had done, she wasn't going to let them off so easily.

21

Evie had barely managed to catch up with the Claxians as they entered the nearest building. Despite her improved speed, it was still a challenge as they could cover great distances in a short amount of time. Esterva came up on her left, her face showing the barest hint of a flush, despite the fact she tried to hide it.

"Where's—?" Evie asked, turning.

Xax was still a good hundred meters away, trotting as fast as she could. Evie had to remember Yax-Inax were not known for their speed. But Tos was nowhere to be seen. "I guess the Arc-N'gali stayed with the ship."

"Finally had to use the restroom," Evie quipped. She would have preferred Tos stay with them, but that wasn't her priority now.

They stood in the center of the atrium of the closest building to the landing pad, but it wasn't like any atrium Evie had ever seen. For starters, everything was sized to fit the Claxians, which meant doorways and ceilings were much higher than she was used to. But the structure also seemed to have been sculpted in a way, instead of constructed. As if some ancient mountain had once stood on this spot and the Claxians had delicately carved the building from it over millennia. The architecture was simple and understated, but also seemed to have been done with great care.

The three Claxians had stopped with the gurney holding Sesster. They moved him into the middle of the room, where a circular device rose from the ground. Was this where they were going to try and revive him? It seemed very much out in the open, with no privacy. Doors and archways led to other parts of the building, and above them balconies overlooked their position every thirty meters or so. On them, Evie could see other Claxians moving about. Though some had stopped in their places and held still. She couldn't tell if they were "looking" at Sesster or not. But she figured a species who couldn't see in the same way she could might not care about something like privacy.

Xax came huffing up on her right, placing her two lower hands on her knees as she bent over and gathered her breath. "Too...old," she managed to get out.

"Where's Tos?" Evie asked.

Xax shook her head. Evie didn't like the fact that he could leave at any second and strand them here, but then what would he do? Return to Rutledge empty-handed? It was in his best interest to take them back to Sil space. And for the moment, it was worth the risk. She had to make sure Sesster was okay first.

We thought he was lost to us. It wasn't the voice of R'resst, but one of the others. *I am Jissell*, she said. *I knew Sesster long ago. We told him leaving would end up killing him. It turns out we were right.*

"Does that mean...he's dead?" Evie asked.

"What?" Xax exclaimed, her eyes going wide.

Not yet, said R'resst. *We must not give up hope until we have attempted a connection. Don't be so dour, Jissell.*

Evie put her hand on Xax's heaving shoulder. "Not yet. They're still trying."

"Gods, I wish I could hear Claxian," Xax said. "It would make this so much easier."

"So do I," Esterva said.

Jissell and the other, smaller Claxian lifted Sesster off the gurney and on to the circular divot in the middle of the floor. It had raised three meters and stopped. Once he was inside, they took great care to unfurl his five appendages, splaying them out in different directions. To Evie, it seemed very intimate, as if they were witnessing something private.

Don't worry. We Claxians are not modest. Think your thoughts, and do not be ashamed. What we do, we do to save our fellow.

Evie could feel her face turning read. She herself had been intimate with Sesster in a different kind of way, when he'd helped her with her hallucinations. What would he say when he found out their root cause was now standing right beside him? Evie hoped she got the opportunity to find out.

Each of the Claxians took two of Sesster's appendages with their own, their small "fingers" on the ends of their tentacles interlacing, except for R'resst, who only took one. They then reached out for each other and once they were done, each Claxian was connected to the other in a circle around the body of Sesster. Evie's mind had gone quiet. She wasn't sure what to make of the strange scene. All she could do was hope they were doing the right thing for him and whatever this ritual entailed, it would be successful.

Xax, having finally caught her breath, watched with eyes wide. Evie was sure she'd never seen anything like this before. But when she turned to her mother, Esterva wasn't paying attention to the ritual at all; she was shifting her focus from one area of the building to another. When she glanced up, Evie did the same only to see at least all the Claxians on the balconies above standing perfectly still. Whatever this was, it was solemn. But despite R'resst's assurances there were no

Athru on this planet, Evie couldn't help but share in her mother's paranoia. Did they really leave the planet alone? Were there not plenty of natural resources here as—

Evelyn.

"I heard him!" Evie shouted, her voice echoing through the cavernous space. The name had come across her mind clear and easy, just like she'd remembered. It had been Sesster, she was sure of it.

"He…spoke?" Xax asked.

Each of the Claxians shuddered in unison, and Evie got the impression something was wrong. Something in the air felt…off. "What's happening?"

Too many…

The images are…

Turmoil and anger. I…confusion…and…

Evie held her hands to her head, they were all trying to speak at once, and she couldn't discern what any of them were saying. "Stop, one at a time," she said through the pain in her head.

He's trying to communicate directly with you, R'resst finally said once the crosstalk had calmed down.

What would he want with her? Jissell asked.

"Does it matter?" Evie asked.

"What? What's happening?" Xax asked.

"He's alive," Evie replied. "And he's trying to reach out."

He's been under for too long. Waking him is…dangerous, R'resst said. *If we're not careful, his body could go into shock before it has had a chance to fully wake. We need to calm him.*

Evie tried reaching out with her own mind to find a way to reach him, to let him know everything was okay and to keep him calm. But if the other Claxians couldn't do it, what chance did she have? She wasn't sure if it mattered or not, but she decided it was better to try than not. She closed her eyes and concentrated.

Sesster. I'm here. Everything is okay.

A bright, white light filled the room and Evie lifted her arm to shield her face from the light and the ambient heat. Once she was sure she wouldn't burn her retinas out, she opened her eyes to find she was no longer in the cool Claxian atrium. A soft wind blew against her skin, but the heat from the sun shone down on her and hard dirt crunched under her boots. She glanced around, realizing she was alone beside a long road. A road she recognized. "I'm back," she whispered as the images of Sissk coalesced for her. This was the same place she'd come in Sesster's *mind-place* before.

Still shielding her eyes, she turned around to find the road desolate, except for snow-less Selasi Mountains in the distance. Just as she was about to call out, a gossamer-white shimmer appeared in the distance. As it grew closer it coalesced until it took the white-robed form she recognized as Sesster's mental projection of himself in this place. Once he was fully solid, his feet settled on the ground and he opened his eyes, which were still white and pupil-less.

"Sesster?" Evie asked, wanting to make sure this was still him and not one of the other Claxians.

"Captain," he said. "You're alive."

Evie's composure broke and she ran to him, attempting to wrap him in a hug, but when she reached him, there was nothing but air. "I am sorry, my *mind-place* is not still whole, like most of me."

"That's okay," she said, feeling tears well up in eyes that were only a mental projection. Even if they weren't real, they felt real. "And I'm not a captain anymore. Just plain Evie."

"What is going on?" Sesster asked.

"You've been in a coma—or whatever it is your people experience. Zenfor said one day you just…stopped. You curled up and we haven't been able to wake you since."

Sesster pitched forward, then righted himself. "Yes. After we'd returned to Coalition space. After we'd seen—what they did. The destruction—"

She reached out, even though she couldn't touch him, she placed her hand where it barely moved through his arm. "It's okay. Volf took the ship back to the planet to get us. Most of us came back. We made it back to *Tempest*. We're still together."

He furrowed his brow. "But we're not on *Tempest* now. I'm getting…flashes…of memory. Strange images. A woman missing an eye. And…you, with one of the Athru."

She nodded. "The woman without the eye is Samiya. We found her and what remained of her refugee camp when we returned. The Athru is my birth mother."

"You're half-Athru," Sesster said, digesting the information. "Then is that…how you knew how to save us back at Omicron Terminus?"

Evie nodded. "Listen, there is a lot to go over and a lot you've missed. But I need you to relax. The other Claxians—"

"Other Claxians?" Sesster asked.

"Yes, we brought you back to Claxia Prime. It was the only way we could wake you back up. Your life signs were growing critical. Xax said if we didn't bring you back home, you would die."

Sesster pitched forward again. "Wait…no…something is wrong. Something I must...remember." His face strained and for a moment, his white eyes glowed. "We arrived…with an Arc-N'gali."

"We couldn't bring any humans. The Athru have Claxia Prime surrounded and have bioscanners on their ships. It's a—"

"No, no, that's not what I mean," Sesster said, straining. "I can't read Arc-N'gali; they are closed off to us. But there

was someone else. Someone whose thoughts came to me..."
He inhaled sharply. "Evelyn, the Sargans can't be trusted.
Rutledge can't be trusted. I remember now, I could feel his
subterfuge back on *Tempest*. He means to destroy us all."

Evie shook her head. "No, that can't be. He's been helping
us; he gave us this ship for reconnaissance. So, the Sil would
know how to attack."

"I'm sorry, Evelyn. I wish I could have told you sooner."

Evie blinked and all of a sudden, she was back in the
Claxian atrium, her head spinning. She fell to her knees.

"Whoa," Xax said as she and Esterva jumped to grab her
on either side.

He's stirring, R'resst said. *I detect his brainwaves.*

Evie shook her head to clear it. Could Sesster have been
right? If so they needed to get off this planet and back in the
undercurrent as soon as possible. "We need to go," she
croaked. She would just have to hope the Claxians could finish
taking care of Sesster.

"Go. Where?" Xax asked.

A terrible thought passed through her mind as Evie got to
her feet. Instead of answering Xax she turned on a dime and
sprinted out of the building and back toward the ship. *No, no,
no, no,* she kept thinking in time with the beats of her feet as
she pushed her Athru capabilities to the limit. She covered the
distance twice as fast as she had on the first run, but she
stopped short before reaching the ship they'd arrived on.

There stood Tos in front of it, with a smug look on his face
while two Athru cruisers flanked the ship on either side, and a
dozen Athru had joined him, all of them staring at her with
intense hatred.

She stood there a moment, taking in the situation. Had Tos
given them up as soon as they were out of earshot with Sesster,
or had this been the plan ever since they left, the Athru playing
along with those "inspection stops"? Not that it mattered. Evie

could outrun them, but where to? And what of Xax and Esterva, she couldn't leave them behind. Her only options were to try to fight them off, or surrender. And neither looked to be in her favor.

22

Cas's comm chirped, breaking him out of his trance. He'd been going over battle plans, trying to figure out at least three different strategies they could use once they were close enough to the Athru fleet to engage them. But he wasn't a battle-hardened warrior, nor was he a general. He was an explorer, and up until very recently, a courier. Determining ship positions and battle strategies wasn't his forte. Nor was holding the lives of so many people in his hands. He knew Rutledge was much better at this kind of work, but he hated to go ask the man for help, even if it would mean saving lives in the long run. He supposed he'd just have to swallow his pride and do it.

His comm chirped again, reminding him someone was on the other side of his door. "Come in?" he half-asked, running his hands down his face. Despite the uneventful trip to Sargan space, he still wasn't sleeping well.

Box entered, nearly pushing the doors apart. "What were you doing in here? Having a rub of the ol' knob?"

Cas sighed. "What do you want?"

Box straightened. "Permission to open and inspect Xax's virus collection."

"Her what?" Had he said *virus* collection?

"You mean neither Evelyn nor Captain Greene told you about it?" Box's voice came across condescending. "It's not illegal."

"That's good to know. Do I want to know what it is or is it just going to stress me out further?"

"Probably stress you out. It's a collection of some of the most deadly and dangerous viruses known to exist. And it's sitting in a secure facility in sickbay."

Cas could feel his eyes go wide. "Why the hell would anyone have something like that on board?"

"To create antiviruses to different strains of diseases, of course," Box said. "You can't develop antidotes if you don't know the root cause. She told me they aren't common knowledge but are kept for emergencies."

"And you want to open them up on the ship?" Cas asked.

Box animated his hands in front of him. "I know what you're going to say. But picture this: the Sil weapons don't work on the Athru. We need a backup. I still have Esterva's sample in the lab from where Xax took it when she came on board. All I need to do is subject it to a few dozen of the deadliest viruses in the known universe to see which one is more effective. Then Zenfor can build that into a new weapon! Neat, right?"

"You want to make a biological weapon," Cas said, not asking.

Box held up a finger. "A *dangerous* and *lethal* biological weapon. Don't forget the dangerous part."

Cas leaned back in his chair. "And what are the odds this weapon only affects the Athru and no one else? Can you guarantee it won't hurt any of the species on board if something goes wrong?"

Box gave him a semi-shrug, tilting his head to the side. "I mean there's always the *possibility* something might happen. But trust me, if something did get out, no one would be alive long enough to realize what had happened. You should see some of the viruses in this unit, there are ones in there once airborne will kill a human in less than point-zero-five seconds. Your brain wouldn't even register what had happened to your body before it shut down." He stroked his metal chin. "I wonder if you'd still be conscious in those last few moments? Kind of like a living death as the final electrical signals—"

"Okay, I get it," Cas said, standing. "As appealing as a weapon that could kill all of us in under a second sounds, I'm going to have to say no to that one."

"But—"

"Why don't you tell me the *real* reason you're here." He stared straight into the robot's yellow blinking eyes.

"I'm sure I don't know what you're talking about," Box replied.

Cas shook his head, not taking his eyes off Box. "Uh, uh. You can pull that shit with the rest of the crew, but not with me. I know you too well. And despite any 'improvements' you might have made, I can still tell when you're lying. You knew I'd never approve a request to remove those viruses and if you wanted to do it, you would have without my permission. Maybe you have already, I don't know. So, tell me what's going on."

Box's eyes stopped blinking. "Just so you know, I *didn't* remove the viruses. I wouldn't do that. Anymore." Cas held his gaze. "Okay, fine, you want to beat it out of me? Here. Here it is! I am worried about you. Happy now? Happy you've gone and embarrassed a Coalition medal of honor recipient?"

Cas sat back down. "Worried about what?"

Box hesitated. "Rutledge. You don't make the best decisions around him. It's like you become…this other person. Like you're trying to be the person you thought you should have been when you were still on the *Achlys*. Or maybe the person you think should have stood up to him the first time. Either way, it's not you. He's affecting you in ways you may not realize."

Cas tried to internalize Box's words without reacting to them. His first instinct was to refute everything the robot had said; to tell him he was being ridiculous. But he was right. Just being in Rutledge's presence was enough to set him on edge. And there was no shortage of animosity between the two, that much was clear. "Look, I appreciate you coming down here and checking on me, but you don't have to worry. I can take care of Rutledge."

"Can you?" Box stepped closer to Cas's desk. "In my studies I've downloaded a great deal on psychological stress and the effects it has on a person's psyche. You may be dealing with stressors you don't even realize."

"Of course, I'm dealing with *stressors*. I've got the entire fate of humanity on my back with a species who wants to kill us on one side and another species who would rather step on us than help on the other. It's kind of a lot."

Box's eyes brightened. "You know what this means?"

"What?"

"It means I am now your designated therapist." He sat in one of the chairs opposite Cas, crossing one of his metal legs over the other and tented his fingers together. "Why don't we start at the beginning. Tell me about your childhood."

"Oh, for Kor's sake." Cas stood and walked over to the window. They were still in the undercurrent, and its green glow enveloped everything outside the glass. They would be back in his old stomping grounds in only a few hours and then all they could do was wait for Evie.

"I'm waiting," Box said.

Cas had to admit, he had some trepidation about returning to Sargan space, especially considering he hadn't been back since Evie had first shown up and whisked him away to the Coalition. And the fact Rutledge was back on his ship did make it seem like a lot, mentally. Maybe it wouldn't be a bad idea to take Box up on his offer. He turned back to the robot. "Okay, look. I'm only doing this because I've known you forever, not because you're a *therapist*. If I wanted a good one I'd call Belmont in here."

"Ouch," Box said.

"And when we're done, you're going to help me with battle plans. I need a strategic mind."

"Um, perhaps you've forgotten, but my function is to heal, not to kill."

Cas sat back down. "Then I guess we're both going to do be doing something we don't want to. Okay, where do we start? And don't say with my parents."

Box adjusted himself. "Let's begin with your parents…"

***

Evie winced as the clamps enclosed both her hands, keeping them locked together in front of her. To the left and the right stood Athru soldiers, both of them encased in a type of armor she'd never seen before, and an energy weapon of some sort on their backs. It looked like it might be part of their armor, and automatically deploy in the middle of an engagement, which she supposed was useful if you needed to keep your hands free. And if these Athru were anything like the ones she's met on the planet back beyond Omicron Terminus, they probably ran both on two legs and all four appendages depending on the need.

Esterva stood beside her, also clad in the same manacles, staring straight ahead. She'd been right, the Athru had been here. Or at least they'd been monitoring closer than Evie had thought possible. Xax stood off to the side, kept apart from her and Esterva, but the Athru hadn't bound her yet and Evie couldn't figure out why.

165

"Why don'cha git th' other one too," Tos said, walking in front of Evie, but looking at the Athru. "She's part of their group."

"Athru have no quarrel with Yax-Inax," one of the Athru soldiers said in the Coalition's universal language. "She is free to do as she pleases."

Tos scoffed. "I don' git you people."

Evie didn't either, but she wasn't going to waste this chance. "Xax, make sure Sesster wakes up. He's alive and he's in there. But make sure he's okay, then get off this planet. Get out of this system." Xax nodded.

"She has nothing to fear from us, mutant," the soldier said. "But you are not so lucky." Evie glanced to her mother who remained stone-faced. She wasn't going to give them an inch, and Evie could respect that.

R'resst cartwheeled up to them, coming to a stop only a few meters from where they held Evie and Esterva in front of a small Athru ship that had landed beside Tos's ship.

I am sorry. I've tried to argue on your behalf, but the Athru are insistent you come with them. We didn't know they were monitoring you.

Evie wasn't sure if she could believe that or not, but for the moment it didn't matter. The Claxians were pacifists; it wasn't like they'd fight off the Athru to save Evie and her mother. She couldn't fault them for being who they were.

If I could do more, I would.

"Just make sure Sesster gets better," Evie replied. "You'll have to figure out a way to communicate with Xax, but I expect you'll give her the same courtesy you've shown us so far."

Of course.

Evie turned to Tos, who still had a smirk on his wide, red face. "And just what the hell are you going to tell the fleet when you get back?"

Tos smacked his lips. "With any luck, by the time I git back, th' fleet will be nothin' but spare parts."

Evie's heart jumped into her throat. The fleet. The *Tempest*. "You think Rutledge is that clever?"

"Oh, I know he is. I've seen it with my own eyes." The eyes on his face closed and the eyes on the stalks above his hat seemed to grow with intensity, until Evie felt a pressure in her head. Tos laughed. "Your cap'n is too wrapped up in his own mind to see it. I know." He tapped his own head and the pressure released. So, it was true, Arc-N'gali were telepathic, and resistant to the Claxians. Rutledge had made sure Tos had accompanied them just in case something happened with Sesster, so he couldn't warn them. And yet he had anyway. And just as Cas had suspected, Rutledge was going to turn on him. But why?

"On the ship. Now." One of the Athru guards pressed his fist into Evie's back. She winced again; it was like he knew just where to press to make her back muscles tweak.

"Don't go back to the fleet," Evie called to Xax. "Don't give them a reason to kill you. Just leave this place and go home." She barely got the last words out before she was shoved into the ship, with her mother behind her. She couldn't tell if Xax had heard her or not.

"Sit," the Athru said, pushing her down on a low bench. The other one pushed Esterva down beside her. A magnetic clamp pulled Evie's hands down in front of her, so the manacle clamped down to the shelf, causing her to be halfway bent over. Esterva's did the same.

"Where are you taking us?" Evie demanded.

The Athru said something in their native language but Evie missed it. Before she could say anything else the ship had taken off and she felt the ground drop out from under them. Despite the fact she'd never been on an Athru ship before, the interior of this small craft felt surprisingly familiar, not as alien as the Sil ships. She would have expected their fleet to be different somehow, more advanced. Or maybe something akin to the stone temples she'd encountered on their planet.

"Do you know what's going on?" Evie asked. "Why didn't they just kill us down there?"

"I'm not someone who gambles, but I am pretty sure we are to be inspected before we're killed," Esterva replied. She turned to Evie. "I'm sorry, this isn't how I wanted this to go. But I'm glad I came. If I hadn't, you would have had to face this alone."

"Did you know? They were watching us?"

"I had my suspicions ever since the last few checks the Arc-N'gali pulled us through. There was something…too uniform about all of them. But I've been away from our people a long time, and I didn't want to jeopardize the Claxian. If I'd said something, he might not have made it back in time."

If there was one bright spot in all this, it was the fact Sesster was back among his own people now, and safe. Evie hoped she'd still be able to deliver the information to Cas somehow, but she tried to stamp down any hope she felt at the fact the Athru hadn't killed them down on the planet. She'd known the risks of this mission going in and despite everything, she would do it again if necessary. Although next time maybe she would have Box pilot the ship instead. Whatever the Sargans had planned, she prayed Cas was smart enough to figure it out in time. Otherwise, there was a good chance the Athru could succeed in their ultimate goal. She had to find a way to get a message to Cas, warn him about Rutledge. She wasn't sure how one man could go up against an entire fleet of Sil ships, even with a ship as big and powerful as the *Hiawatha*.

"I know that look," Esterva said. "And whatever you're thinking, don't. It's too late for me, but they may be willing to spare you."

"What are you talking about?" Evie asked.

"I'm a traitor to the cause and they won't hesitate to execute me. Probably in some elaborate ceremony to make an example to others. But you're an anomaly. I'd be willing to bet they'll be as interested in you as the Sil were. You might still be able to have a life."

"You're talking like it's already over," Evie said, furrowing her brow. "Like we don't even have a chance."

"Sweetheart, that's what I'm trying to tell you," Esterva said. "We don't."

23

"I'm surprised the defense net is still there." Evie watched as the small ship flew past the series of interconnected space weapon platforms that were designed to protect both Earth and Claxia Prime in the event of an invasion, not unlike the Athru one. The only problem was the designers of the net hadn't anticipated a species being able to hide within bubbles of time to obscure themselves from detection. Evie imagined the fleet came through the Horus system and the platforms didn't even register a blip until it was too late, and the ships were out of range.

The net itself was a giant sphere of platforms set every hundred thousand kilometers in every direction, which once it was complete, had formed a kind of protective bubble around the orbits of all the inner planets of the Horus system: Ra, Earth, and Claxia Prime. But now they seemed to be sitting out there, dormant, even though hundreds of Athru ships moved between them.

"It's possible they've reprogrammed the net to fire on only Coalition ships. Or perhaps only ships where a human signature is detected," Esterva said. "Or they've disabled them completely."

Another reason Cas couldn't bring the fleet here. She wasn't sure how effective the platforms would be against the

Sil ships, but they would decimate the *Tempest* in a matter of seconds if they were indeed programmed to fire on it. Evie strained to look beyond the window from her bent-over position, trying to see their destination. Out in the distance was an Athru ship much larger than the others patrolling the system. "I think I see where we're going."

Esterva's long neck bent to see where she was looking. "Of course. *His* ship."

"Dulthar?" Evie asked. Esterva nodded. "You actually thought you could get aboard that thing undetected? It looks like a fortress."

Esterva shrugged. "Don't discount the element of ignorance. People often don't look for what they don't know is there."

As they grew closer, Evie took in the size of the massive vessel. It was at least a kilometer long, with a wide oval shape and what looked to be a control tower or perhaps even a tall building rising from the back third of the ship. She couldn't see any propulsion, but if she thought about it, the ship could be a distant cousin to the one that tried to destroy them in the mine field at Omicron Terminus. "Kind of overcompensating, isn't he?"

"The size of the ship has a purpose; it focuses the energy from smaller vessels to annihilate planets. And while some of the larger ships can do that on their own, this is the only ship with enough raw power to destroy stars."

"So that's how they do it," Evie said. "You would think by being able to wield that much raw power they could do something constructive with it instead."

"It's what I've been working for my whole life," Esterva replied. "The ship also acted as my people's home for a long time."

"What do you mean? I thought your people were from that weird planet—the one out of time."

171

Esterva shook her head. "We just developed there. And once our ancestors figured out how to manipulate the planet, how to control how it moved through time, we finally managed to construct something that could sustain us long-term. Something we could live on while being in the same time-frame as the rest of the universe." She stared at the ship through the window. "It took centuries to build."

The city-ship was in full view, taking up most of the window now and Evie could see a series of small ports on the side, which could only be docking ports or ship hangars. She tried to remember what Cas told her about the ship they'd boarded, about how the doors had just melted away. This ship didn't look like it could do that, but then again, she'd seen stranger things.

One of the Athru in the seats ahead of them said something in his native language, and Evie thought she caught the word "docking" but wasn't sure. Perhaps if she focused, she could discern their words.

The small ship came up right beside the hull of city-sized vessel, and the Athru piloted it until Evie was sure they would collide. But instead all she heard was a thump and a small hiss of air before the door on the shuttle did *melt away* to reveal the interior of a corridor which could only be on the mothership. The clamps holding her and Esterva down released and Evie was able to lean back for the first time in an hour and stretch.

"Let's go," the Athru said, taking her by the arm first and leading her through the opening into the corridor. Had he said those words in universal or the Athru language? She wasn't sure. Not that it mattered. As long as she could understand them.

They were led through a few corridors until they reached what Evie could only assume was a main thoroughfare. It was a long space, and the ceiling had to be at least a hundred meters high. Evie couldn't believe a space this large existed on a ship, but here it was. Hundreds of Athru milled about, going about their business, passing them by until one by one they noticed Evie, each of them stopping to stare at her. Before she knew it, everyone in the space had come to a dead stop and any ambient noise had died until it was deathly quiet. She found it incredibly creepy.

The Athru soldier took her by the arm and moved her through the space, the crowd parting before her as if they were all of one mind. Each face was the same: a blank face, with eyes intent and searching. She'd never felt so exposed in her life. And she had to wonder if this was part of a ritual. Surely they could have docked the ship closer to their destination, but was it possible the Athru got some kind of sick pleasure at seeing her paraded in front of them like this?

Halfway down the thoroughfare, the guards veered to the left, where the crowd parted again, and they walked through another large archway into an even taller space. Despite the open door, this room was empty. As if everyone knew not to come in here, which set Evie on edge. The sides of the walls were clad in what to Evie looked like glowing wall panels, each of them pulsing with a blue energy. Above them the ceiling was transparent so she could see the edge of the tall tower that sat on top of the ship, and the stars beyond. She turned back to Esterva only to see her face paler than usual, which meant they must be close.

The corridor was long, but not as long as the one they'd just left. And it seemed to end in a semi-circle, which was a glass wall, bisected by tall columns at multiple points so the windows were thin, but still showed the stars beyond. The columns in between them also pulsed with the same blue energy she'd seen on the walls. But the entire room was so massive, she didn't realize there was a figure standing at the end of the room, with its back to them. The figure turned as the sounds of their footsteps approached. He was an Athru, sharp-faced with hard features and even harder gray eyes.

"Finally," he said. "Welcome home."

"Dulthar, I presume," Evie said.

"Correct," he said, staring them both down. There was no humor in his voice, nor his face. Evie got the impression he was not someone to trifle with. He was as tall as Esterva, but wider in some ways. An alpha among many betas. Evie wondered if all Athru leaders were like this. "I already know your name as well, Evie."

"You'll call me Ms. Diazal. I only let people I like call me Evie." The Athru guard jerked Evie and she tensed, causing the guard's grip to slip on her arm and he stumbled back, unprepared for just how sturdy she was. The guard returned to his position but didn't take Evie's arm again.

"I'll call you whatever I like," Dulthar said. He turned his attention to Esterva. "Your betrayal is complete with your daughter's disrespect," he said.

"Betrayal? I'm trying to save the Athru! This madness has to stop Dulthar. I tried to tell you before, but you wouldn't listen to reason."

"Because there was no reason in your words. Only cowardice. You would have us undo millions of years of planning. Of *searching*. For what? For…this?" He gestured to Evie.

"Searching? You were looking for us?" Evie asked.

Dulthar shook his head. "Haven't even told her the truth yet." He *tsked*. "I'm surprised at you Esterva. I thought you'd at least allow the child to make her own decision in the matter. But when you withhold all the pertinent information from her, it's a little more difficult."

"Mother, what's he talking about?" Evie asked. She didn't like where this was going. Esterva had already lied to her multiple times, and she'd promised there would be no more. But here they were again, just like before.

Esterva gritted her teeth. "She's already made her decision; can't you see that? I know by now you know what happened on Hescal. What her crew did to the planet and those you left behind. And if you ask me, they *deserved* it."

Hescal. Was that the name of the planet out of time? The one the Athru had developed on?

Dulthar threw up a hand. "I received a report from Rockron. It was…inconclusive." He turned to Evie. "Do you remember your old friend? Before you brutally murdered him?"

"I wouldn't call him a friend," Evie said. "Considering he turned me against my own people."

"No. *She* turned you against your own people by creating you in the first place," Dulthar yelled, pointing at Esterva. "She's the reason you are this…hybrid. You should have been Daingne, of the full Athru blood. Instead, you're…whatever you are."

"Daingne is dead," Evie said. "Just like every other Athru you throw in my way. If you're not careful, you'll be next."

"Idle threats don't work on me, girl," Dulthar said. "And you shouldn't spout off when you're backed into a corner. It only shows how desperate you are. We already know your Sil fleet is preparing an attack. It's funny, before your ship came back we never had a problem with the Sil. And now they'll all have to die because of your influence."

"I wouldn't be so cocky if I were you, Dulthar," Esterva said. "I've seen their weapons. Their technology. And if you had been confident you could beat them, you would have destroyed them instead of creating a treaty. Either that or tried to subjugate them like you have all the other Coalition species."

Dulthar glared at her under hooded eyes. "You speak out of turn Esterva, it has always been your most failing characteristic."

"I speak the truth," she replied. "The Athru are diseased. Stricken ill by their own hubris. And your leadership will end up—" The movement was faster than Evie's eyes could track. One moment Dulthar was in front of them, the next he was behind her mother, his hands around her head. In one swift move he jerked, and Evie heard an audible *SNAP*. She watched helplessly as Esterva's eyes lost the light in them and her body crumpled to the floor.

Evie fell to her knees, scrambling over to Esterva's inert body, praying he'd only harmed her but knowing in her heart of hearts it was too late, and the woman who had been her mother was dead. She wanted to scream, to produce a primal yell that would reverberate through the universe, but instead she held her mother, cradling her face in her enclosed hands as the light in the room reflected off the crystal embedded in her forehead.

"My leadership...will fulfill our destiny," Dulthar said.

24

Cas sat in his command chair on the bridge, cracking his knuckles. He'd already been through all of them once, and as he watched the ship come out of the undercurrent he tried to crack them again, finding there was nothing left but silence.

"We've exited the undercurrent, sir," Ronde said. "Right on target."

"Sargan space," Cas said. More specifically, the Vetar sector. Close to Devil's Gate. Though it was almost impossible to tell based on the position of the stars alone, Cas could feel it in his bones. He'd traveled these areas too much, and they'd been ingrained in him. Returning sent an icy chill down his back. It was hard to believe it had been eighteen years since he'd last seen this place.

"Shall we head to Devil's Gate, sir?" River asked.

Cas shook his head. "Hold position here for now, and Zaal, instruct the Sil fleet to do the same. Even if this space isn't the hub of activity it used to be, a Sil armada showing up at the most popular trading port might cause some problems."

"Aye," Zaal said, "transmitting now."

"So now what?" Hank asked. "We just sit here and wait?"

"Sir, our…guest is trying to reach you through the ship's comms. Should I let the message come through?" Tileah asked.

Cas took a deep breath, staring at the view screen. He'd already had his doubts about Rutledge but, with Saturina and Box piling it on, it was hard to ignore the voices in the back of his head. He wished he could just put the man in an escape pod and jettison him out into space. If he could just do that, if he could be rid of him once and for all, he'd feel a lot better. While Box's *therapy* session hadn't done much, it had reaffirmed Cas's belief he didn't make good decisions when Rutledge was involved. He was too compromised. Cas needed a buffer, someone who could act a shield between him and Rutledge if this was going to continue.

He ran his hand through his hair. "Samiya, can I see you in the command room a moment?" She nodded and stood from the Engineering position. "Hold the call for now. Make him wait," Cas said as they passed Tileah's station.

"I guess you heard," Samiya said once they were both in the command room. Cas stopped, staring at her.

"Heard?"

"About my trip down to see him. I'm sorry I went behind your back, but I needed to do it, for my own sanity and I knew you'd never approve of it."

"Wait," Cas said, putting his hands up. "What are you talking about?"

"Rutledge," she said, as if it were the most obvious thing in the world. "Isn't that why you called me in here? I went down to speak with him while we were in route."

"Alone?" Cas asked.

"No, I had Vrij with me." *Fuck.* She'd involved Vrij in this? Now he'd have to interrogate the Bulaq about why he didn't report her activity. What was the point of having a chief of security if he kept things secret?

"Samiya, I don't like to hear this. I need people I can trust on this ship, especially now. Especially after what happened. You can see why this might make me a little worried."

She shook her head. "I know. And I'm sorry I didn't tell you. But it's been weighing on me, like I know it's been weighing on you. I couldn't stand it."

"What did you end up telling him?"

She sighed and took one of the seats. He noticed she seemed to collapse into it with extra weight, as if she was carrying a heavy load. "The only thing that matters. I told him what John and I did to the *Achlys*."

Cas's heart thudded in his throat. "How did he take it?"

She pursed her lips. "I'm not sure. He was mostly quiet."

Dammit. He couldn't blame her for needing to get it off her chest; he had his own issues digging at his psyche. But if Rutledge knew the original experiment hadn't been a failure but instead was the result of sabotage there was no telling how he'd react. Cas tapped his comm. "Vrij?"

"Yes, Captain?"

"Has there been any change at Rutledge's quarters? Anything…strange?"

There was a pause on the other end. "I don't b-believe so. My officers report nothing out of the ordinary."

"Thanks, Vrij, keep me updated." Cas ended the comm.

"Maybe it wasn't a big deal," Samiya offered.

Cas cut her a glance. "You really think he wouldn't take it personally? Especially since he still thinks it's his job to save the Coalition?" It was obvious a barrier wasn't going to be possible. Cas would have to confront him, get over his problems with the man somehow.

Or maybe not. Maybe he should let Rutledge stew in the knowledge everyone had worked against him. Then again, it might just be the thing that could turn him from friend to foe. Cas didn't believe he'd hurt their chances of winning this fight, but he might try to wrest control of the ship somehow. Cas needed to make sure that didn't happen.

Cas's comm rang again. "Yes, Lieutenant?"

"Sir, the message is more insistent this time. I believe he really wants to speak to you. He's trying to use a priority code from his room," Tileah said.

Cas crossed his arms and shook his head, looking at Samiya. "Go ahead and put it through. Might as well see what he wants."

"Aye."

Cas braced himself.

The comm opened with an audible pop and Cas knew something was wrong. "S-sir? Can y-you hear me?"

Cas snapped to attention. "Vrij? What's going on?"

"He's gone, sir. Overrode the doors somehow, I don't know. I w-was on g-guard. H-he…h-he—"

"Vrij, what happened?" Cas asked as Samiya's eyes went wide.

"He t-tore my p-personal comm from my arm, stole my w-weapon," Vrij said. Cas ran back onto the bridge, followed by Samiya.

"We have a breach, locate Rutledge, he broke out of his room," Cas ordered. "And get someone from medical down to the crew quarters to help Vrij." Cas didn't want to think about how a human had overpowered Vrij, with his razor-sharp mandible, but somehow Rutledge had done it. His stomach sank. He never should have allowed him to step foot on this ship.

"I've informed sickbay, Box is sending Menkel to help Vrij," Zaal reported.

"No sign of him on the internal scanners," Tileah said, working her control console. "For some reason he's not registering."

Cas looked at Samiya. "Where could he be going? He wouldn't want to get off the ship, would he?"

She shook her head. "I don't know. There's no telling what he might want to do."

Cas tapped his comm. "Saturina, keep the bays on alert. Rutledge escaped from his room and we don't know where he's headed."

"Acknowledged," she replied without any judgment in her voice, for which he was grateful. She had tried to warn him, after all.

Tileah tapped her personal comms. "All security teams on alert, we have a breach. Human male, approximately two meters tall, one-hundred five kilograms. To be considered dangerous." She watched her console for a moment. "Nothing yet."

"Which means he's not out in the open," Cas said. He had to be using the access corridors in the ship, but for a man as big as Rutledge that would be a tight squeeze. Where could he be going? His gaze snapped back to Samiya. "Have you heard from Engineering?"

She turned to her console. Cas couldn't believe he'd allowed this to happen. He should have kept Rutledge in the brig from the moment he stepped on board, instead of allowing him "freedom". He'd picked up a few new tricks in the past two decades; breaking through a secured door and tearing out someone's personal comm were extreme measures, and for an eighty-year-old man, shouldn't be possible.

"I'm not getting a response," Samiya said. "Just an automated reply saying everything is normal."

"That's where he's gone," Cas said. Whatever he was planning, it had something to do with Engineering. A thought ran through Cas's mind. It was also where the Sil weapon had been located on the *Achlys*. If Samiya had told him what she'd done…he couldn't be that petty, could he? Then again, this was a man who'd court-martialed his junior officer for having the gall to disagree with him.

"Security teams to Engineering," Tileah said, locking down her station. "I'll take care of this, sir."

Cas held out a hand. "No, he'll want me. Keep your people out of Engineering until I get there. We have no idea what he's doing or what he's capable of. He might be able to blow the core. I need to get a read on him before we make a move."

Tileah opened her comm and revised her orders to the security forces.

"You can't just go down there," Hank said. "The man is unstable, and you're the captain."

"I'm also the one responsible," Cas replied. "You have the bridge—and if something happens to me, the ship. I know you'll make sure we succeed in our mission." He ran over to the hypervator doors.

"Wait," Samiya said, locking down her station. "I'm coming too. If he's upset at me it might help take some of the heat off you. Give him two targets to worry about instead of one."

Cas thought about it a moment, then nodded. He didn't want to put Samiya in danger, but she was right, and if they could catch Rutledge off guard then he was willing to take the chance, for now. "Don't let them know we're coming. If he's already in there, I don't want to give him any kind of advance notice."

Tileah nodded as the hypervators doors closed, sealing him and Samiya from the bridge. Even though time was short, Cas needed one thing before they reached Engineering. It was a good thing the armory was on the way.

25

"Monster," Evie said, still holding the limp head of her mother in her manacled hands. She couldn't believe she was gone...just like that. Esterva had always seemed so strong—so in control. Like an immovable object. And she'd helped save them from the Sissk extremists, as well as the Sil. In an instant, Evie was without her parents once more. She wished she could at least close Esterva's eyes, but with the contraption around her hands there was no chance of it. All she could do was clumsily set her mother's head back down. As she did, she stared back up at Dulthar with a piercing stare. He glared right back, a frown on his face.

"She had it coming," he growled. "She betrayed our people, first by allowing those *humans* on her ship instead of eliminating them, and then by creating *you*." She was about to interrupt him, but he leaned down closer to him. "Make no mistake, you are an *abomination*. No matter what anyone else has told you. You shouldn't exist and the only reason you're not laying there dead beside her is because I am *not* a monster. I am going to give you a chance to choose for yourself. You didn't ask to be created or brought into this world, so I can hardly fault you for it, but every decision you make after this point will determine whether I let you live or not. This is a trial basis, and you should be grateful for my generosity." He straightened up and clasped his long hands behind his back. His robe was long like Esterva's though it was a muted navy, which stood in contrast to his grayish skin.

"I don't need your generosity. I want nothing to do with the Athru, or your…crusade. Whatever it is. You have done more damage to me than you can ever know, and I will spend my last breath fighting you."

"A child's words, from a child's viewpoint. The world is bigger than that, Evelyn. There is no good or bad. Perspective is everything, these simple constructs do not exist." He turned and walked back over to the curved wall. Evie stood and the guards behind her tensed.

"I know anyone who uses other people for his own means, who kills because he doesn't get his way, or who decides an entire species isn't worth the air they breathe is evil. There's no other word for it."

He spun on her. "There is. *Justified*. I am justified in everything I do," he spat. "Even sparing your life. And since Esterva never enlightened you to our cause, I can see why you would think that. The fact that she never told you means she was afraid you might agree with us. I'm no fool, I know your power. I know if you really wanted to you could probably kill me. But there is an Athru in there somewhere, and you need to satisfy that part deep inside you that has been yearning for something ever since you were born and left on that wretched planet to grow up in a meager and meaningless existence." He walked over to her, inspecting her. "The least your mother could have done was brought you back to us, so we could raise you properly." He reached out with one of his hands but withdrew it before it touched Evie's cheek. "Have you noticed yet? This entire time we've been speaking in our native language?"

Evie thought about it, realizing he was right. She wasn't speaking universal anymore. When had that happened? Had she just naturally fallen into their language? Was it that part of Daingne that was still inside her somewhere, translating? She hadn't even known she had the ability to speak it.

"You see, it's a natural part of you. And if you'll just stop fighting it…" Dulthar trailed off. "Allow me to enlighten you. Then we'll see if you're still beholden to your precious Coalition." He turned again and raised his arms. Above them a massive starfield seemed to explode out of nowhere. As best Evie could tell, it was a holographic projection, but unlike any she'd ever seen before. The images seemed much more realistic, almost like they were live rather than representations. "Since the beginning of our recorded history, humanity has always been a thorn in our side." In the starfield, one of the stars began to pulse and the field *zoomed* in on that star. To Evie it looked like the star around the Athru planet, Hescal. "Our ancient texts speak of our people crash-landing on Hescal eons ago. Eons for us, but much less time for the rest of the universe. Whether it was fate or just bad luck, we came upon the planet and could not find a way off. It took hundreds of years before we even knew it was out of sync with the rest of time. But our ancient texts told us something else: humanity was not to be trusted. Humanity was a destructive force in the universe, and it was the responsibility of anyone who encountered them to destroy them, or watch them decimate planet after planet."

The image had zoomed in closer to show Hescal in full, its green tinge and rings distinctive against the stars. "This has all been because of some ancient writings? Your entire basis for living?" Evie laughed. "Where did they come from? Who wrote them? Do you even know? Or are you just blindly following what has been written for you?"

"They came from our ancestors, in their journeys through the stars," Dulthar said. "What we know, as it has been passed down through our genetic code, is that allowing humanity to live and thrive is a danger the universe cannot afford. And it is our duty to make sure this plague ends, here and now."

"You can't be serious," Evie said. "Just because it says so in some old book or even because that's what previous generations thought doesn't mean it's true! Where's the proof? What says humanity is so bad? How do you know the information is even accurate?"

Dulthar's face turned stoic. "You already know the answer to that question." The images of the planets and stars moved again, this time everything became a blur until it reformed on the Claxian system. Where they were now. Horus was easy to pick out, glowing a soft orange in the middle of the system, while Ra, Earth, Claxia Prime and the other planets made their elliptical orbits. But it wasn't a live image, as Earth was still blue and green.

"You've witnessed it," Dulthar said. "In the Coalition itself. Who was it who decided to deceive their partners and create secret missions?" Dulthar walked closer to her. "Who was it who covered it all up, keeping all the information from their closest allies, so they could build a weapon of unimaginable power? *Who* in the Coalition were the ones who orchestrated everything that you knew to be wrong?" He was in her face, staring into her eyes. "Who was it, Evie?"

"Humans," she admitted. She hadn't known about it in the beginning, but a group of humans had orchestrated the *Achlys's* mission, without the permission of Coalition Central. She even remembered she and Captain Greene discussing what would happen if the Claxians found out. She'd been *complicit*.

"So, you see, even when they purport to be part of this great Coalition, they work behind the scenes for their own interests, undermining everyone else. They don't deserve to be part of this Coalition." The image of Earth morphed from blue and green to a ruddy brown.

"You're going to judge an entire species—over a trillion people—on the actions of a select few? The Coalition has been in existence for over two millennia. Just because a few—"

"Oh Evie," Dulthar said, shaking his head. "Do you really think this is the first and only time this has happened? This just happens to be the first time it blew up in their faces. Humans are so good at subterfuge; they've managed to keep all their other clandestine operations secret. Trust me, I know. I have an entire history of data on them we pulled before razing the planet." He walked away from her; his hands clasped behind his back again. "You may have heard of one other—and it had to do with your *allies* out there now. About a hundred years ago?"

"The four-days war," she replied, her heart falling.

"Imagine a species so arrogant, they think they can beat a species ten-thousand years more advanced than they are, and they actually send their own people into battle to try. Now you tell me, what could be the impetus behind such a decision?"

Again, she was forced to give an answer she didn't like. "Hubris."

"Precisely. A species that has no understanding of its limits is dangerous. A species who will go out into the universe full of arrogance and superiority will eventually lead to destruction. Whatever they may have done in the past is lost to time, I will admit that. But their behavior since has been less than ideal. A species as volatile and destructive as they cannot be allowed to exist in a galactic community. By coming here, we have *saved* the other species of the Coalition, including the Claxians."

Evie recalled the feelings of hatred and loathing that had flooded her brain when Daingne had taken over the first time. Then there had been no reason or rhyme behind it; it was nothing but unbridled rage. Perhaps she hadn't taken the proper amount of time to explore *why* she felt that way. But if

Dulthar was telling the truth, it at least gave her some answers. "So that's it, then. Everything you've done is to protect the other species of the galaxy."

"To the best of our ability. They had to be stopped. And we know a few small pockets still remain, such as your former ship. But in time we'll find them all. Humans don't live that long."

"And what about the Bulaq?" Evie asked, watching Dulthar's face carefully. "How did you protect them?"

His eyes narrowed. "An unfortunate casualty. Once we'd located our primary goal we couldn't let anything get in our way."

"So, you had to destroy their entire system?"

"By impeding our goal, they were hurting themselves; they just didn't know it. We left enough alive to rebuild their society somewhere else. Their culture is strong, and they are fast builders. They will be fine. And now that we have eliminated most of the human threat, they will be able to thrive in peace, without worry that humanity will one day reach their space and try to take it from them." He sized her up. "It's a lot to take in, I know. But as you're one of us you can handle it. The only question that remains is: shall I remove the shackles, or allow you to join your mother? It's your decision."

Evie took a deep breath. As she saw it, she really didn't have a choice.

26

When Cas and Samiya reached the door to Engineering it was flanked on either side by security personnel. "Do they know you're out here?" Cas asked.

"No sir," Crewman Unak said. "The visual feeds from Engineering have been cut off, so we don't know what's going on inside."

"That's not right," Samiya said. "There should have been an alert if we lost visual."

Cas tapped his comm. "Zaal. Check and see why we weren't notified about the loss of the cameras in Engineering. I want to know if Rutledge did something to them."

"Checking now, Captain. I'll comm you back as soon as I have an answer."

Cas unholstered the boomcannon from under his jacket. Samiya stared at him and he shook his head to say *don't worry, I've done this a thousand times before.* "Stay out here until you hear from one of us," Cas whispered. "If he's in there and he has hostages, there's no telling what he might do." Unak nodded. He turned back to Samiya. "You stay out of sight. I want his attention on me."

"I'm not going to let him hurt anyone on this ship," she replied.

"Then just make sure you include yourself in those efforts." Cas double-checked his boomcannon was set to the particle blast setting, then nodded at Unak to open the main door. It rolled away with a rumble and Cas stepped into Engineering, his eyes scanning the large room and all the corners before coming to rest on his quarry.

Above him, Rutledge stood on the second level, facing away from Cas and toward the primary undercurrent conduits. He was working on one of the automated terminals which made traveling through the advanced undercurrent possible without Sesster. Beside him Tyler was on his knees, his head down, though he seemed otherwise unharmed. The rest of the Engineering crew were still at their stations, but all were looking in the direction of Rutledge. Except for Zenfor, whose face was burning with rage as her hands dug into the sides of her own console, crushing the metal.

"I wondered how long it would take you," Rutledge said, not looking up from the terminal.

Behind Cas the door rolled closed again. Cas pointed his weapon at Rutledge's back. "Daniel, whatever you're doing, stop right now." Faster than his eyes could process, Rutledge had Vrij's weapon touching the center of Tyler's skull. *What the hell?* Cas thought. *How could he move so fast?*

"I'll tell you what I told the rest of them," Rutledge said. "Put down the weapon or lose your engineer. It's that simple."

Cas grimaced, not liking his options. Rutledge had planned for this, and it seemed Cas's appearance in Engineering was little more than a minor inconvenience to the man. Cas stole a glance at Zenfor, who gave a subtle shake of her head. He tossed the boomcannon away, listening to it clatter across the floor.

"Good boy. Looks like you can follow orders after all."

"What do you want, Daniel? And what does Lieutenant Tyler have to do with it?" Cas called out.

"The Lieutenant was in the wrong place at the wrong time. I needed a hostage, he happened to be close to the access port where I came out. Nothing more. As for what I want, I want to finally be done with all of this. With you especially."

"At least we can agree on that," Cas replied.

Rutledge spun around, his eyes burning. "You think this is still all some big joke, don't you? You think you were so clever in disobeying my orders, that you were the savior of the soul of the Coalition. Let me tell you something, *Commander*, since you never officially earned your current title. You did far more damage to the Coalition than I ever could have. And the worst part about it was I thought for a while you might have been right. When the weapon didn't work, and it ended up killing everyone on board the *Achlys* I thought to myself: 'Maybe Caspian made the right call all those years ago'. But it turns out there was a third player, someone working against me behind the scenes, and I never saw it coming."

"Samiya told you," Cas said. His suspicions had been right.

Rutledge barked a laugh. "Of course, you knew. I'm half surprised you didn't put her up to it. You know what the saddest part about all of this is? I was willing to help you this time. For a short while, I was on your side. But you've ruined all of that now. Just like before."

Cas furrowed his brow. "What are you talking about *my side*? You've never been on anyone's side but your own."

"Wrong. I was on the Coalition's side. For as long as I could be. Even when they imprisoned me, I still held them close in my heart. I had spent my life loving and wanting to protect the Coalition, even if it betrayed me." Rutledge raised his weapon into the air and Cas could see the relief spread across Tyler's face. "But when I was faced with certain death, I had to make a choice."

Cas glanced at Zenfor and the other Engineering personnel again. Samiya was nowhere to be seen. Maybe if he could keep Rutledge talking it would give her enough time to get the drop on him. He was glad she'd talked him into letting her come. "What choice?"

"Compromise or remain entrenched in my beliefs. And I chose to live."

"You allied yourself with them." Cas realized Saturina had been right.

Rutledge scoffed. "It wasn't easy. They hate us, you know. With a passion. But I managed to convince them that other human settlements would be much more likely to trust me and allow me in than to let the Athru find them. I could be their envoy and help them root out any remaining resistance."

"You've got to be fucking kidding me," Cas heard one of the engineers say. He turned. It was Lieutenant Denna, her narrowed eyes locked on Rutledge. There were similar sentiments throughout the rest of the crew. Cas glanced at Zenfor; she was practically shaking. If he didn't know better, he'd say she was close to launching herself from her station up to the second level.

"As horrible as that is," Cas said, intent on keeping the man talking. "It doesn't make sense. Because you're right, they hate us. Why would they work with one of us?"

Rutledge laughed. "You make it sound like I'm the only one. I know of a few others, infiltrators who will seek out the pockets of resistance, and alert the Athru to their presence. There are a lot of humans unaccounted for in this part of the galaxy. Little did I know they were using cloaking technology to shield them from Athru sensors; that is a bit of engineering brilliance I'll have to relay to Commander Gysan if I ever see her again. But now that I have the specs, it won't help anyone else." He tapped the console again and a rumble rolled through the room.

"What are you doing?"

"My job. I'm taking care of the Athru's problem for them," he replied.

"He's set the undercurrent generators to cycle their energy through the ship," Lieutenant Denna said. "The forces will tear us into molecules!"

"You should have known this was going to be your future, Caspian," Rutledge said. "The minute you disagreed with me you sealed your fate."

"That's what all of this is about, isn't it?" Cas yelled over the growing din. "The fact your *ego* can't deal with the possibility you might have been wrong!"

"I wasn't wrong!" Rutledge replied. "None of this would have happened if you'd just *listened to me*. And now, all these deaths are on your head." Cas caught a glimpse of Samiya standing behind Rutledge. She'd managed to climb up the rear scaffolding, and gotten behind him, crouching low with her eyes locked on him.

"I've been accused of that before," Cas replied. "And given the chance, I'd do it all over again." He nodded and Rutledge's eyes went wide a second before he turned to see Samiya barrel into him, knocking him off balance and over the railing on the second level. He fell ten meters down to the floor, landing with a thud. Cas ran over and grabbed his boomcannon, turning back to Samiya. "Good work, Commander."

Samiya nodded and checked on Tyler, who seemed no worse for wear. She then began the shutdown sequence for the overload Rutledge had initiated. Cas made his way over to where Rutledge had fallen only to stop short. The man—who should have at least been seriously injured, if not killed from a fall like that—stood up like nothing had happened, Vrij's weapon still in his hand and pointed at Cas's chest. Cas didn't even have time to raise his own weapon. "You didn't really think they'd let me stay a human, did you? As part of the deal I had to undergo certain…modifications so I was no longer like you. So, I was no longer one of their targets."

"What did they do to you?" Cas asked.

"Modified my genetic code. They're good at that kind of thing. More strength, better senses, longer life. And then of course there's this." He reached up and tapped his artificial eye. It began blinking.

Cas's comm crackled to life. "Sir, we've got an incoming Sargan fleet approaching. At least six hundred ships and they all have weapons armed."

"You've led us to a slaughter," Cas whispered.

"Maybe things could have been different," Rutledge admitted. "When I first came to you, I was genuine in my offer to help. Hunting humans becomes tedious after a while. But now I see what the Athru see—humanity is beyond saving. If I can't even trust my own officers…well. Let's just say—"

"*Enough!*" As Rutledge's finger tightened on the trigger, his attention was torn away by Zenfor, who vaulted over her station and in three long strides, each shaking the ground as she stepped, closed the distance between her and Rutledge. With inhuman speed he swung the gun to the side and fired directly into her chest, but she didn't even pause as the blast hit her dead center. Zenfor wrapped one hand around his neck and the other around his hand, squeezing both at the same time and lifting him off his feet. "This is for all the lives you've destroyed, Sil and human alike," she said as Cas heard the crunching of bones in his hand and his neck. Rutledge's eyes rolled in the back of his head and he uttered a small *hurk*. Zenfor released what remained of his bloody hand, now mashed together with broken pieces of Vrij's gun. Her other hand continued to squeeze his throat until there was an audible *pop* and Rutledge's limp body fell to the ground, spasming, as Zenfor continued to hold up his detached head with one hand, blood dripping from the neck. "Justice," she said. "Finally." She winced and his head fell from her hands, striking the ground and rolling a few meters as Zenfor fell to her knees, staring at the black mark in the middle of her chest. She glanced up at Cas before collapsing on the ground herself.

Cas smashed his comm. "Medical emergency! Box, get your ass down to Engineering!"

"On my way, boss," Box said.

Cas ran over to Zenfor, hoping beyond all hope she hadn't just sacrificed herself for him. As he held on to her praying for Box to hurry the hell up, all he could think about was how selfless she'd been, and how it might have cost her everything.

27

Evie could *feel* Dulthar's stare. As if the man had reached out with his gaze and struck her. He was waiting for an answer, but to her, it was obvious.

"You can try to kill me," she said. "But I'm pretty sure you'll fail."

His eyes flashed, but otherwise his features remained neutral. "Pity," he said. "We would have welcomed you, even with your abominable heritage. It's such a waste. But perhaps it is better this way. No human genes left in the galaxy, as it should be." He nodded to the guards behind her.

Evie closed her eyes, inhaling sharply and settled her focus.

So, the voice in her head said. *This is what it's come to. All that effort.*

Leave me alone, I've already killed you, Evie replied to the ghost of Daingne. *Now let me concentrate.* Despite the fact she'd eliminated the sentient part of herself that was Daingne, some of her "essence" remained. Her presence was what made it possible for Evie to speak Athru, because she'd never learned the language. And even though that part of herself was gone, Evie could dig deep and find a silent strength in there. An inner power that was only available to her.

In the half-second all of this went through her mind, Evie felt time slow around her. She curled her hands into fists inside the manacles and smashed them together, the metal shattering as if it were glass, freeing her hands. Opening her eyes, Dulthar's eyes were wide with panic as he shouted something in slow-motion.

What's that he's saying?

He's scared of you, as he should be, the voice replied.

Evie turned and in one swift move, shoved the palms of her hands into the guards' faces, feeling the crunch and crack of bones underneath. The guards fell to the ground before they could even react, and Evie returned her attention to Dulthar. He continued to shout and threw up his hands in front of him, backing away, the folds of his robe rising and fluttering in strange and beautiful patterns. She had enough time to appreciate the physics of the robe itself before she reached for him and scratched him across the face with one hand while planting the other directly into the middle of his chest, sending him sailing backward until he struck one of the glass windows. A sizeable crack appeared from the impact, and Dulthar crumpled on the ground.

Time sped back up and Evie dashed from the end of the room, running at full speed back toward the main thoroughfare. It only took seconds to reach but as soon as she did, she realized she had no clue where she was going, or what she needed to do. Getting off the ship was one possibility, but as almost every Athru in the corridor turned to look at her, she realized that wouldn't be easy. Some of the Athru seemed fearful, but the faces of the rest contorted into snarls. One rushed her and she backhanded him, sending him skidding across the floor. At this, some of the others backed away from her, while more stepped forward, two with large stick-like weapons. She didn't want to find out what those weapons were capable of, but leaving the ship wasn't an option either.

She was on the Athru mothership and despite all their plans, she'd never get this chance again.

Evie turned and ran for the nearest wall, off to her left where there were few Athru standing. The ones with the sticks and a few others pursued, but as soon as she got to the wall she planted her feet and jumped, landing two and a half meters up, then pushed off again, sailing high above the heads of the Athru until she landed eight meters away near the middle of the thoroughfare. The Athru standing around—she could only assume they were mostly citizens as they didn't have any weapons, nor did they seem in much of a mood to fight— gaped at her as she sprinted down the hallway through the crowd. As some brave Athru stepped out to stop her she would either run directly into them, knocking them away or jump over them, watching their shocked faces with glee. Never before had she felt so alive and free to move. Only now did she realize she'd been subconsciously holding back her entire life and now that she knew her own capabilities, it felt good to explore them for once.

But she still needed to find a way to use this ship to her advantage. The most obvious choice was to find the bridge and begin firing on all the other Athru ships. If she couldn't manage that, then a self-destruct. Her mother had said this was the ship that focused the energy of all the other ships, which meant if she could take it out, maybe they couldn't destroy any more planets or stars. Maybe Cas and the others would have a chance, assuming they had discovered Rutledge's deception.

But as far as she could see, there was no way to access any other part of the ship other than this ridiculous corridor. Her best bet was to try and get back to the surface ship she'd come in, perhaps overpower the pilots and then take it up to the bridge, which she figured was near the top of the tower somewhere. She wasn't sure why she thought that was the case, but it seemed to be right in her mind. She had to trust she had innate Athru knowledge she could use to her advantage.

Knocking a few more Athru out of the way, she ran back the way she'd come, cursing herself for not using her abilities in the first place. Maybe if she had, Esterva would still be alive. But she'd been so overwhelmed by the ship and seeing all of these people she'd momentarily forgotten herself. She never should have let them take her and her mother from Claxia Prime. Then again, she was fast, but Evie wasn't confident she was fast enough to outrun weapons fire.

She barreled back into the room she'd first come through with the guards, only to find a solid wall where the door had once been. She glanced around for a control panel, seeing only Athru writing on the wall. She focused her thoughts and her mind began to wrap around the words, discerning their meaning.

No access without proper authorization. Do not open field before connections are complete. Dem. 5.6372 – AC code 2.17.

She wasn't sure what the last words and numbers meant, but she needed to get that door opened. There was a small panel on the wall beside where the door had been, and Evie had to reach back into Daingne's memory to figure out how all this worked. If the memories were accurate, all she needed to do was convince the door she had proper authorization.

"Hey!" Evie turned to see another Athru guard with one of those sticks in his hand. She wasn't sure if it was one of the same ones from before or not, but she rushed him, plowing him back into the wall. He hit it with an *oof* and the cracking of bones somewhere, dropping his stick. Evie stepped back, allowing him to fall to the ground, howling in pain. She grabbed him by the wrist, dragged his body over and placed his hand on the panel. A little indicator turned purple. She took that to mean proper authorization. So why wasn't the door opening?

"Open this," she said to the guard who clutched his stomach.

"You can't leave," he coughed. "There's nowhere to run."

"I don't want to run," she replied. "Now open it or I break your neck."

He shook his head. "No, you don't understand. There's no ship out there. It's nothing but a vacuum."

Damn. Without a ship there was no way up to the bridge without going back through all those people. And even then, she'd be at a disadvantage, not knowing how to move about the ship. She looked down at the injured Athru. "How long can you hold your breath?"

"What?" he asked.

Now she understood, the door wouldn't open because the "field"—whatever it was, that kept the pressure and the air in was active. She just needed to disable the field and she could go outside the ship. She'd managed a few minutes in the depths of space with Zenfor. Maybe she could stay out there longer if she needed to. Long enough to climb up to the tower. "What's the average time we can be out in open space without dying?" she asked.

He shook his head. "No, you are a fool, you're gonna—" she hit him hard enough to render him unconscious, then grabbed hold of one of his arms. She turned back to the control panel and made sure to close the connection to the large corridor, sealing it from the ship. She then used her newfound "authorization" to drop the main field, via the guard's handprint. The indicator went from purple to orange. She had to assume that meant she could pass. Evie drew in a deep breath, and with the guard in tow, stepped toward the wall.

As soon as the portal that was supposed to connect to a ship opened, she and the guard were yanked forward. She barely had time to grab on to the edge of the opening before they were blown into open space, but she managed to hold on to both the side of the ship and to the unconscious guard until all the air had been expelled from the room. Once she was clear of the opening and zero gravity took over, she began a quick climb on the outside of the ship, working her way up the side with one hand and two feet working in tandem. It was surprisingly easy to ascend without gravity dragging her down, but she had to be careful and not get overzealous. One missed handhold and she and the guard would tumble off into nothingness. She could only hope she'd be able to hold her breath long enough to get to another junction point on the tower itself.

Once she reached the edge of the ship, she pulled them over, then flung herself straight forward, skimming the top of the ship until she reached the tower. She glanced up, a kind of dull pain resonating in the back of her brain either from the cold, the lack of oxygen or both. She needed to hurry.

Planting her feet at the base of the tower she pushed off with all her power, propelling them up at a tremendous speed. Without anything to slow the inertia they traveled stories in only seconds, the top of the tower fast approaching. As Evie reached out to slow them, her foot caught on an errant greeble on the side of the ship, sending them spinning out of control. She lost her grip on the guard as she tried to grab on to something—anything to keep her from hurtling into the blackness of space. Her spin was uneven, and she crashed into the side of the ship, bouncing off the sharp plating which cut into her skin and tore at her clothes. She scrambled to find a hold but missed completely. As she felt herself tumble out of control away from the ship she couldn't help but think about what a waste it had all been, and how she'd done nothing but let everyone down. Perhaps it was for the best that her last few moments be resigned to being alone in the depths of space.

A hand reached out and grabbed her shirt, yanking her back toward the ship. Evie looked up to see the guard had grabbed on to one of the small greebles on the side of the ship and because his arms were longer, had managed to reach her just in time. He placed his hand on the side of the ship a few meters down and another portal opened, an explosive amount of air spewing from the opening. Once it was clear, he hurtled them both down and through the portal, closing it behind them. Evie felt warm all over and the gravity inside the room pulled her to the floor as the guard limped over to a nearby control board and tapped a few images. The room was flooded with oxygen again and Evie gasped in lumps of air at a time. When she'd caught her breath she looked over to the guard, also panting and still holding his middle where she'd run into him. "Why?" she asked.

"You could have let me die," he said. "Just let me get pulled out into space. But you didn't."

Evie sat back, still inhaling air. Her hands were slowly regaining their color, which meant the rest of her probably was too. The bio blockers either weren't working anymore or had been turned off. Which could have been a side-effect of the extreme cold of space.

"So," Evie said, staring at the guard as they sat across from each other, neither one moving. "Now what?"

28

"Tell me she's going to be alright," Cas said, running beside Zenfor's body as Box and two of the other nurses rushed it to sickbay on the hovering gurney.

"I can't tell you that," Box said. "But we'll do everything we can."

Cas's comm opened again. "Captain, the incoming fleet," Zaal said. His voice, while still deep, seemed to resonate a bit higher than normal.

"I know Zaal, I'll be there in a minute!" he yelled, then cut the comm. He turned back to Box. "What do you need from me? Resource wise? What can I do?"

"Stay out of the way," Box said. "Let me do my job. And you go do yours. I'll keep you updated, but nothing I do will matter if the ship gets blown into a thousand pieces."

His words struck Cas like ice. Box was right, he wasn't helping by getting in the way. Cas couldn't fall back into his old habits; he wasn't going to be paralyzed by the possibility of loss. He stopped running, allowing them to continue on without him, and he caught one last look at Zenfor's immobile form as they turned the corner toward sickbay. Cas ran back in the other direction to the nearest hypervator. It opened for him—one of the perks of being captain—and he tapped his comm as soon as he was on. "Zaal, I'm on my way up, how close are they?"

"Less four minutes, sir, closing fast. They were hiding on the far side of Devil's Gate."

Fucking Rutledge. For all his talk about wanting to help he'd been doing nothing but leading them to slaughter ever since he'd arrived. Cas doubted he was ever serious about helping them and that this had always been the eventual plan, but he was willing to bet Samiya's talk with Rutledge sent him over the edge early. Otherwise why not wait until the entire Sil fleet was in place before springing this attack? Which brought up another point to consider: if the Sargans were advancing on them, it meant they had to be confident they had the capability to defeat the Sil—something that shouldn't be possible given Sargans were known for notoriously unreliable tech as it was usually cobbled together from dozens of different species. Had the Athru armed the Sargans, after they'd eliminated every human from their space? Or had they just let Rutledge and others like him do their dirty work for them?

The doors opened and Cas stepped on to the bridge. Hank stood from the command chair and stepped to the side. "Captain on the bridge," he announced.

"Give me an update," Cas said. "What's the status of our fleet?"

"They seem—unperturbed," Tileah replied. "They haven't charged any weapons or raised any defensive barriers."

Cas made a face. "What, do they just think the Sargans are coming for *us*? Arrogant bastards. Open a comm to the Sil, I want to talk to them personally."

"But sir," Zaal said.

"Do it, Zaal, we don't have time."

"Aye," he replied. The comm opened.

"Sil fleet. As you've no doubt noticed, we are facing an incoming Sargan armada. Contrary to what you may think, they are not here just for my ship, but for all of us. Prepare yourselves for a battle."

"They're responding," Zaal said. The main view screen changed to an image of a Sil clad in her full uniform, a blue light glowing above her faceless helmet.

"You were told never to contact us in person," she said, her voice rife with fury. "And now you—"

"Save the theatrics," Cas interrupted. "We have a bigger problem. There's a good chance that fleet out there is armed with Athru weapons. They may have the capability to damage or destroy your ships. We can't stay here; we need to move forward into Coalition space now. Call the other half of the fleet still protecting Thislea. We're attacking."

"Preposterous," the Sil said. "We still have no intel."

"And we're not going to either, the shuttle's mission has failed. It's unlikely the occupants are still alive," Cas said, realizing what he was saying as the words came out of his mouth. He wasn't sure a comm had ever gone through to Evie's ship from Rutledge or not, but they'd have to investigate that matter later, when they weren't facing imminent death.

"We demand to speak to our own representative," the Sil said. "Per our agreement. This will not—"

"Listen to me," Cas said, growing frustrated. He leaned forward, to make the Sil pay attention. "Your liaison is missing, most likely dead. Zenfor has been mortally wounded by a rogue Athru operative. Coincidentally he was the same person who attacked your people twenty-five years ago. The person who first made the incursion into your space was behind all of this. He is dead, but we have to deal with this fallout. And we're not going to get anywhere by arguing."

"Two minutes away, sir," Zaal said.

"What's it going to be?" Cas asked. "Do you call the rest of your fleet, or are you going to allow the Athru to arm *another* potential enemy so when they finally do come after you, they'll outnumber you a hundred to one?"

The blue light above the Sil's head pulsed rapidly. It reminded Cas of how Box's eyes would sometimes blink when he was processing a lot of information. They didn't have the luxury to sit around and wait for the Sil to weigh the decision. He could just imagine this information being transmitted back to the Sil Sanctuary and the delegates there arguing over how to proceed. But in this case, they didn't have the luxury of time.

"They're coming out of their undercurrents," Zaal said.

"Ignite the ship's armor," Cas said, "And ready our new weapons." He didn't take his eyes of the screen. He knew the Sil could "see" him and he wasn't going to be the first one to blink.

"You have dragged us into your conflict, human," the Sil said, seething. "And now we will all pay for your foolishness."

"You want to blame me? Fine. But I'm telling you now we were drawn into a trap. If we don't attack the source now, we won't get another chance. We were lured here because the Sargan fleet couldn't get to Thislea fast enough. We can outrun them to Horus, and then we'll only be facing one enemy instead of two."

"They've opened fire," Tileah said.

"Ronde, give us some evasive maneuvers, don't let their weapons hit this ship, even if you have to do an undercurrent jump," Cas said.

"Aye," he replied, exchanging a look with River, who nodded.

"Consul! They have just destroyed the Kitchtall!" A voice said on the screen. The Sil's blue light strobed for a moment.

"Move us out of firing position," she said, then turned back to Cas. "We are agreed, human. But once this is over, you will answer to the Sanctuary for leading us into this trap, whether it was your intention or not. And you will be judged. *If* you survive."

"I've been judged before," Cas replied. "And I'll be glad to go through it again if it means we stop the Athru." He cut the comm and the viewscreen returned to an image of space, hundreds of ships emerging from green-tinged portals in space. Some of them had already begun firing.

"I'm reading five, no, six hundred Sargan vessels still coming out of undercurrents all around us," Tileah said.

Cas took the captain's chair. "Plot a course to the Horus system. Get us out of here as soon as possible."

"Sir, if we breach Coalition space without knowing the locations of their patrol ships—" Tileah began.

"We'll run into them on the way, I know," Cas replied. "We'll just have to stay on guard until we can reach the Horus system. And we'll have to expect the patrols will become more frequent the deeper we get."

"Course plotted and laid in," Ronde said. "We better go, it's getting dense out here."

Cas pulled up a tactical overlay of the system on the screen. A quick analysis showed the Sargans outnumbered their fleet almost two-to-one. And they'd already taken down three of the Sil ships. "Ronde, punch it before we lose anyone else. Maximum speed."

Ronde nodded and in an instant they were inside the undercurrent. "Samiya reports the generators down in Engineering are working fine, Rutledge didn't do any permanent damage," Hank said, reading from his display.

Cas let out a breath of relief. "Drop armor and disengage weapon systems. Looks like we'll have to wait until the main event before we get a chance to test them out." He turned to

Tileah. "But I want you running drills every four hours. We're going to run into these bastards and my bet is it will be sooner rather than later. Let's make sure we're ready for them."

"Yes, sir," she replied.

Cas glanced over at Zaal. "Is everyone with us?"

"Two more of the Sil ships were damaged before the fleet could get away," he replied. "I have to assume they'll be captured and stripped for parts."

"Maybe," Cas said, but he wasn't so sure. Knowing how the Sil felt about their ships led him to believe they might end up sacrificing their lives rather than risk capture. Either way, they were down five ships and based on what they were about to face, they couldn't afford to lose anyone. Which reminded him.

"Where are you going?" Hank asked as Cas headed for the hypervator.

"I need to check on Vrij and Zenfor," he replied. "That man did a lot of damage, and it's my responsibility to see that it's all undone. I'll be in sickbay if you need me."

Hank nodded as Cas stepped back inside the hypervator. The short battle had told him one thing they hadn't known before: the Athru had the capability to fight back. Which meant this was going to be a very costly battle, no matter the victor.

***

The doors to sickbay slid open, revealing two groups of people. The largest, including Box, were still hovering over Zenfor's limp body, working furiously. Box didn't even look up to acknowledge Cas's presence, which was just as well. He'd promised to stay out of the way and that's what he was going to do.

The other group, comprised of only two people—Vrij and Nurse Menkel—were over on one of the non-surgical beds. Vrij was sitting up, rubbing the side of his ribcage. Cas walked over with what he hoped was a non-threatening smile on his face. "How is he?"

"Surprisingly good," Menkel said. "From what he described I would have thought his injuries would have been more severe."

"Bulaq are s-sturdy," Vrij said, wincing as he spoke. He turned to Cas. "I'm sorry. I failed in my job. You need a n-new head of security." He slapped his left cheek with his right hand. Cas took this to mean he was upset with himself.

Cas shook his head. "No. Rutledge had capabilities we couldn't anticipate. The Athru genetically modified him to be stronger, faster. It wasn't your fault; it was mine for allowing him to come on board. When you're well enough, I want you to return to your duties. That's part of the reason I wanted to come down here." Cas nodded to Menkel who seemed to get the point and gave them some privacy.

"I a-appreciate that, Captain," Vrij said.

"We've run into a…hiccup. Rutledge had a Sargan armada waiting for us, he was working with the Athru." It physically hurt Cas to admit he'd been so wrong about the man, but there was little time for regrets. Even though the trip to the Horus system would take some time, it felt like they barely had any at all.

"That's a big hiccup," Vrij said.

"But it got me thinking. For the Athru to have made a deal with him, they *must have* boarded Starbase Eight, rather than just fired on it from space. Which means we might be looking at the possibility of boarding parties."

"You want us to b-be combat ready," Vrij said.

"I hate to say it, but yes. I'd rather we be prepared than not." He shot a glance over at the group working on Zenfor.

"I don't want to lose anyone because we were caught with our pants down."

"Pants down?" Vrij asked.

"Unaware," Cas said, turning his attention back to Vrij. "I want you to get started as soon as they clear you from here."

"I understand. M-may I also make a suggestion?" Vrij's eyes were wide, almost as if he was afraid Cas might hit him for daring to ask.

"Of course."

"The prisoners—the pilots in the custom holding cells. Y-you may want to reconsider their long-term imprisonment. T-they aren't the same anymore."

Cas leaned back, considering it. The entire reason they'd been imprisoned in the first place was because they had backed Chief Rafnkell in an attempted coup against Evie and him for control of the ship. But that had been nearly a season ago and even though they'd been living in comfortable habitats constructed in one of the cargo bays, they were still in a prison. He also couldn't ignore the fact they might need as many spacewing pilots as they could get their hands on when they reached Earth. The spacewing ships were notoriously hard to hit with conventional weapons fire and they might provide ample distraction to the Athru at a crucial moment. "I'll take it under advisement," he replied.

"Thank you, sir. I-I've gotten to know them. They aren't all bad."

"Most people rarely are," he replied. Cas placed a reassuring hand on Vrij's shoulder, then left him be as he took another look at the group surrounding Zenfor. Despite wanting to know what was happening, he managed to leave sickbay without interrupting their work. Box would comm him when there was news. For now, he had other matters to attend to.

29

Even in the dim light, Evie knew her skin had returned to its normal color. Not as if any of the Athru had been fooled before when they'd seen her paraded down on the thoroughfare, but now it was obvious she was of human heritage. She pushed herself up off the floor, struggling to stand. It seemed the exertion in the vacuum of space had really taken it out of her. She had to steady herself against the closest wall.

The guard stood as well, just as shaky, but didn't take his eyes off her. She couldn't very well kill him, not after he'd saved her life. But at the same time, if she allowed him out of her sight, she'd probably find herself dead at the hands of a hundred Athru.

"What do you plan to do up here?" he asked in his native language. Evie found she still had no trouble understanding it.

"I can't tell you that," she replied. They were in a stalemate, staring each other down but neither one of them strong or confident enough to engage the other. "You know they'll just kill me, right? You could have saved everyone a lot of trouble if you'd just let me float away."

"I know who you are," he replied.

Evie pursed her lips. "Don't tell me you're part of some underground resistance group."

The Athru shook his head. "I'm a loyal officer. But...my living sister...she is more opposed to the will of our people. If I'd let you die...she never would have forgiven me."

The Athru had familial units? She'd never heard of them forming bonds in that way, other than how Esterva spoke of their relationship. Evie hadn't considered *how* the Athru lived, she had just assumed they were all part of the same collective group, with their single-minded goal.

"What happens to those who aren't willing to follow the will of your people?" she asked, wondering if the punishment was as harsh for everyone else as it had been for her mother.

"It's best if they aren't found out," the guard replied.

A smile formed on Evie's lips. "You mean to tell me even with all that genetic knowledge passed down through our genes, some people still decide to disagree with it?"

"It's more common than you might think," he replied.

"And the people, on this ship. They're not all warriors, are they? They're not even all part of a military."

"No," he admitted. "This ship has served as a portable home for my people for generations. Many of those here are civilians."

"By Garth," Evie said under her breath. Well, she had been curious about the Athru as a people, and now she'd seen it for herself. She'd tried to convince herself they were all the same: ruthless killers who would do anything to accomplish their goal. But what if that was just the case of their leaders, and those in charge of their fighting forces? "How many of your people feel this way?"

"Trust me, it's a minority," the guard said, annoyance creeping into his voice.

"So. What are you going to do? You turn me in, I die. You let me go and there's no telling what I could do."

"They'll be looking for you, tracking you," he replied. "They know you're on the ship somewhere. Eventually they'll figure out what you did."

"That's convenient," Evie replied. "Just let someone else deal with the problem."

"What choice do I have?" he asked. For the first time he seemed genuinely desperate. Perhaps he was new to the job, or perhaps he'd been in this position so long it had worn on him, but Evie couldn't exactly fault him; he was the first semi-decent Athru she'd met, and that included Esterva.

"You could help me," she replied. "Your people have already killed most of mine. Or, what I used to think of as mine. I'm just trying to save what little is left."

He shook his head, his large eyes squinting. "I can't do that. My duty—"

"—is to ensure humanity is eliminated, yes, I know. I got the full speech from Dulthar." He didn't move.

"They'll be coming soon. All I have to do is keep you here until the rest of them arrive. And then—"

"—and then you end up betraying your sister anyway," Evie finished for him again, driving the point home. "No matter how you cut it, *your* action is what matters here. But what's more important to you? Your so-called duty, or the respect of your family? And you don't need to say it, because I already know. The question is, have you figured it out yet?"

He screwed up his smooth face, which looked strange on an Athru. It wasn't something she was suspecting. "What am I supposed to do? Get you off this ship? They'll know I helped you."

"I don't want to get off, I want to get to the bridge," Evie replied.

"Why?" he asked.

"The less you know, the better," she replied. "But it would probably make your sister happy."

He shook his head. "You can't go to the bridge. It's too heavily guarded, not to mention I don't want to be accused of treason."

She instinctively glanced up. "It's above us, isn't it? If I could just find a way up there…"

"It's below us, about nine levels. You overshot it. There are only observation levels and scientific equipment above."

She stepped away from the wall. "That's fine then. I'll just be on my way."

He moved to step in front of her, his height causing her to look up. "Did you not just hear what I said? It's too heavily guarded. You'd be killed before you even got close."

Evie smiled. "So, you do know your choice after all."

The guard turned away from her, shaking his head. "I…can get you off the ship. Maybe. If I call up one of the—"

"No," she replied. "I'm here, I'm not leaving. I'll never get this opportunity again. I don't want—" A strange sensation came over her and Evie felt the room tilt at a strange angle. She felt time do that strange thing again where it seemed to slow down, but in this case it crawled to a virtual stop.

Evelyn.

"Sesster?" She glanced around, looking for him, thinking she had gone mad.

Can you—hear me?

"Yes, where are you? Are you on the Athru ship?" In the past the only time he'd been able to contact her was when they were in close proximity. Had the Athru taken him and the others and brought them aboard this ship as well?

No. I'm still on Claxia, he replied.

"Claxia, how is that possible?"

I'm still not sure, but in speaking with the others here, we think it may have something to do with my self-imposed exile. I had not reached out for so long that now my ability to reach is even further than before. But it is only with people I'm close to. I...I can't find Zenfor.

Evie's heart dropped. Did that mean Rutledge had ambushed them and maybe even destroyed *Tempest*? "What about Cas, can you find him?"

I'm still trying. But I found you. Where did they take you?

"I'm on the Athru's main city-ship, I think. I'm trying to figure out how to get to the bridge, maybe blow this thing up so it's one less weapon they have against us."

Evelyn. I know this is not the time, but I must know. Was there a concerted effort to keep Caspian's mission into Sil space secret from the Claxians?

Evie closed her eyes, cursing her younger self for keeping that secret from him. He was right, this *wasn't* the time, but she couldn't lie to him. Not that she would anyway, but she'd hoped this would have been something they could have talked about in person. "Yes," she replied. "They knew if the Claxians found out it could undermine the stability of the Coalition."

She didn't hear anything in her mind for a moment, but the world remained semi-frozen around her. She watched the Athru guard's form moving as he walked, albeit much slower than normal. Had he been standing still; she wouldn't be able to tell time was still going forward. "Sesster?"

You are right, they wouldn't have approved. Thank you for being honest.

The room sped back up and Evie realized she was in the process of falling and her face hit the cold floor. The Athru turned to her, surprised. "What happened?"

She pushed back up, shaking her head. "I...don't know." She rubbed her head. Had Sesster cut the line between them on purpose? He'd reached across over two hundred million kilometers to speak with her, maybe something had happened to his ability. Or perhaps he was angry. And if so, what did he intend to do? Either way, she didn't have a good feeling about it.

"You don't want what?" The Athru said, inspecting the small panel full of words that looked completely foreign to Evie now.

"What?" she asked.

"You just said you don't want—something, then you fell on the floor."

"Oh," she said, trying to recall their conversation. The incident with Sesster had unnerved her. "I don't want to waste this opportunity. I'm here, now. I can't leave."

The Athru studied the information before him. "You're not registering as human on the scanners, which explains why they haven't found you yet, but it won't be long until they do a ship-wide scan and find there is a person here that shouldn't be. If you're not coming up on the bioscanners, you'll show up on the heat maps. You don't have a choice; you need to get off this ship."

"*No*," she replied. So, the bio blockers were still working in some way. But her human self was reasserting itself. "Is there somewhere I can go—or some way you can fix the sensors so they can't find me?"

"I'm no engineer," the Athru replied. "I'm just a soldier. And I won't help you commit espionage on my ship."

"No one is asking you to. All I want to know is if there is something that can be done until the heat dies down. Without me leaving the ship?"

He huffed, the puff coming from his small lips. "There is only one place on this ship that doesn't register a life sign, but it's dangerous, and illegal."

"Whatever it is, it's better than waiting to be hunted down. If I can just stay low for ten or twenty hours, I'll have a better chance at getting in the bridge. They'll think I'm gone." She knew even if Cas had somehow escaped Rutledge the fleet

216

would be days away, assuming they were still coming at all. It was better to lull the Athru into a false sense of security and make them think she'd been killed trying to escape. It wasn't much, but it was all she had at the moment.

"You're familiar with our time bubbles?" he asked. Evie nodded. "It's a technology we adapted for our own use. But there's a chamber on this ship, accessible by Dulthar and some of the other leaders. It's his…crypt, I guess you could say."

Evie shook her head, some of the words were slipping out of comprehension. "Did you say crypt?"

"Dulthar has been leading our people for almost one hundred and ninety centuries. Some of my people consider him a living god, but it's due to a miniature time chamber built into this ship. It harnesses the same energy from our home planet to severely slow down time for the occupant. He will spend fifty or sixty years in there at a time and it's as if no time has passed at all."

"A miniature time chamber?" Evie asked, fascinated. "And it doesn't register life forms inside?"

The Athru shook his head. "It is outside of normal time, so scanners can't scan the inside. If you were in there, they'd never be able to detect you."

"What about Dulthar? What if he decides to go back inside?" she asked.

"I doubt he would. He's been gearing up for something big lately, came out of the chamber months ago. He won't go back in until he's sure all is well. It could be another year. And you only need to be inside for a few days." The Athru stared at the ground, as if he'd just given up all his people's secrets in one fell swoop.

"Thank you for telling me," she replied. "Where can we find this chamber?"

"It's in the bowels of the ship," the Athru said. "On the complete other side."

"Which means we'll have to go back down, and we can't be seen. Otherwise, someone might figure out what we're doing." Evie tried to think; could she stomach another trip in the vacuum of space?

"Wait, what do you mean we? Like I said, I'm not a traitor. I serve the Athru cause—"

"Apparently not, otherwise you would have let me die," Evie replied. "I'm not asking you to shoot your own people. But I do need help finding and getting into this chamber. Once I'm inside you should be able to relax. All you have to do is come get me in a few days. And then you'll never see me again."

"And what do you plan on doing to my ship when you're out?" he asked, sizing her up.

"Maybe it is better you don't know the details." Evie was conflicted. Before it had been a simple matter of blowing the ship up, ridding the universe of a bunch of Athru at once. But if some of them were decent—enough to warrant her respect—she'd have to come up with a new plan. Destroying the ship was off the list of possibilities. "But I promise I won't put the people on this ship in danger. I—I know what it's like to care for the people you serve with."

"Alright," he said. "I can accept that."

"Good." She walked over to the wall they'd come through. "Now get ready to hold your breath again."

30

Cas stared at the screen in front of him. It had been almost seventeen hours since they'd left Sargan space and Rutledge's "surprise" behind. He was exhausted, dirty and short-tempered, but refused to return to his quarters until they ran into the first patrol in Coalition space. They had to find a way to keep whatever ship they ended up encountering out here from transmitting their presence to anyone else. Even the smallest ping could give them away, which meant they needed to be fast but *careful*.

"Sir?" Zaal said from his station. Besides Cas, he was the only other one who hadn't been relieved by one of the other shifts yet.

"Yeah." Cas rubbed the stubble on his cheek as he snapped his eyes back open.

"I'm happy to report the Sargan fleet has fallen far enough behind it will take them a month to catch up to us."

"Good," Cas replied. That was one thing Rutledge hadn't counted on—their speed. Maybe if he'd been able to execute his plan properly it wouldn't have mattered. He might have found a way to cut them all off at once, wrangling them like steer for the slaughter. But his temper had betrayed him, and he hadn't been able to hold himself together. Cas always suspected hot-headedness would be his undoing. He imagined the man standing over a dirty drain grate, a Sil judge staring over him from a pedestal and pointing at him, yelling something in their language.

Cas's head jerked up as he realized he'd fallen asleep right after Zaal's report, and it took him a split second to remember the man was finally dead. "Anything on the road ahead of us?" he asked.

"Nothing on long-range scanners," Ensign Olguin said.

"Captain, you need rest," Zaal said. "A few hours, at least."

Cas rubbed his eyes. He was right. He was no good to anyone if he couldn't think straight. Maybe he could set up a small bed in the command room, stay close in case they needed him.

"Boss?"

Cas snapped to attention. "Box, go ahead." His heart was thundering and all thoughts of sleep had been dispelled as if they'd never existed.

"I need you to report to sickbay," he said, his tone somber.

Fuck. Cas glanced at the faces of his second shift, then relinquished control of the bridge to Zaal. "If anything happens, you'll know where I am," he said.

"Yes, sir," Zaal replied.

Cas stepped inside the hypervator, dreading what he was about to face. He wasn't sure he could do it; he still hadn't come to grips with what might have happened to Evie and the others. If Rutledge was dirty, then that Arc-N'gali Tos was too. He might have just flown the ship into the nearest star and ejected at the last second. Cas never should have trusted him to take them to Claxia. Was it worth breaking radio silence to warn Evie? Or would that just tip off Tos? Regardless, he wasn't sure he was ready to face sickbay. He needed some help.

He tapped his comm. "Saturina?" he asked, his voice cracking.

"What's wrong?" she replied.

"Can you—would you report to sickbay please?"

"Of course. Are you there now?" Her voice was full of concern. She was too good to him.

"I'm on my way," he replied. "I'll see you in a bit." He ended the comm. Cas let out a long breath, trying to slow his heartrate. Given the number of stimulants he'd taken and the lack of sleep, the last thing he needed at the moment was a shock, but this was part of the job. You had to take the good with the bad. Even when it was the worst thing imaginable.

He stepped off the hypervator on level fourteen and made the short walk down the empty corridor to sickbay. He paused a moment outside the main door, hoping to give Saturina time to catch up. But he also couldn't put this off any longer. He needed to get in there to see Zenfor for himself. Cas took one last deep breath and stepped inside.

Box sat at Xax's desk in her office, while Zenfor's body lay off to the side, on the same surgical bed she was on when Cas was in here last time. Vrij was no longer here, having been discharged ten hours ago. Or was it fourteen? He couldn't keep track. But a few of the nurse staff still milled about. When Cas glanced back over to Zenfor, he noticed the monitor hooked up to her system showed a heartbeat.

"Box!" he called. The robot jerked his attention up, then walked out from around the partition. Behind Cas, the sickbay doors opened and closed again and Saturina was by his side.

"What's going on?" she asked.

"That's what I want to know," Cas replied.

"Oh good, thanks for coming down so quick," Box replied, his eyes blinking in rapid succession. "You'll be happy to know I've managed to stabilize Zenfor."

Cas gaped at him a minute then rubbed his temples. "Then why the hell did you sound so dour on the comm channel? I thought she was dead!"

"Oh," Box said, glancing over to Zenfor, then back to them. "Nope. She's in great shape, thanks to my extensive knowledge of Sil anatomy. It's fortunate for you I've been secretly taking her biological samples for study, the Coalition records on Sil are woefully incomplete."

"Wait, so is *that* why you've been taking samples from me too? And Evie? How many people did you take samples from?" Cas asked.

"Oh," Box said, his eyes blinking in surprise. "Um, yes, that is *exactly* why I took them from you and Evie. Exactly."

"Box," Cas warned.

"Okay,   fine.   I   was justtryingtocreatehumanlifebutitdidntwork." Despite the fact he ran all the words together, Cas still caught it.

"You were trying to create *life*? As in a *baby*?"

"Yes," he said proudly. "That's what Box does; he creates!" He raised a hand as if he were grasping for something.

"No, it isn't, and don't refer to yourself in the third person," Cas replied. "Why…how on—?"

"See, I knew you'd react this way, which was why I didn't tell you. I collected samples from many of the couples on board, in the event they might want to conceive one day and would need assistance."

Cas's eyes slid to Saturina. "And why did you think you needed samples from me and Evie?"

"Be*cause*," Box said, exasperated. "It was obvious you were hot for each other, and you were the perfect match. I've said that from the day you met."

If he wasn't positive he would break his hand, Cas would have slugged Box right there. Instead, he took a deep breath and tried to reset himself. "Let's just…you were able to repair the damage to Zenfor?"

Box didn't skip a beat at the change of subjects. "Yes. Though, had she been human she probably would have died within seconds. The Sil are a sturdy bunch. Like a walking tank."

"I know," Cas said, "I've felt the effects before."

"Box," Saturina said. "You understand why Cas is upset, right?"

"Yes," Box replied. "His insecurities about his own sexual prowess as a man have often led him to make rash decisions. Belittling me over just trying to help him with his love life is one of his defense mechanisms. Though I am happy to say since the two of you have begun your relationship, I've put all of my research on hold." Cas's hands had balled into fists.

Saturina sighed. "I mean about Zenfor."

"Oh. Not really. Though my skill has been exceptional. Did you know the team and I have been working for almost a full day on her? There were some close calls, but I think with proper rest, she'll make a full recovery."

"Is she awake?" Cas asked.

Box made a buzzing sound in the back of his head somewhere. "Of course not. Would *you* want to be awake after someone had been inside your chest cavity for twelve hours? I don't think so. I have her sedated so she can rest. And let me tell you, it took a *lot* of sedative. Like, *a lot*. You know Humarian Pessooks? Twenty meters tall and all muscle. I used more sedative on Zenfor than it would take to knock out one of those things for a week! Her body does this thing where it can absorb and soak up certain substances; I've never seen anything like it."

"I think it's how they connect to their ships," Cas said. "Or it allows them to connect better, through their suits." He shook his head. "No matter. Was there anything else?"

"No," Box said, his voice chipper. "Just wanted to let you know what a good job I did saving her life. Perhaps even worthy of another commendation? I can make space right here." He tapped a space on his chest beside the medal of honor.

"I'm not giving you a medal for doing your job," Cas said. "Look, I need to get some sleep. Let me know when she's awake."

"You got it, boss," Box replied. "Sweet dreams."

"And burn that research, that's an order." Box made a whining noise, but Cas turned his back to it, leaving sickbay. Saturina followed him into the corridor. "One of these days he's going to give me an aneurysm, I know it."

"I wouldn't put it past him to give you one, then fix it just so he could say he did," she replied, a smile playing on her lips.

He grinned. "I hope you know to ignore him. He's…eccentric. Is everything okay in the bays? I'm sorry if I've been preoccupied, it's just after everything that happened with Rutledge, and now Zenfor clinging to life..."

She reached up and ran her fingers through his hair, brushing it off his forehead. "When was the last time you slept?"

Cas didn't bother to check the time. "Sometime yesterday. Before everything in Engineering."

"Go to my quarters," she said. "And turn your comm off. No one will look for you there. You need a good seven or eight hours at least."

"I can't afford seven or eight hours." He appreciated the gesture though. Just the thought of laying down in her sweet-smelling bed made him feel better.

"You can, and you'll do it or I'll go back in there and tell our Chief Medical Officer the captain is unfit for duty and needs a sedative." Even though she was still smiling, he thought she might be serious.

"Damn, bringing out the big guns," he said, putting his hands out.

"It's what I do." She narrowed her eyes.

"We don't need another mutiny on this ship." He glanced away. "Speaking of which, have you spoken to the pilots in cargo four lately?"

She shook her head. "No, why? Is there a problem?"

"Vrij asked me to reconsider their…internment. He says something about them has changed. Would you mind speaking with them, getting a feel for what he might be talking about? We might need good pilots but not if they're going to endanger the ship with some ill-fated vendetta."

She had turned back to all-business. "I'll go speak to them now."

"Thanks," he said, then headed off in the other direction. A soft bed was sounding better by the second. He might not even make it that far.

31

Regaining consciousness was not easy. It was as if he'd been in a deep cavern, and only the smallest pinprick of light shone at the very end, highlighting the way out. And as he moved toward that light, his appendages became heavier and heavier, willing him to stop and return to his dormant state. But Sesster had been dormant long enough, and even though it was difficult to find his way out, he had to. He couldn't stay any longer.

But upon breaching the end of the cavern he had found himself in an onslaught of information; too much to process. It assaulted all of his senses at once and what he came to realize was he was experiencing the last ten years of his life in only a few seconds. When he'd "voluntarily" set himself into his hibernation state, his mind hadn't been completely closed off. It had continued to absorb events around him. If he concentrated, he found he could remember vivid details of conversations he'd never been privy to but had happened in his presence. And when he finally did wake properly and could stand on his own—with some assistance from his fellow Claxians—he found there was only one person he wanted to speak to.

The one person who had continued to stay by his side, and kept her promise to return him home, no matter the means.

Sesster's mind had reached out for Zenfor, searching far beyond what should have been possible, but instead finding Evelyn Diazal. She had also helped return him to his home, but Evelyn's heart held a deep secret. A secret which had become common knowledge in the days after the ship had returned to orbit around Hescal, and to which he'd been absorbing over the past ten years without even realizing it.

The humans had taken measures that could have sent the Coalition into a war with the Sil, and they had done it in secret, without the council's approval.

Part of him wasn't surprised. They were a child-like race after all, and the Claxians had taken given them everything they had needed. It was funny: human memories were so short. No longer did they remember how they had been on the brink of starvation when they found the Claxians. No longer were they grateful for all that had been provided to them and allowed them to thrive. Sesster had hoped they had grown out of their infancy in the past two thousand years, but it seemed some behaviors were impossible to remove, and it had cost the entire Coalition for them to see that.

And still, the Claxians had known this was a possible eventuality, and they had still given freely. Because the humans hadn't come to Claxia Prime looking to conquer it, as so many other species had before. They came looking for cooperation, and in that single attribute, had earned the respect of the Claxians, despite all the potential dangers. It was easy to see how some of humanity could become complacent and forget, while others worked to make themselves better. Sesster had to believe the people he'd chosen to work with, the reasons he'd decided to leave Claxia aboard a Coalition starship, were because he was helping the best of humanity. But learning of this deception made him question his convictions. Out of everyone, he had hoped Evelyn would have somehow been ignorant to the whole endeavor; that she wouldn't have been a part of it. He could only assume Greene had been part of it as well, considering it had been his ship. How could things have gone so wrong? He'd been so sure about them.

I sense you are troubled, brother. R'resst stood nearby, one of his arms outstretched. Sesster's arm stretched to meet it.

The humans. Did you know about their plan for the Sil weapon?

We found out not long after the fall of the Coalition. It was the Athru who revealed the truth to us. They have not been malevolent toward us; however, they keep a close eye. They know humans hide here, he said.

Here? You allowed them to take refuge on Claxia Prime? He was surprised they hadn't been banished. He recalled something—the memories were fuzzy—but there had been an incident on Sissk. An event where humanity threatened the planet. He wasn't sure, but he had the impression had there been any humans on Sissk, it would have been destroyed. Had he dreamed that, or had it happened in his absence? He wished he could read Dr. Xax, communicate with her, but she'd never been receptive to him in any way. He needed Tyler or one of the others.

Not all of us have given up on the Coalition. I suggest you not either. Not all the humans should be held responsible for the actions of a few.

I spoke with one, Sesster said. *But she was distant. I didn't realize I had the capability—*

You've been under a long time. It is as if your mind has been storing potential energy and now that you are awake, it is being turned kinetic, reaching out far beyond your normal limits.

How long will it last?

R'resst voice came across unsure. *I don't know. But be careful. You are still fragile from your time under.*

R'resst dropped his arm and Sesster felt his fellow Claxian move away. It had been so long since he'd been among his own people it felt strange being back. He could sense Xax nearby, but the pilot who'd brought them here was already gone, his deception complete. He could reach out to Evelyn again, but she wasn't who he wanted to speak with. There was one person he needed to contact and so he focused all his efforts on finding Zenfor. If she had died, he should be able to tell.

All was dark for a few moments as his mind probed further than it ever had. He felt he could reach into a space that transcended the distance between the stars, a place that was only filled with thought. A place—until very recently—he'd thought of as a small box. But now the box's sides had been blown off and it was expanding, like three-dimensional representation of a four-dimensional object—always moving outward across the space-time continuum.

After a few moments, a familiar setting washed over Sesster, and he realized he'd found *Tempest*, with the myriad of minds aboard all jumbled together. A few bright spots remained, including Caspian and Tyler, but he ignored them, instead searching out his quarry. And he found her— unconscious in what he assumed was sickbay. Sesster dipped his mind beneath the conscious plane.

Zenfor, do you hear me?

I—hear...Sesster? You are alive? Where are you?

I am back home, thanks to you. They completed their mission; they returned me home. He couldn't describe how good it was to hear her voice again. To feel her presence near him, even though they were hundreds of light-years apart.

Sesster, you must warn Diazal. The Sargan can't be trusted—they've—

I know, he replied. *It has already happened. They took her and her mother away from here.*

We are coming to you, she said. *To Earth. There was an ambush here, and Caspian has convinced the Sil to engage the Athru. But we need the data from Diazal. We are coming in blind.*

Here? He asked. *You can't, the ship will be destroyed. Why must they be so arrogant?*

He felt her presence shift. *I have never heard you speak of them that way. What has happened?*

I know of the deception, he replied, the memory reverberating through him. *I know what they kept from me. Even those I thought I could trust, such as Evelyn and Captain Greene.*

They had no part in the mission, Zenfor replied. *It was all Rutledge's fault. And I have taken care of him.*

If they had no part, then why did they cover it up?

He could feel her mentally tense, as if she were gearing up for a fight. *They told everyone when they returned from Hescal—the Athru planet. Even though they hadn't made the decisions to make it happen—and Caspian had even sacrificed his career to try and stop it, they knew revealing the truth would seed cracks in the Coalition. They tried to take care of it themselves, but it was too late. By the time we returned, it had been much too long. All those who had a hand in the plan were dead, except for Rutledge.* He felt her swell with satisfaction. *And like I said, he has been dealt with.*

Sesster resigned himself. *I just don't know.*

Do you remember what you told me about them? Just before Volf decided to take us back into open space—to leave the Coalition behind?

I do, he replied.

You need to tell them. You need to help them remember their own past. They deserve to know, and you can show them. If you can reach me, you can reach them.

Zenfor…I don't know how they'll handle it.

They're stronger than you think, she said. *They might surprise you.*

Sesster contemplated the idea a moment. If he was going to tell them, he'd didn't want to do it like this. It needed to be more personal. That was, if it even mattered. *How close are you?*

I don't know. Days, at least.

I need to think it over.

Don't wait too long. The more they know, the better prepared they will be. It might even help find a way out of this.

Sesster took a moment for himself. *I'll speak with you again soon. Once I've made my decision. Will you be awake by then?*

I hope so.

Then I anticipate the next time we are together.

As do I. As he pulled away, he experienced an overwhelming sense of satisfaction and happiness from her, something that was rare for the Sil. He hadn't realized just how much it meant to her that he arrive back home alive. When they'd met, though they'd been kindred spirits, she'd been closed off and distant. But now…

Perhaps she really did love him, after all.

32

"Here, follow me," the guard said, crouching down behind a low barrier in the long room. Evie had managed to propel them back down to the underside of the ship, though they'd had to stop once to regroup and make sure neither one was suffocating. She still hadn't reached the limit of how long she could stay in space and when she'd been out there her skin had gone that ashy gray color again but returned to normal as soon as they were back inside. The guard had led them into an access portal and then into this long room which as far as she could tell was empty, but he knew this ship better than she did.

"I don't even know your name," she said as they low-walked from one barrier to another. Evie shot a glance down the long hall, seeing nothing.

"Kithal," he replied. "Third class Master."

"Evie," she said, "human/Athru hybrid."

"I still can't believe I'm doing this; I should have arrested you as soon as I had the chance." He paused a moment, then motioned for her to follow.

"Sorry, Kithal, I don't think it would have happened. Considering…" She motioned to herself with one hand.

Kithal glanced back at her, his small mouth in a frown. "Right." He stopped them in their tracks. "And you still promise you won't hurt the people on this ship? Most…" He sighed. "Most aren't largely in favor of what we do. Some are. But I think many of my people have become apathetic to our…instructions. Except for our leaders, they are the passionate ones. And we follow their lead."

"It sounds like you're not so sure yourself," Evie replied.

Kithal set his features. "My loyalty is to my superiors and my people. It's just sometimes it feels like those two are in opposition to each other." He motioned for them to continue along the low walls, moving up the corridor.

"Did you know, about my mother and her group?" Evie asked. "Were they common knowledge?"

"After they defected, yes. We were ordered to seek them all out and bring them to justice. As far as I know there were only two left: your mother and the one called Martial."

Evie pushed her feeling back, not wanting to get emotional in front of him. "Now there is no one."

Kithal stopped. "I'm…sorry." He glanced up, his eyes scanning above them. "Come, we're close now. We need to get there before they figure out what we're doing." He broke into a fast walk, staying below the barrier until they cleared the corridor and came to a T-junction with a series of rooms along the adjacent wall. He checked the length of the corridor in both directions and led Evie to the largest of the doors. "This is it. Typically there's a guard posted down here but they must be using everyone they can to find you. And I'll need to report soon."

"What will you tell them?" Evie asked.

"I can make my way back up to our concourse without being seen. I'll say I was rendered unconscious when I tried to stop you. It's the truth. Once I'm confident they've stopped looking for you, I'll return." He pressed his hand on the door and it slid open without a sound, revealing a large black box situated in the middle of the room. Evie approached it and the sides opened like a cabinet, revealing a table inside, tilted at a high angle she could lay up against.

She paused. "How do I know this isn't a trick to subdue me?"

"Because you're right. If they find you, you'll be killed. And my sister would never forgive me."

Evie was struck by his earnestness. It seemed—familiar. Out of all the Athru she'd met, Kithal was the most empathetic—something she thought the Athru weren't capable of. Rockron and Dulthar hadn't had any compassion. And Esterva—she had been too preoccupied with her own goals to see very far beyond herself. Had she never met Kithal, she would have had assumed Esterva was right about the entire species. But now all of that had changed. "Do I just…close my eyes? How does it work?"

Kithal glanced at the door over his shoulder, still standing open. "No, you don't experience the passage of time at all. From your perspective I will literally close the doors and then open them again—you won't even notice anything has happened." He was rushing her inside, but she could understand why. The longer they stood her talking, the greater the chance they'd be caught. Evie stepped into the device and lay back against the upright table.

"See you in two seconds," Kithal said and he closed the cabinet doors. Just as Evie watched the pinprick of light between the two doors diminish, she felt as if she were pulled—no, yanked away as if on a string to another place completely. She landed hard on her hands and knees, feeling a coarse grain beneath them. Everything was still dark, until it wasn't. A purple light shone in the distance, illuminating a pre-dawn sky. Something must have gone wrong—he had tricked her after all. All his talk of having a sister—probably nothing more than propaganda to get her inside this thing, whatever it was. And now she was subdued.

But as Evie stood and glanced around, she realized she was no longer on the Athru ship; instead she was back on Sissk, standing beside the road that led away from Lechal and to her childhood home. In the distance stood the Selasi Mountains, but the whole place had a shimmery quality to it, as if it had been conjured in some way. This couldn't be because of Kithal—somehow Sesster had pulled her back here, despite the vast distance between them.

"Sesster?" she called out. "Are you there?" Evie twirled in place, recognizing this as Sesster's mind-place and not the actual place she'd lived most of her younger years.

Evie turned again and saw a figure walking toward her, but it shimmered as it moved and she had to squint in what little light there was to make out the shape. It had to be Sesster, like before, when they would come to this place together. She was impressed at how far his range seemed to stretch now; there had been a time when she needed to be in the same room with him to experience this kind of connection. "I'm so glad you came back," she said, approaching the figure. "I was afraid after our last conversation—" She stopped short. The wavy figure cleared, but it wasn't Sesster. It was Cas.

"Evie?" he asked, looking around. "What's going on?"

"Is it really you?" She approached him carefully, unsure if this was some kind of illusion or not.

"Of course, it's me, where are we? This looks like—Sissk. But that's impossible, I was just at my desk—on *Tempest*. How can I be…" He trailed off, then stared at her. "Is this…the mind-place?"

She inhaled sharply. She hadn't told anyone but him about this place before, because if there was one thing Cas was good at, it was keeping a secret. "It *is* you," she whispered. She ran over to him and threw her arms round his neck, finding he was as solid as she was. He stumbled back.

"I don't understand," he said. "You're alive."

She pulled back from him. "Of course, I'm alive."

"But Tos—Rutledge—I figured he would betray you—"

"He did," she said. "He was in league with the Athru the entire time. They were waiting for us on Claxia Prime."

Cas screwed up his features and seemed to realize he was still holding her by the waist. He promptly let go. "But why? To what end?"

"The Athru wanted me to join them—they tried to convert me," she said. "Cas. Esterva is dead."

His face fell. "Oh, Evie…I'm—I'm so sorry."

She stopped any tears from welling up. Now was not the time. "I'm just glad you and the ship are okay. I wouldn't let myself think about what might have happened—"

"I know how you feel," Cas replied. "But don't worry. We're coming to get you. The fleet is on its way to the Horus system, intel or not."

Evie's eyes went wide but she couldn't suppress a grin. "How did you make *that* happen? The Sil—"

"—are pissed, but they just needed proper motivation," he said. "Are Sesster and Xax—?"

"Fine," another voice said, startling them both. Evie turned to see what she had come to think of as the humanoid projection of Sesster came into being beside them. He didn't so much appear as he dissolved into place, white robes and all.

"*Sesster?*" Cas asked, dumbfounded. "What the hell?"

"Captain," Sesster said, his completely white eyes staring at Cas, "I have the ability to reach across vast distances, but I do not know how long it will last. I brought the two of you here while I still could…on Zenfor's advice."

"You spoke to Zenfor?" Cas asked. "How?"

"Why? What happened?" Evie echoed, concerned. "What's wrong with Zenfor?"

He shook his head. "She'll be okay. She just…had to exact some revenge on a certain former admiral we both know." The way he said it made Evie think Zenfor hadn't held back, for which she was glad.

"First I'd like to congratulate you on your promotion," Sesster said to Cas.

"Sesster—" Evie began, not sure where to begin after their last short conversation.

"It's alright," he said softly. "I didn't fully appreciate your position before. But I think I understand now."

"What is he talking about?" Cas asked, concern in his eyes.

"He knows about the Coalition's attempts to hide your original mission from the Claxians." She faced Sesster. "I'm assuming all the Claxians know." He nodded. "I never wanted to keep that from you. But I was foolish," Evie said. "I believed what I was doing was for the good of the Coalition. I believed Rutledge when he told me it would make the Coalition a stronger organization. And yet, deep down, I think I still knew it was wrong."

"You were trying to keep the peace," Sesster said. "The truth is I first sensed something was amiss when Caspian came aboard at Starbase Eight." Sesster's white eyes settled on Cas. "You had so many secrets hidden in that mind of yours; it was hard not to listen to them all. I knew there was something wrong, and for a long time I managed to willfully ignore it. But during my…exile…I couldn't ignore the truth any longer."

Cas stiffened. "It was never my intention to drive the crew apart. Or undermine what you had. My issues with the Coalition ran deep. I was so blinded by hatred I couldn't see how that hate was affecting those around me. I never should have put either of you in that position."

Evie reached out to him, taking hold of his hand. "I'm glad you did. Neither of us would still be here if it weren't for you."

He smiled, squeezing her hand before it dropped away. "Sesster, we're on our way to the Horus system. We're coming to end this."

"Cas, there's something you should know," Evie said. She'd been trying to find a gentle way of saying this, but for the life of her couldn't figure out how. She just needed to get it out. "The Athru—they've...*terraformed* Earth. It doesn't look anything like it used to. I think they've been strip-mining it to build their fleet here. Over seven thousand ships. I don't know how the planet could come back from something like that."

"What?" Cas's face had gone pale. "How can that be?"

"They're determined to annihilate you," Sesster said. "And what better way than to strike a blow at your home planet?"

Cas took a few steps back, apparently in shock. Evie stayed close to him, in case he collapsed. "All those people—everyone I've ever known—"

"Esterva seems to think they were amassing some kind of weapon here, but I haven't seen it yet. Just the ships. But all Coalition outposts in the system have been destroyed," Evie added. "Except for the defense grid. It's still there, just no longer operational."

"I—I can't..." Cas trailed off. Evie had nothing but sympathy for him. Had she been raised on Earth she'd probably feel the same way. Though, she wasn't sure she'd feel much pity if Sissk had been destroyed.

"Captain," Sesster said after Cas had a minute to process the shock. "Part of the reason I brought you here was to discuss this."

"Discuss what?" Evie asked.

He stared at her, his demeanor calm and measured. "The fact Earth is not your home planet. And it never was."

33

"I'm sorry?" Cas barked, the incredulity of what Sesster had said reverberating through his mind.

"It's true. But humanity's memory is so fragile. Or sometimes, you forget your own heritage because it suits you. About fifteen hundred years ago, there was a concerted effort by humanity to 'lose' records of your initial journey to Earth. The idea was humans would feel more protective of a world they considered their own."

"But that's...that's insane," Cas said. He glanced to Evie who had gone silent. "Right? I mean what about geological records? And...and I don't know, archeological digs...and...Evie, help me out here."

"I don't know, Cas. Sesster doesn't lie."

"I'm not saying he's lying; I'm saying he's mistaken. Humans are from *Earth*. That's just a basic fact."

"Fact," Sesster said, allowing the word to reverberate among them. "Facts can be distorted, even changed, through the lens of time. When you first arrived to us you were...lost. And even though you were desperate, you didn't try to deceive us; you were more interested in learning about us, about exchanging ideas. And you weren't the first."

"What are you talking about?" Cas asked. This didn't make any sense. Humans had been on Earth since the dawn of time—they'd evolved there, then left for the stars, only to find Claxia Prime, their closest celestial neighbor, was inhabited. "The discovery of Claxia set off a renaissance among humanity. It's what pushed us into the stars, beyond the borders of the Horus system."

Sesster shook his head. "No. You *came* from the stars."

Cas couldn't believe what he was hearing. He was about to throw his hands up and walk away when he caught Evie's gaze. "Hear him out," she said. "You owe him that much at least."

Cas gritted his teeth. She was right. "Okay. But with a *healthy* amount of skepticism."

Sesster nodded, folding his hands inside his long robes. "Almost three millennia ago, humanity came to us from deep space on a city-sized ship. By the time you reached us, your population had dwindled to less than fifty-thousand, and many of your people were in stasis, with little promise of ever being revived." Cas stifled an objection. "Back then you didn't travel by the undercurrents. You didn't know how. But you came to us from some place distant, having been in transit for tens of thousands of generations."

"But," Cas said, unable to hold himself in. "Where did we come from then? If we *arrived* here as you say…where is our home?"

"I don't know," Sesster replied. "That information was lost to time and the fact your ship had imprecise navigational records. It was impossible to tell where you'd come from. But one word remained in your vocabulary—a word that had always meant home: *Earth*."

"I don't understand," Evie said. "We came to a system that just happened to have a planet named the same thing?"

"No," Sesster said. "Before you arrived it was known to us as *Menlasa*, which meant blue ball in our language. We knew without help; humanity would not survive but another

240

few centuries. Menlasa was without sentient life, so we allowed you to settle there, to make the planet your own. It was better suited for a species like yours, instead of mine. Your ancestors renamed it—as you did all the planets in our system, and our star—except for Claxia. You settled there, making the planet your home and taking care of it, as part of our original bargain."

"I can't believe this," Cas said. "I need to sit down." Behind him a chair appeared from thin air and he took a cautious seat until he was sure it wouldn't disappear again. "So, we just stayed on Earth then? Made up our entire history?"

"In the beginning, no. It took years to wake all your people and ensure everyone had enough food and supplies to live. But you had ingenuity. You disassembled your ship to create your first settlement—New Phoenix—and you thrived on Earth. Within less than six hundred years, you'd reached into space once more, eager to explore. Eager to expand."

"The beginning of the Coalition," Evie said.

"Correct. It was humans who first proposed a celestial alliance, even after some had splintered off to explore other parts of the system, a group eventually settling on one of the moons of the gas giant Isis."

"The Val," Cas said, the pieces beginning to fall into place. "I knew they'd been human once—"

"—and they still are," Sesster said. "Albeit they just look a little different now. A few millennia on a gravity-heavy world will do that to a species."

Cas supposed he was right. Genetically they were very similar, despite the Val's insistence they were not to be considered human or human-esqe in any way. He'd just come to accept they weren't part of the same species, even though as he heard Sesster talk now that seemed ridiculous.

"This is wild," Evie said. "So, from there did everything follow like we learn in school? About the founding of the Coalition?"

"More or less," Sesster said. "The Claxians eventually gave humanity the ability to travel in undercurrents, as is taught, and from there we expanded together to build an alliance of worlds. It was the first time in the long history of the Claxians a visitor had come to our planet looking for peace, rather than to conquer. Had humanity tried to overtake us, we just would have allowed you to stay until you went extinct on your own. But because you arrived with a message of friendship and cooperation, we were happy to become your allies and partners."

Cas stood from his chair, frowning. "That's why it was so hard for you to hear about Rutledge's subterfuge," Cas said, reaching out for Sesster. But his hand passed right through the robed figure. "That's why you went into hibernation."

"I think I knew, intuitively, something had gone wrong deep within our alliance. But without any of my brothers or sisters around, it was too difficult to bear," Sesster admitted. "I tried to maintain my composure as we observed the destruction brought on by the Athru, but in the end, it was too much. The mental stress was overwhelming."

"And it was easier to hide yourself than try to face those of us who betrayed you," Evie said. "So, when Volf announced she was taking the ship back to Hescal—"

"—I did the only thing I could to preserve myself," Sesster said. "It was not the right decision, and it put you and the ship in danger."

"It wasn't your fault," Cas said. "It was ours. For allowing a small group of humans in power to make all the decisions for us. To put what we'd built and kept for thousands of years at risk. I guess…" He glanced out at the horizon to the rising sun just beginning to peek over the bald mountains. "I guess

242

when humans become complacent, they forget who they truly are." He glanced at Evie. "Comfort has a way of doing that to people. You forget how hard it is to struggle."

"I suppose," Sesster said. "I only wish we'd found out before this invasion. Perhaps we could have done something to prevent it."

"So now what?" Evie's voice wavered. "What are we supposed to do with this information?"

"I needed you to know, because I don't want you to feel like Earth is irreplaceable," Sesster said. "Do not feel like you have to fight to your dying breath to save it. Humanity can live on. You've done it once before. But if you are looking to eliminate the Athru threat—they have set up their primary operations on the surface of the planet."

"What are you saying?" Cas asked.

"I know what he's saying," Evie said, her eyes hooded. "He's suggesting we use the Athru's own weapons against them—to destroy Earth."

"What?" Cas felt a wave of nausea pass through him. "You can't be serious."

"I would never advocate for the complete destruction of another species," Sesster said. "But I am also conflicted about these creatures. They seem determined to stay and have vast resources. My people will be subjugated forever. And all of the other members of the Coalition—sequestered on their planets, cut off from everyone else. It's an imbalance of power." Cas couldn't detect any emotion on his "face", but that only meant he wasn't letting Cas see how he was really feeling. The intent in his words was clear enough.

"And therein lies a new problem," Evie said. "I've had a chance to get to know one of them—a local. He tells me most of the Athru don't care for this war, never have. That it is a few at the very top, in power, who follow the strict doctrine of their own genetic code, which tells them to destroy humanity, no matter the cost."

"Evie, he's lying to you," Cas said. "It's a ruse, to get you to trust them. Remember Rockron? Remember how he said nothing bad would happen?"

"Maybe. But you should have seen the way most of them shied away from me when I escaped. As if they were afraid and wanted nothing to do with me. It was very unlike the Athru we met on Hescal, chasing us down and mercilessly killing us, piling our bodies into strange forms. I'm afraid if we commit genocide on these people, we are no better than those who tried to take control of the Coalition for their own means. It's just not that simple."

"What are we supposed to do?" Cas asked. "The fleet is coming, Evie. We can't not do anything."

She turned to Sesster. "How long has passed in the real world while we're in here?"

"Milliseconds," Sesster replied. "Almost instantaneous."

"Good," she replied. "Because I'm going to need all the time I can get. I'm inside a time chamber. The Athru brass use it to extend their lives far beyond what they should, which means they stay in power forever. This entire crusade could be nothing more than the whims of an overzealous madman. If I can get close enough to the head and chop it off, maybe everything else will fall apart. Surely there will be others and we'll have to do some cleanup, but it might be enough to stop this occupation."

"And make them leave Coalition space?" Cas shook his head. "I don't believe it. They didn't travel all this way and kill all those people just for us to roll over because of a few bleeding hearts. If the Athru truly didn't want this to happen, they would have stopped their leaders."

"Apathy is not a crime," Evie said.

"It is when it involves the destruction of an entire species!" Cas yelled. "By Kor, have you forgotten they have literally killed ninety-nine percent of the population? We don't have a choice here, Evie. We don't have the resources to infiltrate and try to separate the good from the bad. They'll find us all long before that happens. I agree with Sesster, we destroy Earth and we deal a crippling blow to them."

She worked her jaw for a moment. "You just said a minute ago Earth was your home!"

"But that Earth is already gone," he replied. "You said it yourself. And they'll just keep stripping the planet to build more and more ships. For the good of the Coalition—the *original* Coalition, not this monstrosity it had become lately— we have to act while we can. You're on that ship now, we'll never have a better chance."

Evie sighed. She couldn't fault his logic. But she didn't want to see Kithal and others like him killed either. She refused to judge an entire species by the actions of a select few. "*If* we decided to do this, what happens to Claxia? The planets are only two hundred million kilometers apart. Surely the loss of a planet in the system will have dire consequences."

"No doubt," Sesster said. "We will most likely deal with severe weather problems for centuries. And it will alter the orbits of all the planets in the system. We could face a global climate challenge here on Claxia. But it is better than allowing the Athru to stay and build up their armies. Cas is right, even if it isn't the will of the people, enough Athru support these decisions to fill their ranks and enable their leaders to continue. We must put a stop to it."

"Fine," she said, dejected. She *did* have to consider all the other species in the Coalition: the Yax-Inax, the Untuburu, the Husmus-riza, the Goruffians, and all the others. They had been unfairly sequestered on their own planets during this…occupation. It couldn't continue.

"My hold is loosening," Sesster said and the world shimmered around them.

"Don't worry," Cas said, trying to give Evie a reassuring smile. "We're on our way to help. As soon as we get there, we'll provide enough of a distraction for you to use the weapon. Then we'll get you off that ship. Trust me." There was something in the way she looked at him. Something that gave him a pit in his stomach.

"Cas, if this doesn't work…"

"It will, *trust me*," he said, trying to reassure her. He *had* to believe it could work. What other choice did they have?

She paused as the world shimmered once more, glancing around, as if realizing something. "There's so much I need to say," she said.

"You can tell me once you're back aboard," Cas replied. He didn't like where she was going with this. He didn't want to think this might be the last time he ever saw her.

Evie shook her head, the sadness seeming to envelop her. "It can't wait. I know how you feel. I know you love me."

Cas's heart was hammering hard, despite the fact he wasn't even a real being. For all of this being some kind of non-corporeal dream, it sure felt real. "Evie—"

"It's okay," she said. "I've known for a while. I just want you to know I love you too, even if it isn't in the same way."

Cas felt the tickle of tears at the corners of his eyes. "I tried—I mean I did my best to make sure you never knew. Despite—I only ever wanted a friend; I never wanted to make you uncomfortable."

"You didn't," she said. The world shimmered again. She walked up and wrapped him in a hug, holding him tight. He did the same, relishing the moment as if it were his last. He wanted to hold on forever, to bring her back to *Tempest* with him, just so he knew she was safe. He could feel her shuddering beneath his grip and Cas did everything he could to cement this moment in his memory. The feel of her next to him, her smell, even the softness of her braid against his shoulder. When she finally pulled away, she took hold of his hand with both of hers and brought it to her lips, placing a light kiss on top. She smiled. "See you," she said, and the world dissolved.

Cas shot straight up from his desk, his eyes wet and his heart thundering. He had to give himself some time to collect his thoughts. He played their last moment over and over again in his mind until he was sure it would never leave. He was determined to make sure she didn't die alone on that ship. Cas stood and headed back to the bridge. They had a job to do.

34

No sooner had she said her final goodbye to Cas—and that's what it had been, a final goodbye; there was no way she was getting out of this alive, even if *Tempest* was coming. But as the last words had escaped her lips, she found herself right back in the temporal box, the sliver of light disappearing as Kithal finished closing the doors. The light completely disappeared and then the doors were flung open again with such a fervor, Evie knew something was wrong. She shielded her eyes just a second before lunging forward.

"What's wrong? What happened?" she asked. But when she uncovered her eyes, she saw it was no longer just her and Kithal. Twenty Athru guards stood around the box, while Dulthar stood in the middle, holding a limp Kithal by the neck. He was dead as he hung at an unnatural angle; his neck had probably been snapped. Dulthar threw the guard to the ground, his limp body making a thump as it landed.

All thoughts of her conversation with Cas and Sesster left Evie's mind as she lunged for Dulthar. "Ah," he said, holding up one hand. Evie stopped, noticing each of the guards was now armed with the same kind of weapon she'd seen on Claxia Prime. "You've forced me to return to a kind of warfare I don't like," Dulthar said. "The kind that uses weapons. But sometimes it is important to keep your enemies at a distance, especially if they can kill you with one touch." He had a scar over his face from where Evie had scratched him, but it seemed to have healed unnaturally fast.

"I don't understand," she said. "How did you get in here so fast?" Her eyes fell back to Kithal and she realized he had on a different tunic than before.

"I can't believe I ever thought you had the potential to be one of us," Dulthar said.

Of course, how could she be so stupid. Kithal said being in the box was instantaneous, as if no time had passed at all. But something had gone very wrong. They weren't supposed to be looking for her anymore. "How long was I in there?" she asked. She didn't want to consider the possibility it could have been seasons, or even years. *Tempest* might have already come and failed.

"One of your weeks," Dulthar said. "Though I do have to admit, you had me fooled. I thought you'd died in your last escape. Until this traitor here…" He motioned to Kithal, "…decided he couldn't stand the pressure and came clean."

"He…betrayed me?" Evie asked.

"Don't feel left out, he betrayed me as well. He was a very conflicted individual. But I alleviated that problem for him." Dulthar kicked the body of Kithal and it flew to the other side of the room, hitting the far wall and crumpling into a pile. "Now, remove yourself from that box."

"Why don't you just shoot me and pull me out yourself?" she challenged.

Dulthar held her gaze a moment. "You are an arrogant little shit; I'm not surprised your mother sent you off. The *reason* I'd rather not kill you is my business. Now get out or I will have my men blow your legs off and we *will* drag you out."

Evie considered not doing it, but if Dulthar wasn't prepared to kill her yet it was better she cooperate for as long

249

as possible. It would give her more opportunity to escape. She had to assume Cas and the others hadn't arrived yet, as Dulthar would have no doubt thrown it in her face. She stepped over the threshold and outside of the box while the guards kept their weapons trained on her. She couldn't believe Kithal had betrayed her…after all that. Maybe Cas and Sesster had been right. Maybe eliminating all of them was the right call. But it was still a hard pill to swallow.

"Keep her ten meters away from me at all times," Dulthar said.

"Just how old are you, Dulthar?" Evie asked. "Have you been around since the beginning?"

"Don't ask foolish questions," he said, turning away from her as the entourage moved down the corridor. Evie felt silly with so many people training weapons on her, encircling her. If she could just get them to fire at the right time, they'd all hit each other.

"No, seriously. Ever since I found out about your little time bubble I've been curious. You must be ancient. How old? Ten-thousand years? A million?"

"It's none of your concern," he replied.

"Well, it kind of is," she continued, pressing. "I've just happened to learn my people weren't originally from Earth. That we came here on a massive city-ship, not unlike this one. Which begs the question, when did your people meet mine in the past? And what did you witness that was so terrible you decided to hunt us down? You said you had a duty to protect the galaxy from us—but what caused that? Because all this time I couldn't figure out *why* the Athru pursued us. Or even how you'd even encountered us. Back when I thought my species had come from a planet in the Claxian sector it didn't make sense. You would have had to come upon a deep space reconnaissance vessel, deeper than we'd ever sent before. But armed with this new information—"

"You speak too much," Dulthar said, continuing to lead them through the ship. They walked up a wide ramp into a larger section of the ship.

Evie began walking faster to catch up to him. The circle of guards moved quicker too. "And you owe me an explanation. For the death of my mother. Seeing—as you said—she never thought to inform me."

"Slow down," one of the guards said in their own language, but Evie understood him fine. She stopped in place.

Dulthar faced her. "Even now, your arrogance seeps through. I owe you nothing. Esterva betrayed me. As did Kithal. Be glad you're not sharing their fate…yet." He began to turn away.

"What are you afraid of? That I won't agree with your actions once I know the truth?" Evie was tired of being jerked around. If he'd really wanted to harm her, he would have done it already and saved himself the trouble. He needed her alive for some reason, though she wasn't sure why. But she was willing to bet it had something to do with her enhanced abilities.

Dulthar eyed her carefully. "You want the truth. Very well. Our species *have* met before, long ago. On another planet, much like the one you used to call Earth." He scoffed. "So arrogant, naming your new home after your old one. So *predictable*."

"Wait," Evie said, screwing up her features. "What are you saying? Humans came from another planet Earth? In the distant past?"

"Oh yes," Dulthar said. "Third planet in its system, around a yellow-type star. It had…one moon I believe."

"That was our home?" Evie asked. "Where we came from?"

Dulthar approached her, grinning. "Yes. It's where we're *both* from."

251

***

Cas sat at the head of the conference table, tapping his fingers in rhythm as Hank and Lieutenant Tileah laid out the battle plans on the holo screen in the middle of the table. He was having a hard time concentrating. It had been almost seven days since his 'experience' with Evie and Sesster and yet he remained shook. No matter what happened, they had to get her out of there. He wasn't going to leave her to the Athru, even if she'd already given up hope, which is what that had been. He'd seen it in her eyes.

Cas listened to the rest of the presentation, which was mostly made up of diversionary tactics.

"So, if I understand this correctly," Samiya said. "We're not actively trying to destroy the Athru ships, at least not a lot of them."

"Correct," Hank said. "Based on the captain's intel and conversations with Ms. Diazal, we need to give her as many diversions as possible so she can claim control of the Athru weapon and destroy Earth."

"I still can't believe we're discussing this," Tyler said. "Is it really that bad?"

"She said the entire planet is a factory husk," Cas said, his voice emotionless. "There's nothing left there to save. If there are pockets of resistance on the planet—there's nothing we can do for them. We have to cut off the Athru's supply chain if we want a chance of defeating them."

"By Garth," Ronde whispered.

"Something you want to add, Lieutenant?" Cas asked.

"No sir, I just can't believe they're all gone. It's one thing to see a few colony worlds destroyed, or the others cut off. But to see our home—"

"It's not our home," Cas cut in. He'd had a hard time relaying the information from Sesster but given the Claxians were prone not to be deceptive he had no choice but to accept it. Half of their history had all been a fabrication, and somehow, deep inside, it made Cas even angrier at the Coalition.

"Yes, sir," Ronde said, his head down. Next to him, River reached over and patted his hand. It didn't escape Cas's notice how close they'd become. And he supposed he couldn't blame them. With so few humans left, it was only natural.

"The Sil won't like it," Zenfor said. Cas turned to her. For the first time since she'd come on board, she was seated in one of the conference chairs, a small device on her chest. Box had explained it was to help repair the damage and monitor any abnormal activity. And technically she still hadn't been released yet. She was only allowed a few hours outside of sickbay each day until she was fully healed. Box told him he had to continue to sedate her to keep her immobile, as she was too energized when she was awake and couldn't lie still for hours at a time unless she was sleeping. Right after they were done in here she was due to report back to go under again.

"What do you mean?" Cas asked.

"They will want to destroy their enemies and move on. We—*they* don't tiptoe around a problem, they face it, head on."

Cas couldn't help but smile. "Right. Well, assuming the weapons even work, and the rest of the fleet joins us at Horus, we'll just have to hold off until Earth has been destroyed. Once that's done, they'll have my blessing to destroy as many of the Athru ships as they want."

"Does that include the city-ship?" Zaal asked.

"Not until we get Evie," Cas said. "Since *Tempest* is physically the weakest ship, but also the fastest, we have the best chance of getting in there and grabbing her."

"Are we sure she can even do this?" Hank said. "It's been seven days since you last spoke with her. *And* she said their fleet outnumbers ours ten-to-one."

Cas nodded. "I'm sure. She was hiding out on board, *and* she had an ally. I trust her ability to get this done." He didn't miss Samiya and Hank exchange glances. "As for the number of ships…we'll just have to trust the Sil are as good as they think they are. Unless you have a better idea?"

Hank shook his head. "No, sir. Just covering all the bases."

"Dismissed," Cas said. As everyone filed out, Cas stood, approaching one of the windows. Outside the green tint of the undercurrent colored everything. But beyond the stars flew by in such a blur. All those people out there, all those civilizations were counting on him for their futures, even if they didn't know it. Cas had never wanted this; all he'd ever wanted was to go off and explore, not fight an intergalactic war. But it seemed fate had other plans for him.

"I trust her too." Cas turned to see Zenfor standing, though somewhat wobbly on her normally powerful legs. "She'll get the job done."

"I know," Cas replied. "No matter what gets in her way…I know she will."

35

"What are you saying?" Evie asked as she faced Dulthar in the wide corridor. The guards still had all their weapons trained on her but as far as she was concerned, it was just the two of them now. Whatever he was talking about, she needed him to clear it up before she took another step.

"I wasn't there originally, but when the information was still available in our computers—before it had degraded, before we'd learned to encode our genetic material—I learned all about *our* home planet. Though my people have been away far longer than they have."

"They?" Evie asked. "You mean the humans."

"I mean the imposters," Dulthar said. "They call themselves human, when they are anything but. They are nothing but genetic fossils, having survived long past their time. A stepping stone that should have been wiped out long ago."

Evie shook her head. "What are you talking about? Are you saying they shouldn't be here?"

"Of course, they shouldn't be here," he spat. "It was by nothing more than blind luck that they came up on this system and the Claxians. That ship—the one carrying all of humanity to this place—it never should have survived."

"Why not?"

Dulthar grimaced. "Astronomically small odds. There were four ships originally. Humans…humans had driven their planet to the brink of destruction. And they faced a choice: stay and die, or leave and take their chances in the stars. A century was spent constructing the ships that would take them to the undiscovered country to find new homes. Four ships in four different directions, with the hopes one would eventually find a place to settle." He paused. "There was little chance of survival. An entire species moving at sub-light speeds? It's hard to fathom. It took them fifty years just to leave their own system. And it was known if one ship made it, the others never would as it would take too long to communicate between distances and even longer to travel those distances."

"And yet. they did it," Evie said. "They reached Claxia, or—at least one of the ships did. But that still doesn't explain you. You said both humans and Athru were from the same place. Did you mean the same system? Another inhabited world? Was that why you are so bent on their destruction? Because they treated their first planet poorly? It's hardly unique, there are tons of species out there who decimate—"

Dulthar shook his head. "Oh, you stupid girl. Put it together already." His gaze burned on her face. "Athru and Human are the *same species. We* were one of the other ships."

Evie took a step back. "How is that possible?"

Dulthar moved closer and Evie felt the guards tense their weapons. But she wasn't going to lash out at him. She needed this explained, if for no other reason than her own self-satisfaction. "Didn't you wonder how your mother and father managed to mate so easily? How within the span of a few months you came into being? It's because they had the same base genetic code."

"But—there are interspecies children all over the Coalition," she said. "It's…nothing rare." She'd seen plenty of children of multiple species. Though now that she thought about it, she had to work to think up examples of successful pairings and found they were rarer than she'd naturally assumed.

"Those children are the product of centuries of genetic testing and work. Years and years of failures. Your mother did this in only a few weeks."

"But—" Evie began again, though she wasn't sure what she was objecting to. Perhaps if she'd taken more time to think about it, she might have realized he was right—the genetic combination of two species was nothing easy, or fast. And yet, her mother and father had created her in such a short amount of time—*and* she had been the first attempt. Or at least, that was what she had been told. She had originally assumed it was because of Esterva's exceptional genetic skill.

"No," Dulthar said, stepping even closer. "No more buts. This is the reality of the situation, Evie. Humans are nothing more than the ancient ancestors of the Athru. You are looking at your future. Or, I should say one possible version of your future, shaped by one set of specific circumstances."

"How?" she whispered.

"Hescal." Dulthar said. "The ship my ancestors were on was *lucky* enough to find it, after spending thousands of years traveling between stars. Little did we know it was a planet out of time. We investigated, crashed and once we recovered, discovered we couldn't leave."

Evie recalled how their ships had lost power upon reaching the planet, and how they'd all almost been killed going into the atmosphere. "Because of the dampeners," she said.

"An ancient technology, created by a race we neither know nor could understand at the time. We were much like your crew, except we had no idea the structures on the planet existed. It took almost a thousand years to discover the first ones."

"So, you stayed on the planet? Because you couldn't leave?"

Dulthar's eyes narrowed. "We stayed because we wished to. Over the years we deciphered the technology, found ways to use it for ourselves. At first my people thought of it as a detriment, until we realized what a powerful advantage we had—because the planet was out of time. We'd already spent thousands of years on it, but celestially, less than a few months had passed. Do you understand? We saw an opportunity and seized on it. What better way to fulfill our mission than to continue to grow and evolve—not only ourselves but our technology as well? We managed to live and thrive on that planet for over two million years. Can you understand what that would do to a society?"

Evie scoffed. "Apparently it made you all a bunch of assholes."

"No," Dulthar said, drawing out the word. "It made us grow up. As we grew and evolved, we realized just how dangerous we had been in our youth. How dangerous a young humanity was. We recognized that and confined ourselves to the planet until we reached a point where we had outgrown our childish ways. Greed, lies, deception, war—we eliminated them all. We became what humanity always should have been. But we knew there were three other ships out there. Which meant humanity was infecting other parts of the galaxy—spreading the worst of us. It became our credo to put a stop to them, and to eliminate any humans who had not evolved to our advanced state."

Evie took it all in, trying to process everything he'd said. "Do you really have so little faith in your own ancestors that you'd rather destroy them than allow them to try and develop on their own?"

Dulthar laughed, though it was forced and clipped. "Have you not been paying attention? The humans of your Coalition

258

betrayed the other members. And not just once, there have been many, many times. They couldn't control themselves, and risked fracturing everything you had for their selfishness. We have solved that problem. The *human* problem. And when we find your ship, we'll take one more step to completing the process."

"Surely you're not so stupid to think humanity is the only species with those attributes. Look at the Sil, or the Erustiaans. Or even the Yax-Inax; they were involved in more wars than they're willing to admit."

"I didn't say we were trying to eliminate the undesirable traits across the galaxy," he replied. "We are just cleaning our own house. Taking care of our own mess. When other species reach this level of sophistication, perhaps they can join us once more on the intergalactic stage."

"So that's why you've confined them all to their own planets," she replied.

Dulthar shrugged. "They're free to leave, if they wish. They're free to join forces. But they already know what it is taking you a painfully long time to realize: no one is equipped to stand against us. No one has reached our level of technological sophistication. And thus no one is worthy."

"You sound like the Sil," she replied.

His face darkened. "Funnily enough, the Sil were the one species close to us on the evolutionary scale. They were the one species we were willing to partner with. And yet, somehow, humanity came in and screwed that up too. But it doesn't matter, they have made their choice and they will die by it. We will not be stopped."

This was madness, an advanced form of humanity bent on revenge of its past self? No wonder they'd been so clinical in their targeting. With one glaring exception. "And what about the Bulaq? We saw you destroy their entire system. Don't tell me they're another one of the lost human ships."

259

"The Bulaq were…regrettable. But tests needed to be made. And a backward, religious-based society was a perfect training ground. We ensured enough of them would survive to rebuild." He said it as if destroying an entire world was nothing more than a slight inconvenience.

"You're insane," Evie said. What reservations she'd had about these people had just disappeared. She didn't care if they had once been human or not. She was the only thing standing in the way between them and their destruction of the last of the human race, and she wasn't going to allow it.

He turned to the guards. "Let's go."

"Wait," Evie said and Dulthar, his face colored with anger, turned back to her. "You said there were four ships in total. If you were one and the humans who found Claxia were another, what about the other two?"

"Yet to be found," Dulthar said. "But don't concern yourself with that, we will find and purge them." He turned away, sauntering down the hall with purpose while the rest of the group followed. "All in good time."

36

Cas sat in the captain's chair, his pulse quickening with every passing second. Each of those seconds brought them that much closer to their destination, and their destiny. He still wasn't sure if they would be successful or not, but they had to at least try, and with the Sil fleet at his back he at least felt like they had a chance. Had this been nothing but Coalition ships they wouldn't have had a chance, but the Sil were the most powerful race he'd ever encountered. They just *had* to be victorious. Otherwise, what was the point of it all?

"How close?" Hank asked, sitting beside him.

"Distance or time?" Zaal asked. Cas turned to him; an eyebrow arched. "I apologize. It was my attempt at a joke. Considering the seriousness of the situation, I thought it might be warranted."

"Time," Cas said, nonplussed.

"Four minutes until we reach the Claxian system," Zaal replied.

"Four minutes," Cas repeated. It felt like both an eternity and the blink of an eye.

"I never thought it would come to this," Hank said, his gaze straight ahead. "I thought after the Athru invaded we'd be on the run the rest of our lives. I never thought we'd be actively engaging them in war."

"It's a war they wanted," Cas said. "And one we're not going to let them get away with. Ignite the armor."

Tileah nodded from her station. "Armor up."

"Weapons?" Cas asked.

"Charged and ready."

"Status on the other half of the Sil fleet?"

"Last update they were on their way," Zaal said. "They should be right behind us as soon as we enter the system."

Cas tapped his comm. "Bay two, status?"

"We're ready to deploy down here," Saturina replied. "I'm happy to report all ten spacewings are locked, loaded and prepared to engage the enemy."

Cas had been hesitant about using the pilots who had defected at first, but it turned out Vrij had been right. In the face of an insurmountable enemy, they'd rather fight the Athru than their own crew. Cas hadn't met with them personally as he thought it was better to let Saturina handle her own people, and any confrontation with him would probably only sabotage the situation. But he trusted her judgment—if she trusted Linkovich and the others, then he did too. "Good luck, Chief," Cas said. "We'll send battle instructions down as soon as we formulate our attack plan."

"Acknowledged bridge, thanks and good luck." Saturina cut the comm.

Even though the spacewings were small with limited range, they could team up and with their new weapons systems, hopefully disable some of the smaller Athru ships while *Tempest* and the Sil fleet went after the larger targets. Cas just wished he had a comm directly to Evie. They would give her as long as possible, but if things went south quick, he'd have to send the team over to grab her and get back. Cas hit his comm again. "Belmont, Harcrow, are you ready?"

"Ready, Captain," Belmont replied. "As soon as we have her location and get the go ahead."

"Good, keep the shuttle on hot standby," Cas replied. He'd chosen Samiya and Hank's two most experienced officers for the job of retrieving Evie. They'd had a decade's worth of experience in avoiding the Athru so if anyone could do it, they could.

"Thirty seconds from the system, sir," Ronde said.

Cas steeled himself. "Keep in mind, they may be obscured in their time bubbles. It's our job to draw them out." He nodded to Zaal and the Untuburu nodded back, tapping one of his controls. "Sil fleet, prepare to engage."

"They've sent a standard reply," Zaal said.

"Good enough for me," Cas replied. The viewscreen lost its green tint as the ship came out of the undercurrent in the Claxian system, close to the defense grid, just inside Osiris' orbit.

"Holy shit," Samiya said. The space in front of them was littered with Athru ships.

"They're not even trying to obscure themselves," Tileah said. "Diazal's readings are confirmed—almost seven thousand ships." A current of nervousness rippled through her voice.

"Then we shouldn't have any problem finding a target," Cas said. "Lock on to the nearest ship and fire."

"Aye."

Cas held his breath. He wasn't sure if the reason they hadn't hit any patrols on the way in was because they'd just been extremely lucky, or because the Athru *wanted* to draw them in and he didn't care. All that mattered was the Sil weapons worked.

A purple blast erupted from the ship below the viewscreen and flew toward the closest Athru ship, who hadn't even yet turned to investigate *Tempest*. "Arrogant bastards," Cas said under his breath as he watched the purple blast find its target. At first nothing happened, it was as if the blast had just disappeared. But then the side of the Athru ship exploded in a blast of white light and while it didn't destroy the ship, it did knock it of its axis so it began to free-float through the system.

A cheer went up across the bridge as Cas smiled. "All ships, battle plan beta-seven. Spread out, high and fast. Hit as many of them as you can, and search for the city-ship!" As he said the words no less than a dozen plasma blasts launched from different Athru ships, all aimed at *Tempest*. "Mr. Ronde, do what you do best," Cas said, keeping his calm.

"Yes, sir," Ronde said, then nodded to River, whose mechanical hands were already split into two dozen fingers, working the navigational controls. The ship dived down the z axis, avoiding most of the fire but Ronde had to maneuver to keep any of the hits from the ship's new armor. Cas wasn't sure but based on what they'd seen back at Devil's Gate, the armor might not be as effective as the weapons. Which meant any hit on *Tempest* could be its last. They need to stay fast and maneuverable. He brought up a small 3-D image of the battlefield on his personal console.

Above them, Sil ships were still emerging from the undercurrents, each of them opening fire as soon as they were out. He noticed there was nothing very innovative about their attack strategy—that it was more or less straightforward. As if they'd forgotten what it was like to be in battle. "Zaal," Cas said. "Make sure the Sil know they can't just attack head-on. They're going to get slaughtered that way."

"I have transmitted the battle strategy, but I'm afraid they aren't interested in much of what we have to say," Zaal replied. "As evidenced by their attack patterns."

"By Garth," Cas said, watching as the Sil fleet was quickly cut down by the advancing Athru forces.

"We've got six ships on our tail!" Ronde said. "I'll do my best to lose them."

"Let's give them something extra to worry about," Cas said. He tapped his comm. "Chief. See those six ships on our asses? They're all yours."

"Acknowledged bridge," Saturina said. Beside him, Hank pulled up the rear viewers on his personal station and Cas watched as all ten spacewing ships launched in groups of two, each going after one of the pursuing ships. The pursuing Athru ships were thrown by the spacewings' small size and maneuverability as they were peppered with hits from smaller Sil weapons. They didn't do the same amount of damage as *Tempest's* weapons, but it was enough to make them peel off and try to fight off the smaller ships. Which meant there was only one left on *Tempest's* tail.

"I think we can eliminate that one," Cas said.

"Yes, sir," Tileah replied, launching four purple bolts at the pursuing ship. It was too fast and tried to peel off as soon as it realized what was coming, but only managed a half turn as it tried to slow its inertia before all four hit along its side, causing the ship to be engulfed in flames as each one detonated. What remained of the ship broke apart as the oxygen aboard burned in space until there was nothing left but debris.

"I'd say they work," Hank said.

"Damn right they do," Cas replied. He was feeling triumphant, like this might be possible after all.

"I've located the city-ship," Zaal said. "It's stationed just outside the defense grid, close to the prior location of outpost Alpha."

"How many ships over there?" Cas asked.

"At least a few hundred," Zaal replied. "But most are moving to converge on our location. They're coming in force and as soon as we're outnumbered our advantage won't hold."

He was right. Which meant they needed to do as much damage as they could. "Get us back into the thick of it," Cas ordered. Ronde nodded and the ship flipped on its axis, heading back the way it came. "If we can get the other half of the Sil fleet to converge on the city-ship, it should provide Evie with the distraction she needs to take them out. Are they close?"

"I haven't received any further updates from the Sanctuary," Zaal said.

"None?" Cas asked. His last conversation with them had been contentious, but after they began receiving updates from Thislea he'd figured it was all ironed out. "Let me speak to the Sanctuary back on Thislea. Now."

Zaal nodded and the comm line was opened. The main viewer kept an overlay of the overall battle so the bridge crew could coordinate. An image replaced the 3-D layout of the battle on Cas's personal comm system. It was a Sil male, without any armor. He seemed—old, but Cas wasn't certain of it.

"Sanctuary member?" Cas asked.

"Dracsal," the man replied, his face impassive.

"Am I to understand you're the representative I'm to communicate with?" The bridge rocked in one direction.

"Sorry," Ronde said. "Close call, the negators took a second to catch up." On the viewscreen the battle had entered the full fray.

"*You* may communicate with whomever you want," Dracsal said. "It makes no difference to me."

"I'm trying to get in touch with the Sanctuary," Cas said, heat rising in his face. "I need confirmation of the location of the other half of the Sil fleet. When can we expect them?"

Dracsal stared into the camera a moment before his lips pressed into a line. "You can't."

"Look, I need to know. We're facing a slaughter out here in a few minutes. Based on the speed of your ships they should be close. We can only hold this for a few hours."

"Then I wish you luck. Because you will not be receiving any more help from us."

Cas's heart dropped into his stomach. "What?"

"We have received telemetry from the battle and analyzed the Athru capabilities, as *you* had promised us before we began this engagement. If we cannot overpower them with the ships we have engaged at the moment, we will be pulling out of the battle, cutting our losses."

"You can't do that," Cas replied. "That will leave *Tempest* alone and defenseless. We have a plan to stop them, but you have to give us the time."

"And sacrifice even more Sil lives to a hopeless cause? I don't think so. Our goal was to prove the weapons work against the Athru. Now that we have done that, our job is finished. We will regroup in our own space and launch our own offensive when the time is right."

"Don't be an idiot, Dracsal. The only reason your ships are losing people right now is because they're not fighting strategically. I've given them a plan of attack; all they have to do is *follow it*."

Dracsal shook his head. "You should have held to your original agreement and obtained the intel for us. Then we would have known this was a doomed venture without losing any of our people. But now, their deaths are on your head." He cut the comm.

"Sir," Zaal said. "I'm getting a wide-band transmission." Cas nodded for him to continue. "It's from the Sil, telling their people to pull back and return to their own space. Immediately."

37

The guards led Evie into another long corridor, however this one seemed to end at a drop-off with only a thin railing keeping anyone from tumbling over. On the far side of the chasm a flat wall went as far up and down as Evie could see. She couldn't even tell which part of the massive ship they were in anymore, but it seemed like somewhere important. All around her Athru worked on their specific systems, sneaking glances at her and Dulthar's cadre as they walked by. The space had an acrid smell to it, like something had been burned and she glanced up again, realizing the ceiling was so high it disappeared into a fog. Was the ship so large it generated its own weather inside?

"Over here," Dulthar said indicating a chamber with an indention identical to the shape of an Athru. The guards kept their weapons on her, indicating she should do as he said.

"What's this?" Evie asked.

"It is a reconstitutor. It will seek out all your human attributes and destroy them, molecule by molecule, leaving only the Athru. It will then reconstitute you, from scratch, into the being you were meant to be."

"Wait, what?"

Dulthar glanced down at her. "I'm not willing to give up on you yet. There is an Athru in there somewhere, and if I have to go inside and rip it out, I'll do it. Everything else is collateral."

"So you're going to pull my molecules apart and strip me of my humanity?"

"Not just your body," Dulthar said. "We'll scan in your mind and remove everything human. Everything that wasn't a product of your mother's genes. Once all those thoughts and beliefs are gone, I believe we can extract the nascent Athru personality you said you 'killed'."

Evie shook her head. "Not happening. Daingne is dead. Forever. She's not coming back." Even though deep within her mind she knew it wasn't true.

"That's not what our scans of you indicate," Dulthar replied. "She's in there somewhere. Perhaps you think you killed her, but all you did was suppress her. You've done nothing but prolong the process. And maybe you'll lose some of your new 'attributes', such as your enhanced strength and speed, but at least you'll be a decent being."

"Decent beings don't commit genocide," Evie snarled.

"I agree, they don't. We're not killing off the entire human race, just the obsolete part of it. Like a vestigial tail, we don't need it anymore. It's lost its purpose."

The guards indicated Evie move toward the machine, but she stayed put. "I'm not getting in that thing. I'd rather you kill me than be turned into some monster. Rockron already tried that on me once and failed. I'm not going back."

"Rockron was nothing but a simple clerk with no tools at his disposal. He did the best he could with what he had, which admittedly, was very little. You were never supposed to reach Hescal. We never would have predicted you'd ally with the Sil, use their technology to your advantage. But things are different here. We have the capability to turn you into whatever we want." Dulthar stepped back, indicating to the guards to force her inside. One made the mistake of reaching too close to Evie and she yanked him forward by the weapon and before he could fire, wrenched back and threw him as far as she could. He landed with a thump twenty meters down. "Stop!" Dulthar said, holding up his hand to the rest of the guards. "Get her in there, but don't kill her. We've already had enough losses for today."

"Something not going your way?" Evie asked.

Dulthar scoffed. "You don't know because we haven't allowed you to be close to any windows. But your friends have arrived and are currently facing a losing battle against our forces. It will only be a matter of time before they either retreat, or are annihilated."

"They're here? Now?" Evie asked, looking around as if she could have found a way to see outside. But they were deep in the bowels of the ship somewhere. He might be lying to her to try and catch her off guard. Sure enough, as soon as she glanced around, two more guards approached and tried pushing her back into the machine. As swift as she could, she hit them both dead center in the face, causing them to crumple into piles on the ground. She didn't know if they were dead or not and she didn't care. "I told you. I'm *not* getting into that machine."

"This is exactly what I'm talking about. This foolish stubbornness; this infantile display against insurmountable odds." Dulthar said. "Humans love playing the hero." He grabbed a weapon from one of the guards, it detached easily. "I am done with heroes. Now get in there or I will kill you, and we'll hope the reconstitutor can bring you back before it's too late."

Evie scanned her surroundings, looking for a way out. She didn't see one. But if Cas and the others were here it meant she needed to use the ship's weapon, and now. The longer she waited the more of a slaughter it would be. Why hadn't Sesster warned her? Had he lost his ability to communicate with her?

Stepping into the machine was certain death—at least as the person she was. But getting herself killed didn't help her cause either. She needed a miracle.

***

"Sir, it looks like some of the Sil ships are already in retreat," Zaal said.

"You've got to be fucking kidding me," Cas said, running over to his station and inspecting the feeds for himself. Sure enough, the counter showed at least ten Sil ships had already left the battlefield via their own undercurrents.

"Some are still putting up a fight, but it may just be long enough to clear some space for them to leave," Tileah added. "It's not clear what their strategy is."

"These ungrateful bastards," Cas said, seething. "We gave them a way to win this and their solution is to run away with their tails tucked between their legs."

"Sir, the spacewings are reporting they've managed to disable all five of the previously pursuing ships," Tileah said.

"Great." Cas slumped back into his chair. A tiny victory was something, but until Evie blew that planet, there was nothing they could do except watch all their 'allies' run away. "Pick them back up, I want them to be on board in case we need to do a short jump to the other side of the system."

"Aye," Ronde said.

"How should we proceed?" Hank asked.

"Zaal, try to get the Sanctuary back on the line. Maybe I can convince them—"

"I'm sorry sir, they've blocked incoming transmissions."

Cas slammed his fist down on the armrest. "These *fucking* idiots!" Not even Zenfor could get through to them now.

"But," Zaal said. "I am receiving a transmission from one of the local ships. They have committed to seeing this thing through with us."

Cas glanced up. "Really? Why?"

"I couldn't say. They have just transmitted we can count on their support. For as long as they last."

Cas shifted in his seat. "That's something at least. Please transmit our gratitude." Zaal nodded. What was taking Evie so long? Did she even know they were there? Was she even still alive? Cas focused hard, thinking about Sesster, calling him into his mind. He had to find a way to get in contact with her if there was any chance of salvaging this. If she could destroy Earth, the resulting gravity distortions would disrupt the entire system, and give them an edge. The Sil might not be so willing to retreat after that. But even if that were the case, the other half of the fleet wasn't coming, and without those additional reinforcements, there was little chance they could win in a numbers game. They needed something that could tip the scales.

Cas closed his eyes and prayed for Sesster to answer, but there was nothing. And the battle was still raging on.

"Orders sir?" Tileah asked as they approached the fray.

Cas's eyes snapped open. They couldn't wait on Evie, not any longer. This called for something drastic. "Lieutenant," Cas's breath hitched. "I need you...to prepare the trans-dimensional missiles."

"You can't be serious," Hank said.

Cas turned to him, his eyes on fire. "Do I look like I'm kidding?"

"But...that will cut the Claxian system off from the rest of the galaxy!" Samiya said. "No one will be able to use undercurrents, in or out. And it will open up another—orifice to those creatures."

"I know it," Cas said, surprised by the edge in his own voice.

"I can't let you do it," Hank said. "It's not—"

"What you do propose we do? Hand over everything to the Athru?" Cas asked. "Most of their forces are concentrated here. If we use the trans-dimensional weapon, they are stuck…*here*. It won't matter if they can obliterate worlds, they won't be able to use faster-than-light travel. And—" He turned to Tileah. "How wide is the terminus shock?"

"A hundred light-years, minimum," she said.

"Which means it would take them at least a thousand years at sub-light speeds to even get out of the system," Cas said. "Not to mention they hate those creatures. Let them focus their energy on something more powerful than they are for once."

"And it would take close to ten thousand years for space to repair itself—to use undercurrents again," Hank argued. "You can't do that to one of the founding worlds of the Coalition."

"I don't see another option," Cas said. "Because if we do nothing, they'll only continue to build up their forces. At least this gives us more time to combat them."

"It's not a solution!" Hank yelled.

"It's the best we've got. Lieutenant, arm the weapons." Cas took his seat again. "Are all the spacewings back on board?"

"Yes, sir," she replied.

"Caspian," Hank said in a low voice, taking his seat beside him. "I have always supported you; I think you're a man of high integrity. But this…this is unconscionable—you're willing to cut off the Claxians from any further contact with anyone else in the galaxy. Perhaps for good. And what about the Val on Valus orbiting Hathor? What happens to them?"

"Hank, there's no perfect solution here. We had a plan A, and…it fell apart. I don't even know if Evie is still alive. A long time ago I made a judgment call that ended up getting a lot of people killed, even though it was the right thing to do. This time, I'm making the hard call. The Claxians and the Val will be stranded, yes. But the Athru will be crippled, and with most of their forces here, we can pick off the rest, drive them from Coalition space. It's either that, or submit to them. From my conversations with the Sil, I don't think we'll be allowed back in to their good graces. We're out of options."

Hank sat back, disappointment on his face.

"Ronde, keep us out of the main battle lines, I want to launch that missile right at the main city-ship," Cas said.

"Two minutes until it's ready," Tileah said.

Cas had an urge to laugh. What was once so forbidden had almost become routine. Had it not been for Zenfor they wouldn't even have trans-dimensional weapons on board. But she'd helped them build a small arsenal, back when it was the only weapon that worked against the Athru. "*Shit*," Cas said, jumping from his chair.

"What?" Hank asked.

Cas ran to the hypervator. "Don't fire until you hear from me!" he said, pointing to Tileah as he stepped on the lift.

"Aye," she said, looking somewhat worried.

"And River, I need you to plot us a course as close to Claxia Prime as you can get, and step on it!"

"Sir?" she asked.

"Just do it!" The doors closed on him, cutting him off from the bridge. "Sickbay!" Cas yelled at the computer. He tapped his comm. "Box."

"Yeah Boss?"

"Is Zenfor awake?"

"No, I had to sedate her again to let her heal," he said. "She'll be awake in another two hours."

"We don't have that long," Cas said. "Wake her and prepare to move her to Bay One. I'm on my way down."

"What? I can't move her until the cycle is complete. She's hooked up to stuff!"

"Then *unhook* her and get something portable. I swear to Kor, Box, do not argue with me. We are out of time. No games."

Box must have heard the desperation in his voice. "Okay. Yeah, um, yeah just give me a minute."

"That's all I *can* give you." Cas cut the comm and tapped it again. "Belmont, do you still have that shuttle prepped and ready?"

"Yes, sir, just waiting on your orders," Belmont replied, his voice full of excitement.

"I need you and Harcrow to disembark. Keep the shuttle ready to launch though, change of plans."

"Yes, sir," he replied, though Cas could hear the disappointment in his voice. Right now that wasn't important. The hypervator doors opened and Cas ran down the corridor to sickbay, its doors sliding open for him just in time. Box and two of the nurses stood around Zenfor, changing out her equipment to a mobile gurney.

"What's going on?" Box asked.

"Emergency transport," Cas replied. "Let's get her to Bay One."

***

Less than five minutes later they'd moved her into the shuttlebay. Outside the open bay doors Cas could see the battle continuing to rage on, even though most of Sil were still departing. It had taken time to get all those ships into the system; it would take time to get them out. Which gave them a very small window for him to pay a debt he owed.

"Load her up on the shuttle," Cas instructed. "And make sure she's secured." Box nodded as he and the nurses went about their business. Harcrow and Belmont stood outside the ship, watching.

Cas heard footfalls behind him, turning to see Saturina run up, her face flushed and helmet still in-hand. "What's going on? They told me you're launching a shuttle."

"I'm sending Zenfor down to Claxia Prime," Cas replied. "She'll never be happy here and we're about to lose the ability to return to this system. She's done more for this crew than anyone realizes. She deserves some happiness."

"Why?" she asked. "What are you…" Realization dawned on her face. "Is there no other choice?"

Cas shook his head. "If Evie is dead, and I suspect she very well could be, then we're out of options. We're losing our forces and the Athru are already closing in on us."

As if on cue, Cas's comm beeped. "Captain. The weapon is ready, and we've lost over half of the Sil ships. Twenty-five more have committed to staying, but it won't be enough. The Athru are in pursuit of *Tempest*," Zaal said.

"She's all loaded up," Box said. "But I can't wake her until the cycle is finished. It could damage the repair process."

"Now what?" Saturina asked. "Who's going to pilot the shuttle down there?"

Cas faltered. He didn't know. He couldn't ask Box—with Xax gone he *needed* him. But being captain meant you made sacrifices for the good of the crew. In this case, Zenfor was only one person, and this was more of a personal favor. "I'll take her down."

"You can't," Saturina said. "You're the captain, and the ship needs you. Is there no chance of coming back?"

Cas shook his head, his hands beginning to shake. She was going to volunteer to go in his place, he knew it. "We don't have the time. We need to fire the weapon and get out of the system before they destroy the ship."

"Captain," Zaal said again, more urgent this time. "If we're going to proceed, now is the time."

"I'll go," Saturina said, tossing her helmet to the side and climbing into the shuttle.

"Saturina..." Cas said, reaching for her, then pulling back.

"It's okay," she said. "You're right. She deserves this. And I've heard good things about the Claxians from Ryant. It's a good place to settle down."

"I can't ask you to make that sacrifice. What about—" He cut himself off.

"It's the right thing to do, isn't it?" she asked. He nodded.

Box stepped out of her way and descended with the nurses, but Cas noticed Box didn't take his gaze off her. "I've included instructions for Xax to help her continue to heal," he said. "It's all there on that device."

Saturina gave him a terse smile, her eyes going misty. Cas had never seen her cry before. And he couldn't help but think back to Suzanna...and Grippen. He had a shitty track record in the shuttle department. A shockwave of emotions hit him all at once. He didn't want to let Saturina go, but he didn't see another choice, not if he wanted to do right by Zenfor.

"*Captain*," Zaal said. Cas winced, glancing at Saturina, then at Box again. Outside the bay he could see the bluish glow coming from Claxia Prime's rings.

"I'm on my way," Cas said, fighting back his emotions. Saturina put one hand up and mouthed *bye*. Cas did the same, then turned and ran out of the bay, passing the rest of the spacewing pilots who'd gathered at to see what was going on. Cas couldn't watch her leave, not after everything they'd already been through. It was too much. "Hold your fire, Zaal, wait until I get back up there."

"Sir, they're converging on us, Ronde doesn't think—"

"Hold on, just a *minute* longer." Cas wiped his eyes and took off toward the closest hypervator, forcing himself inside without looking back. At least she would be safe on Claxia. Once they detonated the weapon, the Athru's attention would be focused on the creatures that came from the tears between dimensions. It would give Saturina and Xax enough time to get into hiding with the other pockets of humanity still on Claxia. It wasn't an ideal life, but it could still be a full and satisfying one. As long as the Athru never came looking for her. He shook his head; he couldn't take responsibility for her actions. She'd made the choice; she knew the consequences. But that still didn't make him feel any better about it.

The hypervator doors opened back up on the bridge and Cas stepped out. "Status," he said, trying not to let his voice crack.

"The shuttle is away, headed for the surface," Zaal said.

"We have sixty Athru ships headed our direction," Tileah added. "With more on the way. Estimate is twenty seconds until they reach us. The Sil are doing their best to distract them but losing ships quick."

"Ronde, get us to that city-ship. *Fast.*"

Ronde turned in his seat? "Are you asking what I think you're asking, sir?"

Cas nodded. "Inter-system undercurrent. River, I know you can make that calculation. Do it quick."

"Yes, sir," she said confidently. Her fingers moved as if they had minds of their own, inputting the specific coordinates.

Goodbye, Saturina, Cas thought as he watched the shuttle enter the upper atmosphere of the planet. Only a few more moments and she'd be safe. "Hit it."

Ronde activated the undercurrent and for half a second the screen turned a greenish color before returning to normal space. The massive city-ship hovered in front of them, looming in its presence. "Boom," Ronde said, sharing a quick fist-bump with River, whose hand returned to its normal configuration for the bump, then split back open so she could continue to work the controls.

"Lieutenant, prepare the weapon," Cas said.

"Ready to fire on your order, sir."

"Are the Sil ships clear?"

"Our allies are clear," Zaal said. "The others will be out of the system by the time it hits."

"Okay. Then we do this just like last time. Stay ahead of the wave that collapses undercurrent space. Everyone ready?" He got affirmatives from all of his senior officers, though Hank's face was still full of worry.

This one's for you, Evie, Cas thought. He stared at the ship for one last beat. "Fire."

38

Evie bared her teeth. It was better to take her chances with attempting to escape this torture device rather than let them try and rewrite her brain and body. She'd rather die.

"I'm tired of waiting." Dulthar lowered the weapon he held to her knees.

Two of the guards did the same. She was just about to jump when the ship shuddered, knocking most of the guards off their feet, Dulthar included. Evie managed to brace herself.

"What is happening?" Dulthar yelled.

Evie didn't care what was happening. This was the chance she'd needed, and she wasn't going to squander it. She leaped over the guards, grabbing Dulthar by the neck and dragging him to the edge of the massive chasm. "For my mother," she said, snapping his neck in one quick move and tossing him over the edge. His eyes were wide with fear as he fell, and she couldn't be sure he'd even realized what had happened.

A blast from a weapon connected with her shoulder, causing her to cry out and fall to the ground at the immense pain. It was like her entire arm was on fire and she barely jumped out of the way before another blast hit the railing beside where she'd just stood.

"Take her down, she's killed the Head!" one of the guards yelled in Athru. Despite the pain, Evie ducked and dodged around the barriers and columns running parallel with the massive chasm to her right.

Okay, she thought. *I need your help. I know you know the layout of this ship and I know you're still in there somewhere so help me find the primary weapon controls.* At first there was no answer, but then a rough voice answered, coming up from the depths of her subconscious.

You just love throwing people off high things, don't you?

"There you are," Evie said.

I accepted defeat. I stayed gone, as you wanted. The ship shuddered again and above them Evie saw something crumble from the ceiling, falling down into the deep chasm. What was happening outside?

"Where are the primary weapon controls? The ones that will allow me to blow up a planet?" Another blast of energy shot by her, singeing her ear and she ducked away, increasing her speed. She might be able to outrun the Athru, but she couldn't outrun their weapons.

You're close. That chasm—that's the primary weapon conduit. All the energy flows through there.

"Great," Evie said. "So where—?"

Head back to the left, and circle around until you come to a room that will be suspended above the chasm, connected by a catwalk. That's primary control. But there will be a lot of guards in there.

"Guards I can handle," she said, flexing her damaged arm. It was painful, but not enough to stop her. She wasn't sure if that was because the Athru weapons were crap, considering they rarely used them, or if she was just strong enough to withstand the blast.

Claxons rang out all around her, causing Evie to jump. *They're tracking your heat signature,* Daingne said. *You need to hurry.*

"Why are you so helpful all of a sudden?" Evie asked. "There was a time when you couldn't stand me."

Still can't, the voice said. *But you won the battle. You won control. I won't fight you anymore.*

"Good enough," Evie said, following Daingne's instructions and rounding her way to the control room. She spotted it, at the top of a long set of wide stairs, which she took three at a time. As she crested the top, she peered over to see six Athru, all at the controls in the room. In an instant she sprinted forward and caught them by surprise. Her fist slammed into the first, knocking him back and over the far edge of the platform, where he screamed all the way down into the chasm. The others barely had time to prepare themselves, but Evie dug deep and went hand-to-hand with three of them at once. Someone landed a blow on her ribs and she felt the bones crack, but she didn't falter, kicking that individual so hard in the face it collapsed in on itself. The other two redoubled their efforts as more alarms sounded. Evie gave up a block to grab one of them by the shoulders and threw him into one of the only two Athru who weren't fighting. They both fell back in a sickening thump, but the move had opened her up to the sharp claws of the Athru that was still engaged in combat, which sliced across her midsection, spilling blood all down her front. She cried out and collapsed to her knees and held her stomach as the Athru advanced on her. When he moved to swipe again, she blocked it, wrenched his arm back until it broke, then pushed him away from her into one of the consoles. Just as he turned to fight again, she put all of her power into one last punch, snapping the Athru's neck with the force of the blow. Before he could fall to the ground, she tossed him over into the abyss.

Only one Athru remained, watching her from his station. She stood, calmly and walked around Evie, giving her plenty of space, and descended the stairs, disappearing into the ship.

"Okay," Evie said, confused. Though, it reminded her what Kithal had said—not every Athru was a fighter. But that didn't matter now. He'd betrayed her—and this whole endeavor had felt a little too much like when she'd been brainwashed on Hescal. She had to double-check to make sure Daingne hadn't shown her another false vision.

No tricks this time, Daingne said.

"Good thing." Evie winced as she picked up the remaining Athru and tossed them over as well. It took an extra minute, but she needed to focus and couldn't do that if there was a possibility of being stabbed in the back. "Now how to I activate this weapon?"

You're really going to do it. Destroy the humans' home planet.

"It was part of the arrangement," she replied. "It's how we stop your people."

Very well. First you have to unlock the receivers. That will allow this ship to pull energy from nearby ships to consolidate. Evie listened to the instructions, and despite the wailing claxons, managed to follow Daingne's lead to prepare the weapon. She was just about to input the final sequence when the alarms stopped sounding.

"Thank Kor," she said. They'd been giving her a headache.

"I'm not sure if you know what you're doing or not, but I'd advise against it."

Evie turned to see Dulthar standing at the top of the stairs, his hands clasped together in front of him. "What the—didn't I kill you already?"

"You think I've survived hundreds of thousands of years by being stupid?" Dulthar asked. "I just finished explaining to you we have the ability to copy minds. What do you think we use that technology for?"

"You're a clone," Evie said.

"And you are very stupid. Whatever you think you're planning on doing, don't. Not only do my men have a hundred different weapons trained on you from places you can't even see, but it won't be successful. The ship has been damaged."

"By what?" Evie asked.

"Your…friends have used a trans-dimensional weapon." The ship shuddered again as if to confirm his statement. "A portal is forming in the middle of this ship. I've ordered a full evacuation."

Evie laughed, but it hurt her stomach and more blood seeped from her wound. "A trans-dimensional weapon! That's brilliant. And now you're stuck here, aren't you? It will take centuries to leave this place now without faster-than-light speed. They did it, they *beat* you." Evie slumped back.

"Oh yes, they're very clever," Dulthar said, not impressed.

Evie frowned. Something was wrong. If *Tempest* had really used a weapon like this Dulthar should be scrambling to get his people out of the system, or as far away from this ship as possible. Even if he had clones, why would he be standing there taunting her?

He has a trick card, something he's not revealing, Daingne said.

"What's really going on, Dulthar?" Evie asked, staying close to the controls. His eyes flashed.

"It is no concern of yours, hybrid," he spat. "Now move or be shot."

Evie searched the surrounding area, seeing no other Athru, at least none that had taken up positions anywhere around her. Those that she could see were scrambling in a dozen different directions, panicking at the thought of the ship being torn apart by an interdimensional portal. *Scan the system*, Daingne said. *That control there. See what's going on.*

Evie did, tapping the control to give her a readout. It confirmed the detonation of an interdimensional weapon which had collapsed traversable space, but the Athru ships hadn't taken any action to try and leave. They were staying close to the city-ship, which itself was moving closer toward Earth. She remembered Esterva saying something about the Athru having faced down the interdimensional creatures before. How they'd managed to contain them. She performed another scan of Earth, on a hunch. Evie gasped.

"*Move*," Dulthar said, but there was panic in his voice. Fear, even.

According to the information translated into her mind via Daingne's capabilities, Earth had been terraformed into some kind of interdimensional lens, capable of collapsing not just one tear, but *all* of them throughout known space. If the Athru could collapse every tear, it meant they would be unstoppable, and the *Tempest's* efforts would have been all for nothing. She glanced up at Dulthar, her eyes wide and saw him flinch.

Do it now, Daingne said.

Dulthar lunged for her and Evie input the final firing sequence for the primary weapon, aiming it at Earth. Just as Dulthar grabbed her, sending shockwaves of pain through her body, she confirmed the final sequence and the entire room began to rumble.

"No!" Dulthar yelled. The shaking in the room grew stronger and the entire area was filled with a growing din of noise. "You stupid, stupid—" Evie shoved her palm into his face, causing him to fall back, holding his nose and upper lip as they gushed blood. *Red* blood she happened to notice. Evie crawled to the control booth and looked over the edge as a massive beam of energy filled the entire space, cradled on both sides by the chasm. She could only assume this was the planet-killing beam of energy she'd seen destroy Bulaq and its stars. The same beam that had destroyed Cypaxia and Mishtaka. The weapon that gave the Athru all their power, now being fired at humanity's home. But not really their

285

home. She crawled over to the status indicator, and watched on the edgeless monitor as the beam impacted the center of an Earth she no longer recognized. Slowly the planet formed deep, fissured cracks, glowing hot orange. And as flame and fire began to engulf the surface, the pieces began to break apart, large and small, until the entire planet had shattered like a globe of glass. Balls of fire were ejected in all directions, and Evie could only hope Claxia Prime was far enough away they wouldn't see too much damage. But the closest pieces started impacting the ship, causing it to shudder even more.

"You fool," Dulthar said, his voice nasally and wet with blood. "We could have stopped it. We'd built something that could have prevented this. And now you've killed your own people!"

The ship rocked to the side, and as she turned to look down the long side of the chasm, which was empty again, Evie saw the ship begin to separate while a massive black fissure formed in the middle. She could see stars beyond the opening in the hull. A rush of wind pulled at her back and the fog from above moved in that direction, being pulled toward the vacuum.

"If there were any humans on Earth," she said, struggling to stand over Dulthar. "They knew the risks. And by taking away your primary production facility, I've just ensured this system's safety."

"We'll just strip mine another planet," Dulthar said, blood leaking from his mouth. "Claxia or Ra or Valus. There are plenty of opportunities."

Evie shook her head. "Not if all your ships are trapped in the reaches of that thing." She pointed to where the fissure had opened, and a dark tentacle emerged. Followed by another. "Any ship within its radius will eventually be pulled in. And if I'm not mistaken, all of your forces were centered around this ship."

"No matter," he replied, but she could see the fear in his eyes. "There are still plenty of Athru ships outside of this system. Enough so we will survive."

"But none with clones of you, I'm betting," she replied. "Or the people who started this war. Those are all just people out there, following orders. What happens when the orders stop coming?" She winced, still holding her wound. When she glanced down, she realized she was losing an alarming amount of blood.

"At least," he said, his voice growing weak. "I get to take you with me." The ship listed to the side, the stars beyond turning as it did, though the internal gravity kept them in place. Explosions rocked throughout the ship and even more pieces fell from the ceiling, raining down into the chasm. The ship didn't have long.

"And I get to give my life to save the people I love," she replied. "I can't think of a better fate."

He grimaced until the light went from his eyes. Evie stumbled over him, climbing back down the stairs on all fours, trying not to accidentally slip into the chasm. She was leaving a trail of blood behind her.

We're dying, Daingne said.

"Yeah," she breathed, coughing.

You finally get your wish, to destroy me.

"I guess so." Evie pushed up on the handrail, using it to guide herself back down the way she came. No one was paying any attention to her anymore. They were all running past, trying to save their own lives.

What are you doing?

"I need…" She thought she might be able to escape on a support craft of some kind, but with no more undercurrents, she was stuck in the Claxian system. She could always try to make it back to Claxia—Xax was probably still there and could help, but the possibility of finding a way out of the creature's pull was likely impossible. She looked up, staring at the creature as it tore the ship into pieces. The breeze picked up as more air was sucked toward the opening, which had now expanded wide enough so Evie could see parts of the ship had separated from each other. It wouldn't be long now. She slumped back down, sitting with her back up against the railing as Athru panicked all around her.

"I need to rest," she finally said.

At least you're not alone. Evie tried to laugh, but it hurt too much. Instead, she reached up and undid the bun she'd pulled her hair into. She ran both hands through it, shaking it out for the last time then leaned her head back against the railing. She thought back to all her friends on *Tempest*, and all those who still considered her an enemy. She'd never started out to be anything other than a good officer. But at least she could say she'd made an impact. And, hopefully, her actions here made up for her terrible mistakes back at Hescal.

I'm sorry for that, by the way, Daingne said.

"It's not like—" Evie coughed. She tasted copper on her tongue. "—you to apologize."

I think being around my ancestors has rubbed off on me.

"If we can change your mind, maybe it's not too late for all the other Athru out there," Evie said. She was finding it harder and harder to breathe. "But I'll leave that...in more capable hands."

I think you have done right by all those you've lost. All of them would be proud of you.

Evie nodded, her breathing becoming heavier as the wind picked up and the ship shuddered again. At any moment they'd lose artificial gravity and she'd be sucked out into nothingness. But by then she'd already be gone. That was okay, she thought. Not a terrible way to go. At least she got to see the stars one more time.

Her eyelids became heavy and she could feel consciousness fading. "Here…we…go," she finally managed to say before slipping away.

39

Cas held his head in his hands. Just after launching the missile they'd managed to ride the edge of the system before the effects caught up with them, thanks only to Zenfor's technology. He almost wanted to fire three more into the system, just to give the Athru that many more creatures to deal with. But the good news was many of their ships had been focused around the city-ship, and thus would be caught in the creature's pull, just like *Tempest* had been back at the Excel Nebula. One thing was for sure, it was the end of intergalactic space travel for the Athru in that system. An end to their planet and star-killing weapons and an end to all the death they'd brought. He just hoped Saturina had made it safely.

"Sir," Zaal said. Cas looked up. "Long-range scanners report Earth has just been destroyed."

Cas shot up in his seat. "What? How?"

"Seems to be a blast from the primary ship, before it succumbed to its damage."

"*Goddammit,*" Cas said. "She's still alive. We have to go back."

"We *can't*, sir," Hank said. "Even if there was a possibility she was still alive, we're stuck outside the system, a hundred light-year radius. There's no way we could get to her."

"Also," Zaal said, though he was hesitant. "I'm showing the interdimensional tear has consumed the Athru city-ship. If she was on it—"

Cas slumped back down in his chair. They'd escaped virtually unscathed, destroying their enemies in the process. And all it had cost him was three people he cared about. Perhaps that was the *true* meaning of being captain—being willing to take the losses so no one else would have to. But still it didn't make him feel any better.

"And, sir?"

Cas looked up. The rest of the bridge crew were sneaking glances at him. Probably trying to figure out how much stress he could take before he cracked. Samiya's eyes were full of pity, which part of him was grateful for and another part of him hated. "Go ahead."

"We're receiving a transmission from the Sanctuary."

"You've got to be kidding me," Cas said.

"I am not," Zaal replied.

"Where are our allied ships?" he asked.

"Still with us, nineteen made it out of the system." Cas furrowed his brow then made a motion with his hand to allow the transmission.

On the screen ahead of them the image of Dracsal appeared again. "Captain," he said.

"I thought we weren't to have any more contact," Cas growled.

"The evidence suggests you have not only stopped the Athru threat—but you also destroyed the Athru's ability to counteract interdimensional weapons. It was not a feat we thought possible."

"What?" Cas asked. "What ability?"

"When our ships entered your system, they scanned the third planet, the terraformed one."

"We called it Earth," Cas said.

"Our intel indicates the Athru have been busy. They had converted the planet into a lens that could close all of the interdimensional tears at once. Those tears are so deep, it would take the entire force of a planet to focus that much energy back into repairing the space-time continuum. It is the reason none of our ships used any trans-dimensional weapons in the battle. We knew they would be ineffective."

"She did it," Cas whispered. He hadn't even realized the Athru could have countered them, but he should have figured. Especially since *Tempest* had already used those weapons on them once before. Somehow Evie had finished the mission anyway, saving them all.

"It also seems your situation has caused something of a...split among my people."

"You mean the ships that stayed to help, regardless of your orders," Cas replied.

"Yes," Dracsal said. "My people have some discussions ahead of us. The loss of sixty ships, almost two thousand souls—though many escaped into *the space beneath* before it was too late—and the defection of another twenty-five was not something we anticipated."

"Will they be judged?" Cas asked.

"Undecided. But I should tell you we destroyed the other Coalition ship, once the Sargan deception was discovered. There were no survivors."

Cas couldn't blame them for it, and he didn't suspect there were any other humans on the ship anyway. Rutledge had been the only one he'd ever seen, the rest being species from all over the Sargan Commonwealth. "I'm sorry for your losses," Cas said. "Had your ships just listened..."

He made a dismissive noise. "Given these developments, and the fact your species has shown promise, I've been authorized to open a formal dialogue with your people,"

Dracsal said. "However, you are not to re-enter Sil territory. We consider our space sovereign."

Cas couldn't tell if that was good news or not. At least he could be reasonably sure they wouldn't be fighting another war on a second front. "But perhaps, in time, that will change." Dracsal added.

"I hope so."

"Then we will speak again soon," he replied. The comm ended and the viewscreen went back to normal.

"The Sil ships following us have changed course," Zaal said. "Back toward Thislea."

"What the hell was that?" Cas asked.

"An invitation?" Samiya offered.

"Or maybe just a first step," Hank said.

Cas shook his head. "If only they'd stepped up sooner maybe we wouldn't have had to pay such a high price."

"There's an old Untuburu saying," Zaal said. "Best not to dwell on what could have been, but rather what is."

Cas cut his eyes to him. "Are you telling me to shut up and take whatever wins come my way?"

"Perhaps not so crudely," Zaal replied.

Cas rubbed the back of his neck. If they weren't headed back for Sil space they needed to figure out their next move. "Keep us on course for—hell, I don't even know. Just keep us on course. I'm going to get some rest." He stood, walking over to the hypervator. He wasn't even sure what they should be doing. He should be celebrating—they'd just beaten their worst enemy. So why did he feel like a complete shit?

The hypervator doors opened, and Cas had to do a double take. Standing before him, with her hand on her head was Saturina, a grimace on her face. "What—?" Cas asked, his eyes going wide.

"That son of a bitch jumped me," she said. "It took them ten minutes to wake me back up. I'm going to have a huge lump—" Her words were cut off by Cas's lips on hers. He'd never felt so glad to see a friendly face in his life. She returned the kiss, pressing herself into him as if she hadn't seen him in months. He finally pulled away, gasping for breath.

"I can't believe you're still here," he said. "I thought—"

"I thought I was going too," she said. "Even though I *really* didn't want to. But *he* said I deserved happiness, as well."

"Wait," Cas said, his heart falling into his stomach. "Who jumped you?"

***

Zenfor blinked, her eyes fluttering. She felt a quick rush of adrenaline as soon as she realized she wasn't in sickbay anymore. Instead, her eyes had focused on the ceiling of a shuttle. The pain in her chest had subsided, but she could tell she still wasn't a hundred percent yet. She pushed that to the side for a moment and instead tried to sit up.

"Easy." Xax's face came into view. She held one of her hands out to help guide Zenfor up.

"Doctor?" Zenfor asked.

"Just give yourself a minute," she replied. "You're going to be a little groggy."

Zenfor rubbed her head. A cool breeze blew through the end of the shuttle, teasing her fine hair. "Are we on—Claxia Prime?"

Xax nodded. "The shuttle barely made it down before everything went to hell."

"The Athru—" she began.

"Have been taken care of, don't worry. There were only a few on this planet when the tide turned, and they succumbed to the hidden human resistance groups here. I'd be surprised if there is an Athru alive anywhere on the planet."

"Why am I here?" she asked, glancing around. Dusk was just beginning to fall outside. The wind had a bit of a chill to it, even against her normally impervious skin. Beyond the shuttle, an orange sun's light had disappeared behind some distant clouds and a bluish-purple mountain range in the distance. In a way it reminded her of Thislea. "I've never seen this place before."

"It's a beautiful planet, to be sure. The Claxians take care of their home, and they have some of the most expansive libraries anywhere in the Coalition. I've spent most of my time here in one," Xax said. "As to why you're here, you'd have to ask Caspian. He was the one who insisted."

"Caspian?" she asked. "Wanted me here?" She stood on shaky legs. "I never asked—"

Zenfor.

"Sesster," she whispered. A smile had formed on Xax's small lips, but as soon as she saw Zenfor had noticed, she wiped it from her face.

"He's out there, waiting for you," she replied.

Zenfor took a few steps and emerged in the cool, clean air, taking a deep breath. There was an aroma on the air she couldn't place, but she wouldn't call it unpleasant. It wasn't unlike the dosi fields of Rustak Province. She caught sight of him at once and couldn't help but feel joy spread through her limbs. He was really here; he was still alive. After all this time. She walked forward, approaching Sesster and the person she presumed had piloted the shuttle down, who stood just off to the side, gazing at the sunset.

"I suppose I should thank you," she said.

"Oh, yeah," Dorsey Ryant said. "No problem. I've always wanted to see this place." He sighed. "My new home."

"Home? Why not just return to *Tempest*?" she asked.

Because, Sesster said. *Undercurrent travel is no longer possible in this system. In order to defeat the Athru they used a trans-dimensional weapon. It was the only way.*

Zenfor couldn't get over hearing his voice again. *We have a lot of catching up to do,* she replied. But looking at Ryant, she was surprised he would sacrifice his future for her. "You and Xax, you're stuck here."

He nodded and shrugged at the same time. "There are other humans here, so it's not so bad. Beautiful place to live. After a life of flying in the void of space, it's nice to have sunsets to look forward to. And these guys are the best intellectuals in the galaxy!" He gestured to Sesster. For the first time, Zenfor noticed other Claxians standing behind him, huddled in small groups, apparently conversing.

Xax had come out of the shuttle as well and stood off to the side. "And what of you, doctor? Do you not wish to return to the ship?"

"I left it in good hands," Xax said, crossing her top arms. "Plus, I've had enough war. I hadn't exactly *planned* for this, but I find when life offers you an opportunity, you take it. Yax-Inax are naturally curious people, and there's a whole world's worth of information to discover here. I just need to find a translator."

"I'm sure we can work that out, doc. One of these humans has to be receptive to them," Ryant said, clapping Xax on the back. She forced a smile and inched away from the jubilant human.

Zenfor turned her attention back to Sesster. *You came to me in a dream.*

I did. I hope that wasn't too forward of me, he replied.

I am grateful you are alive. And that we have this time together.

He drew closer to her. *So am I. When you're ready, I can show you a place where you will find absolute solitude, free from the burdens of others.*

Zenfor glanced around. It seemed like a beautiful place to live the rest of her life. *That will be nice for a while. But...perhaps not all the time.* Sesster didn't need a face for her to know he was pleased. She could *feel* it.

You have other things in mind? he asked.

Perhaps, she replied. *But there is no rush. For now, let us enjoy our time.*

40

"Not too long ago," Cas said, standing on the dais in front of eighty percent of the crew of the *Tempest*, "Someone told me when they died, they wanted to be returned home. At the time I didn't think anything of it—because I never considered any one place *my* home. I may have been born on Earth, but I've spent most of my life on one side of an imaginary border in space or another." He shot a glance to Saturina, smiling from the front row, Box right beside her. He'd performed a quick check to make sure she hadn't sustained any permanent damage from when Ryant had stolen the shuttle from her. Apparently, the man had literally jumped into the shuttle, knocked her out and then tossed her into Box's arms as the door was closing. There hadn't been time for anyone to do anything about it.

"But today I think about that conversation differently. We all do. Most of us in this room had descendants that originated from Earth, and now we must face the fact that it is gone." He paused, looking at the casket situated beside the airlock. The last time he'd been in this room he'd been unable to speak—unable to articulate what loss meant to him.

"Captain Cordell Greene was the best the Coalition had to offer. He was what we all aspire to be: a model Coalition citizen. But he never knew the truth: that the planet he called home wasn't the place where our people originated. That it was a lifeboat—a saving grace *gifted* by the Claxians over three thousand years ago. And when I think back to his request, I can only hope he'll forgive me for committing him to the stars instead. Out there somewhere is a world that birthed the human race—a world long lost to history. So, it seems fitting that in returning him to the stars, in a way, we are returning him back home—to a place none of us have, or will ever see."

There were a few nods among the audience, and some tears from some of the crew that had been with the ship from the beginning. Tyler looked especially misty-eyed.

"We do this in the hope that he will find his way home, one day." The entire congregation stood, performing the Coalition salute all at the same time. Box's metal hand on his chest clanged through the cavernous room. "Captain Cordell Greene, may your journey beyond be helmed with a steady hand, a vigorous heart, and a sharp mind." Cas nodded to the color guard who guided the casket to the launcher, and ushered it through, pulling a tattered Coalition flag from the top as they did. They folded the flag gingerly, then returned to their original positions. Out the window, the casket floated in the vacuum of space a moment, then took off with a flash, having been outfitted with a miniature undercurrent generator courtesy of the Engineering team. It wouldn't last forever, but it was one hell of a last ride.

Everyone lowered their hands and faced Cas again.

"For the first time in our known history, we have to stand on our own two feet. No longer do we have the safety net of the Claxians, and our allies are scattered and afraid. But we're not going to give up. The Athru tried to take something essential from us, and they failed. It is up to us to rebuild our Coalition and avoid the mistakes of the past." He glanced across the room, staring into the faces of these people who had become his friends, his family, sensing that it was their diversity that gave them their strength. Untuburu, Bulaq, Dorsai, Robot, Human—they all complimented each other. "Knowing our future is in your hands, the hands of this incredible crew that has withstood and persevered through so much, I have to believe Captain Greene would be proud. Thank you all for coming."

Everyone began to file out, but the senior staff stayed behind. "Zaal," Cas said, heading over to the Untuburu who stood beside Samiya and Hank, speaking in low tones.

"I enjoyed your speech," he replied. "It was very…optimistic."

"Did you get in contact with the High Priestess?"

Zaal nodded. "And I sent the evidence you requested. She's ready to speak with us and has agreed not to fire on the ship when we return. I believe in time Untu and its colonies will be receptive to reconciliation."

"I agree," Cas said. Pulling the Coalition worlds back together after having been cut off from each other for so long would be a difficult task, but he didn't think it would be impossible.

"And I received a message from Oxical. They have re-opened their trade route with Takar, which will alleviate some pressure on both those systems."

"Already?" Cas asked. "They must have been desperate."

"Yes," Zaal replied. "But the message is being received well throughout most of what used to be Coalition territory."

"How many more Athru ships do you think are still out there?" Hank asked.

"I don't know, but considering it's been five days and we haven't seen any blowback yet, I'd say they're probably laying low, trying to figure out how to respond."

"And if they come out fighting?" he asked.

"We have the weapons to defeat them, especially now they've lost their primary advantage. Once everyone realizes their planets are no longer in danger of being destroyed, they'll fight back." Cas turned to Samiya. "What of Yax-Inax?"

"They're sending an envoy ship to meet us, to escort us back to their system for the time being," she replied.

"Good. I want to get these weapons on as many allied ships as we can as fast as possible. As soon as the Sargans realize what's happened…"

"…they'll want to take advantage of the situation," Hank replied. "Don't worry. Even with those weapons we'll be ready for them. *Tempest* is still the fastest ship in existence, we can run circles around them."

Cas nodded. "Very good. Samiya, Hank, since you two seem to have the most experience with the old Coalition members—considering you've been through the same things they have—I want you to keep acting as 'ambassadors' to help reunite the Coalition. As soon as we're done at Inax we'll move on to the next closest system, share the technology and so on. The sooner the better."

"Sure," Samiya said. "We can do that. I don't expect we'll get much resistance from the long-standing members." She and Hank headed off to their duties, followed by Zaal.

Cas noticed Saturina and Box standing close by, watching him. *One minute*, he mouthed, then headed over to the figure standing alone, watching out the window. "Lieutenant."

"Captain," Tyler replied, his arms crossed.

"Everything good?"

"Ship is working better than ever," he replied, "thanks to Zenfor."

Cas faced him. "You're upset with me for sending her to Claxia Prime." Tyler's chest rose and fell, but he remained silent. "You two had become close friends."

He scoffed. "She could have been happy here. Things were good."

Cas shook his head. "She wouldn't have ever been happy here. And I couldn't condemn her to a life that I know would have only been mediocre for her. She gave us too much. And she deserved to be where she could truly be fulfilled."

Tyler cast his eyes downward. "She was part of this crew for eighteen years. I knew her better than anyone."

"That's probably true. So, tell me, did I make the right call?"

He nodded, reluctantly. "I'll just miss her."

Cas knew the feeling. "You and me both. But I understand Vrij has been a big help."

A smile spread across Tyler's face. "He's got some…interesting ideas."

Cas placed a reassuring hand on Tyler's shoulder. "That he does. But I don't think he'll steer you wrong." He stood there with his chief engineer for a beat longer before leaving Tyler to his thoughts.

Cas approached Box and Saturina. "A little sappy," Box said. "I would have added a bit more fire and brimstone, you know, to energize the troops."

"They don't need energizing, they need some downtime," Cas said. "This is the first time since we've returned to Coalition space that we can catch our breaths."

"Speaking of which, I memorized the new Coalition charter Wilmoth, Barstow and Amargosa drew up."

"Wilmoth?" Cas asked, looking at Saturina.

She shrugged. "Hey, you said you wanted the most qualified. She used to be in law before she became a pilot. It's part of the reason she rebelled against you. Well…you know…"

Cas tried not to glare. He hadn't sentenced the pilots who had mutinied back to their cells after the battle, instead granting them temporary freedom contingent on good behavior. So far it was going well.

"*Anyway*," Box said. "I was very happy to see a provision in the charter recognizing self-identifying artificial life forms as fully autonomous with all the rights and privileges of any other sentient individual."

"Think that was Amargosa?" Cas winked.

"Regardless of *who*, it's about damn time. I'm going to get that etched on my body, so anytime anyone gives me any shit, I can just point to my crotch and say—"

"*Don't* get it etched on your crotch. For Kor's sake, Box."

"But that's the most effective place!" he whined.

"Give me a medical update," Cas ordered.

Box's blinked rapidly and something clicked in the back of his head somewhere. "Fine. I nominated myself to be the new Chief Medical Officer and with no dissents from the staff I was approved. I put Nurse Menkel as head of medical when I'm away."

"You know I had to approve that order, right?" Cas asked.

"As the new Chief Medical Officer," Box continued as if he hadn't heard him. "I plan to introduce sweeping changes to how this ship is run. I will be requiring each individual to provide biological samples once a month, as well as insist on cognitive scans every six days to ensure everyone is operating at peak efficiency."

"No," Cas said, brushing him aside. "You'll keep things are they are—the way Xax had them set up or I'll find a new CMO."

Box huffed. "Fine. Not even one biological sample?"

The look Cas gave him finally shut him up. "All good in the Bay?" he asked, turning to Saturina.

"Is that *really* what you want to ask me?" she challenged.

Cas hooked his thumb to Box. "With him here, yes."

A smile flickered across her lips. "I've restructured the team—without Ryant we had to make some changes, but we'll manage. I've also spoken with the quartermaster to see about repurposing his ship into something else we might be able to use. I feel like resources will be thin for a while, so we should probably make use of everything we can."

"Good thinking," Cas replied.

"And I finished moving my stuff into your quarters, just this morning."

"Well, *that's* encouraging," Box said.

"See what I mean?" Cas asked.

"Sorry," she said, but the tone of her voice suggested she meant anything but. "I've got to get back to work before we reach Inax." She placed a gentle kiss on his lips. "See you later. Bye Box."

"Goodbye Chief," Box said, waving as she left them alone. Cas glanced around, everyone else had exited as well while they'd been standing there.

"So," Cas said. "Just you and me again, huh?"

"What?" Box asked. "No, of course not. We've got a whole ship of people now!"

Cas shook his head, smiling. Back when he'd first left the Coalition, he never would have thought he'd return, much less come to captain his own ship with such a fine crew. "I guess we're pretty lucky."

"Speak for yourself," Box replied. "What you call luck, I call *fate*."

Epilogue

The door slid open, revealing the small room. Above the desk sat empty hooks, where a sword once hung, and the bed was still a mess from the last time it had been slept in. Cas took a moment, staring at the room as if somehow it might be able to offer some insight to its previous occupant. But it was just a standard room, a space where a life had once been lived.

Cas entered and the doors closed behind him, causing the room to go dark. He watched the stars out the window beyond, bathed in the green of the undercurrent before he turned on the lights. Officially he'd come back to Evie's room to pack it up, so they could use the space for future crew members transferring over from Inax. He'd been pleased with how well the negotiations had gone, and how quickly the Yax-Inax had agreed to rejoin a new Coalition, even without the Claxians. They'd had the same response from Untu, and Zaal was already on his way back, being escorted by the *USCS Winston*. Things were coming back together.

Cas took a seat in the chair beside the desk. "And it's all thanks to you," he said to the ether. "None of this would have happened if it weren't for your determination and grit." He didn't know why he was speaking aloud; it wasn't as if anyone could hear him. But in some way, it made him feel better. Like

305

he could still talk to her and maybe on some plane of existence she might be able to hear him.

"We didn't hold a funeral," he continued. "It didn't seem right. So, we threw a party instead. For those we lost because of circumstance—Xax, Sesster, Ryant. And those we lost from sacrifice, like you, since you were still on that ship when we fired the trans-dimensional weapon." Cas ran his hand over the desk, feeling the smooth metal. He then reached up and activated the small terminal. On it were a list of personal logs and notes Evie had made. He half expected to see a note or a message to him somewhere, but it was nothing but her logs. He encoded all of her data and sent it into the main computer where it would probably remain untouched forever. It was standard procedure to encode and lock down a person's digital imprint once they had died and to keep it for posterity. He would have loved to have spent hours going through all her logs, if for no reason other than to see her face again, but it would have been an invasion of her privacy, and he wasn't going to do that to her, especially not in death.

Cas chuckled. "That person you picked up, the courier back at Devil's Gate, probably wouldn't have hesitated to rifle through someone's personal life, just because he could. Because by that point he'd been so jaded he didn't care anymore. But you pushed me to be better, even if you didn't know you were doing it." He paused. "I never would have made it this far without you, Evie." He stood, taking one last look at the room. She only had a few trinkets around. But on the desk was the Clastus Orb he'd first seen back before they'd even reached the Excel Nebula. He picked it up, finding it detached from the desk quite easily. The door chimed and Cas was so startled he almost dropped it.

"Come in."

"Hey," Saturina said. "Still packing up?"

"It was a little harder than I anticipated." Cas rolled the orb around in his hand.

"Is that a Clastus Orb?" she asked. Cas nodded and held it out to her, but she closed his hand around it. "They're supposed to be good luck for those on a long journey. It's also said those who touch them remain connected, even after death. It's why when they're forged, the forge masters never handle them with their bare hands."

Cas crinkled his brow. "How do you know so much about these?"

She shrugged. "My uncle did a stint on Clastus about twenty years ago. Well, I guess it's been about thirty-eight years now." She stared at the orb. "The entire time he was there, he never managed to get his hands on one. They don't come easily." She indicated his hand. "I think she would have wanted it to go to you." Cas arched an eyebrow. "I know. But I was wrong about her. I was too—engulfed by what she did on Hescal—what the Athru controlling her did—to see the person underneath. In the end, she sacrificed everything for us. *That's* how we should remember her."

"I wish she could see this," Cas said. "The reunification of the Coalition—all of it coming back together to be better than before. A Coalition without all the subterfuge and deception."

"If we can keep it that way," Saturina said.

"We have to," Cas replied. "Otherwise we'll be doomed to face the same fate yet again." He stared at the orb in his palm. "But I have to believe, after all of this, we have *finally* learned our lesson." He smiled at her. "And I'm excited to see what the future brings."

The End

GLOSSARY

Planets/Stars/Outposts

Alpha Onias – core system of the Coalition

Axinal-Illitaica – Yax-Inax moon orbiting a gas giant in the Messer system. Location of a Yax-Inax incursion resulting in the use of biological weapons and the loss of millions of Yax-Inax lives

Cassiopeia Optima – Sargan homeworld (settled by humans millennia ago)

Claxia Prime – Claxian Homeworld

Cypaxia – planet often used for relaxation. The planet is lush with flora, the dominant fauna having been killed off thousands of years ago when the Coalition first settled

Dren – secret Coalition penal colony

Earth – homeworld of the human species. Inside the Horus system

Excel Nebula – stellar nursery deep within Coalition space

Hommel – Class G yellow, primary star to Sissk

Horus – Class K orange, primary star to Earth, Claxia Prime, others

Hutakk Sector – distant area of Sil space

Jurest – core system of the Coalition

Laq – homeworld to the Bulaq, destroyed by the Athru

Marxus – Yax-Inax settlement, used as a refuge after the appearance of the Athru

Mishtaka – a human colony in the Alaria system. Believed destroyed by the Athru

Ocar – a habited planet close to the edge of Coalition space

Omicron Terminus – Trinary Star System including two gas supergiants far outside Coalition space

Opaous – Class H yellow star in uncharted space

Parasatia – home to an ear-burrowing spider, within Coalition borders

Quaval – one of the few charted systems inside Sil space

Rrethal – Class F white, primary star to Cypaxia

Set – outer rim planet in the Horus system

Sissk – border world just inside Coalition space. Unique, as it has twelve sentient species who evolved at the same time

Slatun Incero – home to a human colony settled over a thousand years ago. Believed destroyed by the Athru

Starbase Five – first detected traces of Athru incursion. Location of Samiya & Hank's refugee camp after the invasion

Starbase Eight – Coalition stronghold and first line of defense against Sargan incursions

Thislea – Sil homeworld, much is unknown about this planet

Turn – remote Sil outpost

Us-uu – the system home to the Untuburu homeworld

Zeta Draconis – home to a human colony settled in 2250. Believed destroyed by the Athru

Species

Athru – the true name of the *Andromeda* threat from a distant star system. Determined to destroy humanity at any cost

Ashkas – one of the twelve distinct intelligent races inhabiting the planet Sissk. Prefer to be known as Simmilists rather than *reptiles*, as many off-worlders refer to them

Bulaq – a race of scavengers after their world was destroyed. Resemble one of the species on Sissk known as Ashkasians. No hair and hard plates make up skin. Born with two razor-like mandibles attached to their backs

Chormorph – one of the twelve distinct intelligent races inhabiting the planet Sissk. Chormorphs are descended from living flora on this world

Crilicks – one of the twelve distinct intelligent races inhabiting the planet Sissk. Highly reactive, resemble tall insects

Claxian – founding members of the Coalition and pacifists with advanced technology. Lived as isolationists until first contact by the humans over two thousand years ago. Helped form the Coalition to spread peace through the galaxy

Esook – founding member of the Coalition. Very environmentally aware, all their structures are designed to have minimal impact on the environment of their home planet

Erusitaan – seven and a half feet tall, all muscle. Sharp bone or hoof grows out of their hands. They generally associate with the Sargan Commonwealth and are used as enforcers

Hidre Lagul – paranoid, xenophobic race on the edge of Coalition space. Negotiations to bring them into the Coalition collapsed and all records of the attempts were classified

Human – one of the founding members of the Coalition and central to its operation. Humans can be found on any of a hundred different worlds in the Coalition and often hold high positions of power within the organization. Worked with the Claxians to be the founding members

Husmus-riza – a long-time Coalition species which uses flowing words in their written language

Goruff – one of the earliest members of the Coalition

Lek-Makal – member of the Coalition. Victims of a planet-wide plague originating from a civil dispute

Maxians – member of the Coalition. Most Maxians do not allow physical contact with others

Orungu – one of the twelve distinct intelligent races inhabiting the planet Sissk. Of the twelve, the Orungu are closest in appearance to humans, though with more fur

Sargans – generally human but can also pertain to other species who have joined the Sargan Commonwealth. Sargans are humans who want to be lawless, or at least out from under the thumb of the Coalition

Sil – species of great technological advancement. The Coalition has reached a tentative treaty with the Sil not to violate their borders under any circumstances. Their empire is large. Sil seem to share symbiotic relationships with their ships but not much is known about this phenomenon at this time

Untuburu – early members of the Coalition. Highly religious to their god Kor. Untuburu are the only Coalition members not required to wear uniforms as their religion requires the sacred blue robes be the only garments worn off world. Wear metal exoskeletons to help them integrate with Coalition society

Yax-Inax – early members of the Coalition. Studious, have perfect memory and can retain huge amounts of information. Often integrate themselves into other cultures to learn as much as possible. Easily identified by their six eyes and four arms

Miscellaneous

Alchuriam ore – an obsolete type of metal

Calorcium – a medical material filled with nanobots, injectable into wounds in order to repair/rebuild

Centraxium – a type of metal used by the Coalition in fabrication

Courant – a type of poisonous insect on Thislea

Cyclax – a type of metal used in ship reinforcement, mined by the Coalition

Durax – Sargan construction material

Firebrand – liquor much like whiskey

Galvanium – a type of metal used in ship construction

Gla – Sil word meaning "cousin"

Grande-Grande – a large spaceborne creature

Guursel – a docile four-legged animal native to Thislea. In ancient times was used to pull carts

Heavy Pyron – Sargan construction material

High Town – capital city on Claxia Prime

Kantor Province – home province of Zenfor, situated near the equator of Thislea

Krulak – a harmless spider native to Bulaq society

Magenest – material discovered to block Athru signals

Menlasa – Claxian world for "blue ball"

Palithasol – drug used to reduce blood toxicity

Pessook – large, lumbering animal from Humaria

Rulag – a type of canine on Procyon Four. Often found in people's homes

Rustak Province – an area of Thislea known for its unending beauty

Selasi Mountains – one of five mountain ranges on the planet Sissk

Tetrean Rhino – a large, multi-horned mammal from Tetras Prime

Vurn – rodent-like creature

Author's Note

Dear reader,

This is it. The end.

There was a time when I thought I might not ever be able to write those words. A time when I considered allowing this series to continue as long as I could sustain it. But I realized every good story needs an ending, and these characters deserved that.

I've had such an amazing time writing this series—something I wasn't even sure I could do when I first set out. I knew nine books in a row would be daunting, and there were times in the middle when I wasn't sure I could finish it, but then I would think about you, the loyal reader who has stayed with me this entire time, and I would find a way to make it work. This series is complete because of you, and I can't thank you enough for supporting me along the way.

Of course, I have to give a big shout out to Dan Van Oss and Tiffany Shand for shaping this book into the final product. They both have been consistently awesome through this entire process.

To my beta readers, Meenaz, Kay, Katie and Lori, thank you for all your help and hard work to make this series better. Your polish makes this series sparkle.

Finally, thank you to my wife for her unwavering support in a process that lasted seventeen months. I know it took a lot of patience, and I am eternally grateful.

Sincerely,

Eric Warren

About the Author

I've always been an author, but I haven't always known I've been an author. It took a few tragic events in my life and a lot of time for me to figure it out.

But I've never had a problem creating stories. Or creating in general. I wasn't *the* creative person in any of my classes in school, I was always the kid who never spoke but always listened. I was the one who would take an assignment and pour my heart into it, as long as it meant I could do something original.

I didn't start writing professionally until 2014 when I tackled the idea of finishing a novel-length book. Before then I had always written in some capacity, even as far back as elementary school where I wrote pages of stories about creatures under the earth.

It took a few tries and a few novels under my belt before I figured out what I was doing, and I've now written nineteen novels. I am thrilled to be doing this and couldn't imagine spending my life doing anything else.

I hope you enjoy the fruits of my labor. May they bring you as much joy as they bring me.

Having lived in both Virginia and California in the past, I currently reside in Charlotte, NC with my very supportive wife and two small pugs.

Visit me at www.ericwarrenauthor.com

Made in the USA
Monee, IL
20 April 2020

26717524R00185